A WHIRLWIND OF COLOR

IVY SMOAK

To my husband. I wrote the first book in this series when you were still my fiancé. And I'm so happy to be able to call you my husband now. Our love has been a whirlwind of color since the very beginning.

PART 1

CHAPTER 1

Tuesday

The incessant beeping of Melissa's alarm clock was driving me nuts. Why was she getting up so early? I was the one with a 9 a.m. final. I tried to ignore it, but now that I was awake I couldn't fall back asleep. "Melissa, turn it off," I groaned.

"Penny? Penny, thank God." But it wasn't Melissa talking. It was definitely a man's voice.

My eyes flew open and I stared at the man leaning over my bed. Why was there a man in my dorm room? Why was he so close to me? My heart started pounding in my chest. *Jesus, where did I leave my pepper spray?* I reached toward my nightstand but my fingers came up empty.

The room came into focus and I quickly realized that I wasn't in my dorm room at all. And the beeping was coming from the machines surrounding me, not from Melissa's alarm clock. Was I in the hospital? I sat up and silently cursed when the IV tugged against my skin.

"You're awake," the man said.

I turned back toward him. He was my doctor I presumed. But he looked like one of those doctors you'd see on primetime TV instead of in real life. He was almost too perfect looking. He wasn't wearing a white coat, just a freshly pressed suit. And he was much too close to me.

"What happened?" I asked. "Where are my parents?" I felt fine, but panic was setting in. I didn't remember how I got here. Why didn't I remember what was wrong with me?

"They're in the waiting room." The doctor reached for my hand that wasn't attached to the IV.

I pulled away from him. What was he doing?

"Penny." He lowered his eyebrows slightly.

The way he was staring at me made me uncomfortable. Like he could see right through my soul. I tried to inch away from him, but I was already close to falling off the side of the bed. "Can you get my parents for me?"

He just stared at me like he couldn't comprehend my words. Maybe he didn't speak English well or something. Lots of doctors came to America for work, right? That was a thing.

"Where is my mom? Can you get her for me?" *Comprendo?*

"Penny, I know I fucked up. If you'd just give me a chance to explain…"

"Please." Tears started to prick the corners of my eyes. What the hell did he need to explain? I must be dying. *God, I'm too young to die!*

He looked so dejected. He opened his mouth like he was going to say something, but then pressed his lips back together.

"Please."

"Okay. I'll go get them." But he didn't move. He just stood there staring at me.

I didn't want a stranger to see me cry. I turned my head away from him. I didn't turn back until I heard the door close. He didn't seem like a very good doctor. He hadn't even taken my vitals.

My mom came running into the room, quickly followed by my dad.

"Sweetie, thank goodness you're awake." She grabbed my hand and squeezed it.

It was so good to see her.

"You gave us quite the fright, Pen," my dad said and took the seat next to my bed. "How are you feeling?"

"Fine. I feel fine."

"James said you wanted to speak to us right away."

James? Was that the doctor's name? "I don't even know why I'm in here. And I definitely need a new doctor. He..."

"We've already taken care of that, sweetie," my mom said and squeezed my hand again. She reached out and pushed some of my hair off my forehead. "It's all going to be okay."

I exhaled slowly. They must have sensed that my doctor had no idea what he was talking about either. I was so glad they were here. What would I do without them?

"But what happened?" I asked. "Am I dying?"

"No, no, no," my mom said. "You're fine. You're awake. Everyone was worried that you might not wake up." She paused. "But the baby..." her voice trailed off and tears started to well in her eyes.

"Was I babysitting or something?" Why couldn't I remember?

My mom glanced at my dad and then back at me. "Sweetie, what's the last thing you remember?"

"I was studying for my sociology final. I must have fallen asleep in bed."

She stared at me. "Sociology? Didn't you take that freshman year?"

"Um…yeah." I laughed awkwardly. "Just a few more exams and I'll officially be done my first year. Oh no…do you think I missed any of my finals while I've been here? What day is it?"

My mom looked back at my dad. "Peter, get the doctor." Her voice sounded so serious.

My dad practically flew out of his chair. I had never seen him move so fast.

"Why?" I asked. "What's wrong?"

She squeezed my hand. "You're not in college anymore. Don't you remember?"

"Of course I'm still in college. It's not like I dropped out. I'd never do that. I love school."

She stared at me. "Penny, you're 26 years old."

I laughed. "Mom, I'm 19."

She dropped my hand and covered her mouth before her sob escaped.

"I'm 19," I said again. *Right?*

CHAPTER 2

Tuesday

A different doctor than the first one came into the room. He looked much more professional with a white coat, hair graying at the temples, and a stethoscope dangling from his neck. I instantly trusted him more than the other man. And he didn't hover unnecessarily close or make me feel uncomfortable in any way. Except for his onslaught of questions.

"And what's your name?" he asked. The way he was staring at me made me think this was some sort of trick question. But I had only ever had one name.

"Penny Taylor." Maybe I didn't like him that much after all. He was treating me like a child. I knew my own name. "Do you want me to spell that for you?"

He chuckled. "No, that won't be necessary." He looked down at his notebook. "And the very last thing you remember is studying?" he asked.

I nodded, my mind stuck on what my mom had said. *Penny, you're 26 years old.* I shook my head. I'd think I'd remember if seven years of my life had flown by. "So can I get out of here? I really do feel fine and I have exams to study for."

The doctor jotted something down in his notebook. He looked up from his pages and smiled. "We'll get you out of here as soon as we can, Penny. You have my word."

"You can't release her like this," my mom said. "What's wrong with her?"

Her words stung. There was nothing wrong with me. She was the one that had lost her mind. I glanced at my dad for reassurance, but he was staring at me with just as much worry etched on his face.

Penny, you're 26 years old. The words swirled around in my head, refusing to settle. *I'm 19.*

"I'm going to go talk to your family in the hall," the doctor said. "We'll be back in a minute. Sit tight, alright?" He tapped my blanket covered foot and walked out the door with my parents.

This was just some sort of bad dream. I hadn't been sleeping that well. Austin had blown me off the past few nights, claiming he was studying for finals. But he never studied, his GPA was proof of that. I knew what he was doing behind my back. *Who he was doing.* And he was slowly driving me insane.

I was fed up with his shit. I was so sick of being his second choice. We needed to have a serious conversation about what we were. Again. How many times had we talked about the same issues over and over again? But I refused to go home for the summer without knowing where we stood. That would definitely drive me mad.

Wake up. I patted the sides of my face but the hospital room didn't magically transform into my dorm room. Melissa would know what to do. She could tell everyone what was going on. I looked at the nightstand for my cell phone but it was nowhere in sight. The chairs by the bed were empty too. *Damn it.*

I looked down at the IV stuck in my arm. I was just contemplating how much it would hurt to pull it out when the door flew open.

The first doctor came barging in, his eyes blazing with anger.

"Penny, we're leaving. I'm taking you home."

I shrunk away from him. Why would he take me home? My parents could do that. I didn't like this doctor.

"Everything's okay. Let's just get you unhooked from these." He looked at the machine I was attached to, like he was trying to figure out what to do. How inexperienced was he?

"Mr. Hunter," my new doctor said as he came into the room. He was so flustered that his cheeks were red.

"Penny, you know I'm sorry. You know that. You know I'd never hurt you."

I opened my mouth and then closed it again. Who was this guy? "I don't know you."

He ran his hands down his face. "Baby." He sounded tormented.

But I was more focused on what he had said rather than how he had said it. Was he talking to me? I looked at my parents. I didn't think he was talking to them. When I turned back to him, he was on his knees by the side of my bed.

"Baby, just let me take you home. We can't trust any of the doctors here. They don't know what they're talking about. We're going to go home and everything's going to go back to normal."

"To normal?" My heart was racing. What normal was he referring to? And how did it involve me?

He grabbed my hand. "Yes, baby. Tell him you want to go home."

I pulled my hand away from him. "I want to go back to school. I have finals."

"Penny." His voice broke. "You're not in school anymore. You know that. I know you remember. You have to remember." He lifted up my hand again, tilting it toward me.

I stared down at my hand. There was a tan line on my ring finger. A line that would have formed from years of wearing an engagement ring. Or a wedding ring. Or both. I looked back at the man on his knees, with the desperation on his face. There were small crinkles around the corners of his eyes. Lines that came with age. He was...old. Not old like my parents. But certainly older than me. Too old for me.

"I need you to remember." His Adam's apple rose and fell. "I need you."

I felt like I was going to throw up. How many times had I wished Austin would look at me the way this stranger did? So why did his gaze just make me feel sick to my stomach? I pulled my hand out of his grasp and shifted away from him on the bed.

"Mom, Dad. Can't you just take me home? Please?"

"Penny, the doctor thinks it's best if you just go back to your normal routine," my mom said.

"Then take me back to school..."

"Your normal routine with James. And Scarlett. Here in New York."

"But not for a few days," my doctor interjected. "We'd like to monitor your progress. Despite what your husband thinks, not every doctor affiliated with this hospital is out to get you. You're safe here. And hopefully your memory will come back before you even head back to your apartment."

I barely heard him. I was completely focused on one word he said. *Husband.* I glanced down at the tan line on my finger. *I was married?* I looked at the man on his knees again. *To him?*

"Does that sound good?" the doctor asked. "In the meantime, there are a bunch of people in the waiting room ready to help jog your memory. Familiar faces and stories will be good." He cleared his throat. "Not angry, harsh moments. Pleasant fun ones." He was staring at…my husband.

I swallowed hard. "You're not a doctor?" I asked him.

For a moment it looked like he was going to cry. But then he lowered both his eyebrows. He stared at me in a way that no one ever had before. Like he hated me and loved me at the same time. Goosebumps rose on my skin.

"No. I'm not a doctor," he said.

"What's your name?"

"James." He pressed his lips together and stared at me for a moment, like he was willing me to remember. "James Hunter." He looked at me expectantly, like his name alone would trigger a memory.

But I didn't feel like I had anything to remember. I felt like everyone here was wrong. The doctor. My parents. This man kneeling beside my bed. This beautiful, broken man. I didn't need to know anything more about him to know that he was so broken. And even though I didn't know him, I hoped to God it wasn't my fault that he was like this. Because I had no clue how to fix him. I had no idea who he was. And as soon as I was out of this hospital I was going back to school. I had finals to take. School was my number one priority.

CHAPTER 3

Tuesday

One couple at a time came into my room and pretended to know me. A me that didn't exist. A fabrication in their minds. I knew who I was. And I didn't belong in this hospital bed surrounded by strangers.

They told me story after story, all which sounded made up. And almost all the stories featured the man standing in the corner of the room, staring too intently at me. James. My make-believe husband. Not once did a smile cross his face at hearing any of the funny memories. Not once did his scowl disappear.

I tore my eyes away from him and stared back at the couple in front of me. A blonde with a kind smile and a man with dark eyes and dark hair. They both looked tan like they had just been on the beach. And they definitely looked older than me. Cleary I wasn't really friends with all these old people. If this was some sort of prank, they should have hired younger actors.

The woman glanced nervously at the man and both their smiles disappeared. I had been tuning them out. Had they said something funny? Something I should have laughed at or remembered?

"First you two ruined my proposal and now my honeymoon too? What am I going to do with you?" The guy named Mason winked at me.

That explained why they were so tan. They had been on their honeymoon. But it didn't explain anything else he said. Or who he was. Or why I was friends with either of them in this fantasy world.

"You just got married?" I asked. "Congratulations." *How the hell can I get out of here?*

The woman started blinking fast, like tears were threatening to spill. "Yeah, Penny. You were my matron of honor."

Matron of honor. I stared at her. So we weren't just friends in this made up reality. We were really good friends. Best friends, possibly. I shook my head. I already had a best friend. Where was Melissa anyway?

The woman put her hand on my blanket covered shin. "Don't you remember?" Her smile wavered when I didn't immediately respond. She removed her hand like I had burned her and looked up at her husband.

He cleared his throat. "I know Rob is desperate to see you. He's probably here by now. We'll go let him know it's his turn."

I would have asked who Rob was, but I didn't want to hear another story. The two of them walked out of the room, leaving James and me alone.

I didn't know where to look so I settled on my intertwined fingers. I wished he would leave. Then I could find a way to get out of this room. The silence was heavy between us. I could feel his eyes on me. But I didn't know what he wanted. And even if I had known, I doubted I could give it to him. I wasn't who he thought I was.

But the silence was driving me insane. "How long have we been married in this scenario?" I asked, while still staring at my hands.

He hesitated, his eyes boring into me. "A little over four years."

That was a long time. Four years that I couldn't remember because they had never really happened. I wished he would stop staring. I wished he'd leave me in peace. "Did we date for a while before that?" I asked, trying desperately to vanquish the awkward tension in the air. I had never been good in situations filled with awkwardness. My mouth usually filled the silence with incoherent nonsense. Or I'd just stay mute until the awkwardness felt physically painful.

"We were engaged for two and a half years."

That was an odd way to answer that question. I looked up from my hands. "But how long did we date before our fake engagement?"

His eyes locked with mine. "I proposed to you two months after I met you."

I laughed.

He didn't.

I bit the inside of my lip. We'd been married for four years. Engaged for two and a half. And my mom had said I was 26. *Yeah, right.* I stared at him. That would have meant that he proposed to me when I was 19. The same age I actually was. I racked my brain, trying to remember him. But there was nothing there. Because none of this was real.

Besides, who gets engaged when they're 19? Not me. Certainly not me. I had never even officially had a boyfriend.

Austin and his stupid lack of labels. He was an idiot and surely even he wouldn't propose to someone when he was 19. But James was older than me. That was obvious. There was no way he had been 19 when he proposed in this twisted fairytale he was spewing.

I stared at him staring at me. "How old are you?"

"Thirty four."

Thirty four? "You're fifteen years old than me!"

The corners of his mouth turned up ever so slightly. "Penny, you're not 19. You're 26. And you'll be 27 in a few months. You've always been pretty adamant about the fact that I'm only seven years older than you."

"That doesn't change the fact that you fake proposed to a 19 year old when you were what...27?"

"Yes, but you were 20, not 19. It was after your birthday. And none of this is made up."

"That doesn't make it better."

The small smile had vanished from his face.

"How did we even meet, huh? I'm 19 right now and I'm seeing someone. How could I be engaged to you after my next birthday? And how would we have even met when you're so much older than me? I'm busy studying all the time. None of what you're saying could possibly be true. This whole thing is ridiculous."

"You're not 19."

"Yes I am!" Tears pricked the corners of my eyes. I didn't want to cry in front of him. "I am." I looked back down at my knotted hands on my lap. I blinked fast, forcing the tears to stay at bay. "You didn't answer my question."

"We got engaged because we were in love. That guy that you think you're dating right now? Austin? He's a prick. He never treated you right. You deserved the world and all he gave you were excuses and lies. You're one in a million, Penny. Not one of a million. Is it so hard to believe that you were strong enough to realize you deserved better?"

Yes. Because I still stayed up late at night waiting for Austin's calls. Waiting for some validation that I was good enough. *One in a million. Not one of a million.* That was sweet. James thought I deserved the world. He clearly loved me. The word love seemed to roll my stomach. I felt like I was going to be sick. No, he didn't love me. He was just a good actor. "I meant the other question," I said, trying to distract myself. "How did we supposedly meet?"

He didn't respond, so I looked up at him. There was heat in his gaze. It was like he was willing me to remember. But there was nothing there. No recognition of his features. No feeling when he looked at me. Nothing.

"It's a long story," he finally said.

"I'm stuck in a hospital. I probably have time for it."

He shook his head. "You didn't like our age difference. You're not going to like this either."

"How bad could it be?" Maybe he just didn't remember what he was supposed to say. Actors forgot their lines all the time.

"I don't think it's bad. And neither do you." He stared at me. "Neither *did* you, I mean." But the expression on his face made it seem like it was really bad.

"What, did I steal you from someone else?" I laughed because the idea was absolutely preposterous.

He lowered both his eyebrows. "No."

But for some reason I didn't believe him. Maybe it was the pause. Maybe it was the way he looked offended when

I'd asked. *Oh my God, did I steal him from someone else?* I shook my head. Of course I hadn't. I didn't even know him. He was probably married to some Hollywood actress and obviously someone like me wouldn't be able to steal him away even if I tried. Not that I wanted to. But still, I was curious about why he looked so upset. It didn't look like he was acting.

Before I could ask him any more questions the door flew open.

A man I had never seen in my life ran over to my bed and threw his arms around me. His hair was wet like he had just taken a shower. The t-shirt that clung to his broad shoulders was as wet as his hair. Like he had thrown it on instead of drying off with a towel.

"You scared me half to death, sis." He kissed my cheek before pulling back. "You look okay. Do you feel okay?" He pulled me into another hug. "I'm so fucking happy you're okay."

Sis? I wasn't missing seven years of my life and there was no chance I had a sibling I didn't know about. Especially one older than me who looked nothing like me.

"Really, how are you feeling?" He put both his hands on my shoulders and stared at me intently.

Who the hell is this person? The intensity in his eyes suddenly looked familiar. I studied his features and glanced at my pretend husband. They looked similar. Maybe this was James' brother? Which meant I was this man's fake sister-in-law? "Umm...I'm good. Trying to get out of here as soon as possible." I laughed awkwardly.

"Yeah, I know how you hate hospitals. But you're awake and everything now so you'll probably get out in a beat. I'm just so fucking glad you're okay." He pulled me into another hug. "I never would have been able to forgive myself."

"Robert Hunter!" A very pregnant woman stumbled into the room completely out of breath. "I was trying to talk to you."

"It can wait," he said. He released me from his embrace but kept staring at me instead of the pregnant woman. "Scarlett's doing okay. She's in the waiting room and I know she wants to see you. And we've been looking in on Liam every day. He's strong. I know he's gonna make it. You're all fighters." He tapped the bottom of my chin.

"Who are Scarlett and Liam?"

His lips parted like he was about to tell me something. But then he started laughing. "Good one, sis." The pregnant woman walked up behind him and pulled him away from me with surprising strength.

She started whispering something to him, moving her arms around in agitation.

"No." He laughed. "You're shitting me. Penny tell them what's up. Tell them you know who I am."

Who is this person? "Someone called you Robert Hunter? I'm guessing you two are related somehow." I gestured back and forth between him and James.

He laughed again but it sounded forced. "Very funny. If you're getting me back for all the times I've messed with you..."

"This isn't a joke, Rob," the woman hissed. "She doesn't remember us. She doesn't even remember James."

Rob looked at James and shook his head. "That can't be true. She's just...that's not true. Tell them, Penny."

I didn't know what to say, so I just shrugged my shoulders.

"This isn't funny," he said. "My jokes are at least funny. Cut it out."

"We're just going to take a minute." The woman pulled Rob toward the door. "We'll be back." They disappeared into the hall.

I looked over at James. "Are you related to him?"

"He's my little brother."

"He's...loud."

James smiled. "He is."

"Are him and I supposed to be close? He seemed pretty upset."

"The two of you are really good friends." James left his perch against the wall and walked over to me. "My family and friends became yours."

My heart started racing. What was he about to do?

He eyed the machine that was monitoring my heart rate and smiled. "Everyone you've seen today loves you. But no one on this earth loves you as much as I do." He slowly reached out his hand and brushed his fingers against my cheek.

I flinched and he immediately pulled away.

The look of hurt on his face was palpable. I hadn't flinched when his brother had repeatedly hugged me. Why had I flinched from his touch? I needed to change the subject. I needed to wipe away that look of pain.

"Who are Scarlett and Liam?" I asked.

The hurt seemed to grow tenfold. His Adam's apple rose and fell as he stared at me.

"Two people I should know I guess?" I said.

Tears formed in the corners of his eyes. If I hadn't been staring at him, I would have missed it, because he immediately blinked them away.

He cleared his throat. "If you'll excuse me for one second. I just...I need a minute." He hurried away from me, like he couldn't stand being next to me for another second.

I was left alone in the hospital room. I breathed a sigh of relief. I rather liked being alone.

CHAPTER 4

Tuesday

Visiting hours were over. *Thank goodness.* I wanted to fall asleep, but I couldn't make myself close my eyes. It felt like I was in a horror movie, and as soon as I let my guard down I'd be taken.

Instead, I stared at the closed blinds. All day long as random people visited me, my eyes had been drawn to the closed blinds. Light had streamed through and I so badly wanted to be outside instead of locked in here. I had never liked running, but for some reason I felt like I had years of pent-up energy. I wanted to run around campus with the wind in my hair. It was an unfamiliar sensation and it made me start to wonder if everyone was telling the truth. Because I certainly hated running. But what if time had morphed into this alternate reality where I loved jogging? I shook away the thought. It couldn't be true. I couldn't be missing seven years of my life. I just couldn't.

I continued to stare at the blinds. I knew it was nighttime, but there still seemed to be light streaming through them. How was that possible? And I knew I was in a hospital, but the night didn't sound right. Like the blanket of sleep hadn't reached anyone outside yet. It sounded like there were cars still honking. Like I was on Main Street during rush hour. What hospital was I in? Christiana, probably. That was the closest one to campus.

I slowly stood up. A nurse had unhooked me from everything earlier and said I was free to roam around the room. That it would be good for me to start moving again. That was probably why I felt the need to run. No one had told me how long I had been in here, but it must have been awhile because my legs felt weak as I walked over to the window.

The sounds of a busy street were even louder as I drew closer. I pushed aside the blinds to either side and stared down. And down. And down. To a city street far below. Yellow taxi cabs sped by, cutting off other cars, leaving so many horns blaring in their wake. New York City. There wasn't a doubt in my mind about my current location. What the fuck was I doing in NYC? I took a step back, letting the blinds fall into place.

It's just a bad dream. None of this is real. But when I reached out and opened up the blinds again, the same scene stretched out as far as I could see.

I hated New York. I hated the rude people and the lack of grass and fresh air. Even if everyone was telling the truth and I was 26 and married to an old man, I knew this couldn't be. I would never in a million years move to New York City. I hated it here. I'd never do this.

I put my hand on my forehead. I was losing my mind. None of this was real. None of it. I took a deep breath and walked back toward my bed. I needed to go to sleep. And then I'd wake up from this nightmare. Everything would go back to normal. I'd ace my sociology exam. I'd stand up to Austin. And I'd be happy, albeit alone. I'd much rather be alone for eternity than doomed to a life in NYC with a strange man and stranger friends. I was used to being on my own.

Before I reached the bed, my feet stopped. I looked over at the bathroom door. Looking in a mirror would help me confirm that no time had been lost. That I was still the 19 year old girl I knew that I was.

I felt my hands tremble as I pushed open the door and flipped on the light. I warily stepped in front of the sink and stared into the mirror. I barely recognized my reflection. Not that I looked that different. Just small things that made me not recognize the person staring back at me. My face looked thinner than I remembered, but that was probably just from my hospital stay. My hair looked shinier and fuller than usual. Which was odd because I had been lying in a hospital bed for God knows how long. How did it look so good still? It was also a little shorter. Maybe the hospital staff had cut it. That was something they probably did for patients, right?

I touched the left side of my eye. The small creases that cut through the skin by the corners of my eyes couldn't be as easily explained. I was probably just in desperate need of moisturizer. But really, my complexion looked great. I'd take the creases next to my eyes over the blackheads on my nose any day. I leaned closer to the mirror. My pores had never looked so clear.

Things like that didn't just change overnight. I swallowed hard and closed my eyes. *I'm imagining this. It isn't real.* I took a deep breath and opened my eyes, expecting my 19 year old self to be staring back at me once again.

But it wasn't. I wasn't the same. How was I not the same? I reached out and touched the mirror, like I was about to touch someone else's face. But all I felt was the cold glass. I stared at the tan line on my ring finger and removed my hand from my reflection. My fingers left smudges on the clean surface.

The tan line on my ring finger could be explained. I was terrible with self-tanner. It always left streaks everywhere on my pale skin. This was just one of those instances. A classic Penny self-tanning faux pas. Nothing a little scrubbing wouldn't remove.

I looked down at my hands, arms, legs, and feet. Everything else looked familiar enough. Normal enough. I was still me.

I touched my stomach through my hospital gown and froze. My stomach felt bloated. Very bloated. It didn't feel like my stomach at all. I pulled up my hospital gown and stared in horror at the sight of myself.

I had a small beer belly. That was the only way to describe it. There was a horizontal line with stitches beneath the protrusion. And there were two other smaller lines with sutures on either side of my stomach.

What the hell had I been in here for? I put my hand on my stomach. For a second I thought maybe I looked this way because I was pregnant. But that couldn't be it. I'd feel different. I'd feel a baby inside of me. It was something I'd always wanted, way way in the future. And this was certainly not that time. Even thinking about carrying Austin's baby made me nauseous. No, it wasn't possible. Absolutely not. My parents would kill me.

Just the thought of disappointment on their faces made me know how impossible being pregnant was. I'd never get pregnant out of wedlock. I wouldn't be able to handle upsetting them. That was why I always followed the rules. And got good grades. And did everything I was supposed to do. It was also why I was on birth control and made Austin use a condom. No mistakes. I lowered my hospital gown back down over my stomach.

I must have had something wrong with my intestines or liver or something. Liver. It definitely had to be my liver. I'd drunk alcohol before I was 21 and this was my punishment. When was the last time I had something to drink? When was the last party Melissa dragged me to? I doubted I had more than one beer either way. Could that have made my liver fail? Or maybe it had been two beers. I couldn't remember. Either way, that was probably what did it. And my stomach was swollen because of whatever the doctors did to fix my failing liver. I was fine now. No one said I was dying so they probably didn't have to remove it. They had just opened me up and poked around a bit. Everything would go back to normal soon. How important could a liver be?

Or maybe all of this was a bad dream. A horrid dream and I'd wake up in the morning in my dorm room and everything would be okay. I was just stressed out over finals. Knowing me, I had probably fallen asleep in the library with my head in a book and was just dreaming away.

I stared at my reflection. The reflection I didn't believe. *It's all in your head.* I switched off the lights. *It's all in your head.* I climbed into bed and pulled the covers up to my chin. *It's all in your head.* But I couldn't erase the image of the city street below. Or ignore the sounds of the cars. Or the fact that a woman had stared back at me in the mirror. Not the girl that I knew.

CHAPTER 5

Wednesday

I had never felt so safe and secure in my entire life. Like I was wrapped up in a cocoon of warmth. I squeezed my eyes shut. I didn't want to face today. The nightmare from last night was so vivid. And I was glad it was just that. A nightmare.

Today was a new day. And I needed to get up before I was late for my exam. But I loved having Austin's arms around me. It was the one time when his feelings about me were obvious. When he was sleeping, he clung to me. He held me close. I didn't know why he couldn't do that during the day. Why he couldn't see us as more.

These were the moments I held close to my heart. They were the reason I stayed. The reason why I was patient with him. Melissa said I was a pushover. And maybe that was true, but it didn't take away from the fact that I liked him. I truly did. I was just waiting for him to realize that we were on the same page.

I took a deep breath. He smelled different, like he'd started to wear cologne or something. But I knew for a fact that he didn't wear cologne. For a second I wondered if it was another woman's scent on his skin. The thought quickly faded. This scent was all man. Deliciously male. Maybe it was a new body wash. Whatever the change, I liked it. He smelled like a million bucks. It made me feel slightly dizzy like I was intoxicated by him. I turned in the bed to nestle into his chest.

His arms wrapped tighter around me. "Penny."

That was not Austin's voice.

My eyes flew open at the same time my heart stopped beating. A man's chest I didn't recognize was pressed against my face. I screamed at the top of my lungs.

"Penny, it's just me." The man pulled away, releasing me from his warm embrace.

I screamed again even though I recognized him now. James. The man that claimed to be my husband. The man from my nightmares. The man that couldn't possibly be real.

"It's me." He grabbed both sides of my face and tried to force me to look at him.

I was supposed to wake up from this dream. Why hadn't I woken up? I tried to push his hands away from me, but he gripped my face harder.

"Penny."

"Don't touch me." I clamped my hands on his wrists, trying as hard as I could to fight him off.

"Look at me, baby. Please just look at me. Look at me and try to remember."

"Help!" I screamed. "Someone help me!"

He removed his hands from my face like I had slapped him. And we stayed like that for a moment, with my hands clutched tightly around his wrists. Frozen in the bed staring at each other.

The dark circles under his eyes and the frown on his lips weighed on me. And I had the same sense as before. That he was broken. I wanted to help, but I didn't know him. I couldn't fix him. I immediately let go of his wrists and scooted away from him. "What are you doing here?"

"I can't sleep without you beside me. You know that."

I hadn't meant in my bed. I meant here. In existence. "I know nothing about you." I inched farther away.

"Penny, you know me. If you'd just take a second to truly look at me I know you'll remember."

I kept scooting away from him until my ass was hanging off the edge of the bed.

"Look in my eyes and tell me you feel nothing."

I locked eyes with him. It was true, his arms had made me feel safe. Secure. Warm. But I hadn't known it was him. I thought it was Austin. That was the only reason why I had felt that way. I tried to ignore the nagging thought in the back of my mind. The one that was screaming that when James released me from his embrace, I had never felt so cold in my entire life. My skin pebbled with goosebumps. It was like my body was trying to tell me I needed him. I stared into his eyes, willing myself to remember him. To remember anything that he claimed to be true.

But there was nothing there. Yes, he was handsome. I couldn't deny that. Any woman would be lucky to have him. But he wasn't mine and I wasn't his. Everything he claimed was true couldn't possibly be. I scooted even further away, forgetting that there wasn't any more room, and started to fall off the bed.

He grabbed my waist before I fell, and pulled me back onto the mattress. This time I didn't think his touch was comforting. It was electrifying. Like he had just slapped me with a bug zapper. *What the hell was that?*

I climbed off the bed, pointing at him accusatorily. "You can't just sneak in here and...and...hold me in the middle of the night, you psycho."

He sat up in the bed but didn't respond. His t-shirt was slightly wrinkled, and it somehow made the guilty look on his face even more extreme. He was sad and lost and...I wasn't sure why I cared so fucking much.

I buried my fingers in my hair. "God, this was supposed to be a dream. Why haven't I woken up? What the hell is happening?" I reached down and pinched myself. *Ow.* I stared at the other side of the bed where James had just stood up. I pinched myself again. *Ow.* Why wasn't he disappearing? *Go away!*

I started walking back and forth. "You're not real, and I don't know why I can't make you go back into my imagination. Not that I've been imagining you. I'd imagine someone my own age would want to marry me. At some point. Way in the future. Not any time soon. I'm too young to be married."

"Penny." He started walking around the bed.

"I'm 19. Don't you see that? Don't you see that I'm too young for whatever the hell this is?" I gestured back and forth between us. "You're 34."

"Penny." He stopped a few feet away from me, giving me the space I desperately needed.

I flung open the blinds to see that the city was still below me and started pacing faster. "What the hell am I doing in New York City? I hate the city. I hate it here. I wouldn't choose to be here unless I lost my mind!" I realized I was waving my hands around, but couldn't stop.

"We decided that..."

"We?" I said. "There is no we. And all those people I met yesterday? Those aren't my friends. And you're not my husband. This," I said and pointed to my ring finger. "Was just a terrible self-tanner accident. We're not married. It's impossible. And whatever is going on with my skin," I gestured to my face, "is a weird hospital mirror trick. I don't have wrinkles next to my eyes. Teenagers don't have wrinkles."

"They're laugh lines," James said. "And I love them. I love every part…"

I held up my hand so he wouldn't come any closer. "What, you're telling me you love this?" I gestured to my beer belly. "Am I just fat or did something happen to me? Did I lose my liver? Do livers make you sane? Why can't I remember what the fuck a liver does?" I was screaming now. Screaming, pacing, and flailing my arms around like a maniac.

"Penny, if you'd just calm down I can tell you everything you want to know."

"I don't want you to tell me. I want the doctors to tell me. You're not even real. I've just lost my damned mind."

"Penny, please…" He reached out for me, his hand connecting with my forearm.

I felt the same shock as before. He was strong. And kind and patient. I wanted to be able to lean into him and let him fix everything. But I couldn't lean on a figment of my imagination. "I've lost my mind." I rushed past him toward the door.

"Penny, don't go out there…"

But I had already flung the door open and was running out of the room. I needed fresh air. I couldn't breathe in this hospital.

"Penny, stop!"

I flung open a door at the end of the hall. Strangers turned toward me from their seats in the waiting room. No, not complete strangers. I had met several of them yesterday. Some of James' friends. His father. My eyes landed on my parents. *Thank God.* I was just about to yell for my mom, but someone beat me to it.

"Mommy!"

I turned around to see a little girl with bright red hair running toward me. I saw another reflection of myself. A younger version of me. She looked exactly like I did when I was a kid. And I felt something snap in my head. Like any sanity I had left had evaporated.

I was watching myself from my past. I wasn't actually here. Was I dead? I felt tears start to fall down my cheeks. My life was replaying before me. I stepped out of the way of my childhood self, wondering if she'd be able to just run right through me anyway.

But instead of going toward my parents, she turned toward me. I stepped to the side again, and she altered her path again.

The little girl threw herself on me, wrapping her small arms around my legs. "Mommy, Mommy. I missed you." She peppered kisses on my thigh.

"You have the wrong person, sweetheart," I said as calmly as I could muster. "Your mom is over there." I pointed to my mother.

The little girl pulled back from me and cocked her head to the side as she studied me. "No, you're my mommy. That's Grandma."

What?

"She's your mommy, Mommy. The stork brought you to her. Like he brought me to you and Daddy. And Liam too. He's the most beautiful baby in the whole wide world. Do you want to see?" She grabbed my hand.

I immediately pulled away and took a step back. I collided into a strong chest. The smell of James' cologne engulfed me. It felt like I was suffocating. I stepped away from him.

"Penny." He reached for me, but I backed away.

"No."

"Penny, let's get back to your room." He reached for me again.

"No. No, no, no, no…" I couldn't stop saying it. I needed my parents. Not whatever the hell this was. "Mom!" I started to run over to them. "Mom, Dad, take me home. Tears cascaded down my cheeks. "Please take me home."

"Mommy!" The little girl yelled as she followed me. "Mommy!"

"Would someone get Scarlett out of here?" James said sternly.

"No, I want my mommy!" she screamed at the top of her lungs. "No!" She started crying as James' brother lifted her into his arms. "No!" she screamed. "Mommy! Mommy, Mommy, I need you! No!"

I could still hear her screams as the door closed behind them. Or was it my own screams? Because I sounded just like her. Yelling for my parents. Begging for them to fix this.

"Take me home." I was choking on my tears.

My parents were just sitting there, staring at me like I truly had lost my mind. I had. I knew that I had.

James wrapped his arms around me and started whispering in my ear to calm me down. But his breath wasn't calming. It made my heart race faster. God, I was going to throw up.

"Penny," he said in the soothing tone you'd use for a distraught child. "It's going to be okay. You're going to remember everything soon. Us. Your children."

Children plural? "Get off of me." I tried to wiggle out of his grip. People in the waiting room that I didn't recognize were staring at us. Judging my insanity. "There is no us." I said the word "us" with disgust. "And I don't have any children with you. I don't have any children at all."

James shook his head. "You must have seen the similarities…"

I pushed him off of me. "That was not my daughter. I'm the daughter." I pointed to my chest. "Mom, tell him. Tell him none of this is real." I was barely getting the words out, I was crying so hard.

A doctor rushed in. "Mrs. Hunter, if you would just take a deep breath."

"What's happened to me?" I choked.

James tried to reach for me.

"Mr. Hunter, that's enough," the doctor said, stepping in front of him.

"She's upset, I'm trying to calm her down," James said.

"You're the one upsetting her. Can't you see that? Just give her some space."

I wanted to hug the doctor. But all my fears came bubbling to the surface. "Am I sick? Am I dying? I'm delirious. I'm imagining things. I'm imagining him." I pointed to James, hoping that the doctor couldn't actually see him. Hoping that I was as confused as I believed I was. Hoping that everything was a dream.

"Mrs. Hunter, I need you to take a deep breath."

"That's not my name."

"Okay, Penny, just take a breath. We're going to get you back to your room."

"Make him stay out," I said and pointed to James. "He slept in my bed last night. I woke up and his arms were around me." I started to scratch my skin, trying to rid myself of the feeling of his touch.

The doctor frowned. "Mr. Hunter, how many times do we have to talk about visiting hours? You're not allowed..."

"She needs me," James said, trying to sidestep the doctor. "How can she remember if I stay away from her?"

I started sobbing harder. "I don't need you. I need to get out of here. I need to go home. Let me go home! Mom, Dad, please. Please."

A nurse rushed in carrying a needle.

"Don't hurt her!" James yelled.

But the needle was already being pierced into my arm. The room slowly blurred in front of me. And I entered the dreamlike state I thought I was already in.

CHAPTER 6

Thursday

No matter what I did, I couldn't wake up from this dream.

"Today's the day you get out of here," my doctor said cheerily as he strolled into my room. He sighed when he saw me. "You need to stop pinching yourself, Penny. This isn't a dream that you can wake up from. He put his hand on top of mine to stop me from pinching my skin.

"I know it's not a dream. It's a freaking nightmare."

He lifted his hand. "We've talked about this. You're suffering from amnesia. Your memory should come back."

"My memory is fine."

"You fighting it isn't helping."

"I'm trying to hold on to my life." I felt like I was drowning.

"Getting back into your normal routine is going to help you remember," he said, ignoring me. "Your husband is filling out the discharge forms as we speak. And he left a change of clothes for you in the restroom."

"Please don't make me leave with him."

"From everything I've heard and seen, you two are very much in love."

A forced laugh came from my lips.

"You're one of the lucky ones."

I certainly didn't feel lucky. Everything I knew and loved had been stripped from me. I was transported into this world I didn't understand. With a brooding fake husband and a daughter? I didn't know what was real anymore. Maybe I had imagined the little girl. I probably had. She'd never come to visit me in my room. Maybe I was imagining James. *Please let me have imagined James too.*

"Are you ever going to tell me about my scars?" I had brought it up yesterday after I came out of my forced sleep. But the doctor had insisted that I needed more rest.

He sat down in the chair next to my bed. "You've been having a hard time accepting things as it is. How about we make an appointment for you to come talk next week?"

"So it's bad, huh?"

"You need to take it easy. You were unconscious for two weeks. You can't resume normal activity for at least another two."

"Is it my liver?" God, I just knew it was my liver. I could feel it.

He smiled. "No. Your liver is functioning properly. There's nothing to worry about there."

"So there is something to worry about?"

"No, no. You'll live a full happy life. Come see me in a week." He stood up.

Now that I was about to leave the hospital, everything suddenly felt real. It was slowly sinking in that I was stuck in whatever joke of a life this was. With a man I didn't know. What was he going to expect of me when I went back to his place? I swallowed hard. I couldn't do this. "There's nothing you can do to jog my memory?"

"I know all of this is shocking. And it's going to take some time to adjust. But please, try to accept what you hear. Everyone's just trying to help. That 19 year old that you're holding on to? From everything I've read about you and your family, you turned into quite the impressive young woman. Embrace her. You've been given the whole world. You'll never want for anything."

That wasn't true. I wanted my old life back. But what did he mean by that? Was I rich? Had I robbed a bank? Had I won the Nobel Peace Prize? "Is James famous or something? Or…am I famous? Or…"

"Your husband will fill you in," my doctor said. "In the meantime, if you don't want to embrace this life, how about you pretend this is all real? Make a game of it."

"You're joking."

He shook his head. "It might help. You're going to have quite the eventful day. See you in a week, Penny."

At least he hadn't called me Mrs. Hunter.

***

Make-believe. I didn't have to truly believe it. I just had to pretend to believe it.

I finished dressing and stared into the mirror at the face I didn't recognize. *I can do this. Right?*

The dress I was wearing was sophisticated and uncomfortable. I missed my leggings and tank tops. Maybe they'd be back at my place. *Our place. God.*

How could I play make-believe when I didn't even know what I was about to get myself into? I had no idea where I lived. No idea who I was. I took a deep breath. *Just pretend. It'll all be over soon.*

I smiled at my reflection and tried not to grimace at the face I didn't recognize.

"Penny," James said with a knock on the door.

I opened it and stared at my husband. Just thinking about the word "husband" did make me believe I was in an alternate world. *Accept it.*

"You ready to get out of here?" He looked hopeful. And tired. Or maybe it was something else. The brown hue of his eyes seemed to swirl with secrets. I found myself wanting to know every single one of them before I awoke from this dream.

"Yup. Take me home, husband."

He gave me a strange look. "You've stopped fighting the truth?"

"Sure."

He shook his head, clearly not believing me. But he put out his hand for me anyway.

I slipped my hand into his and felt the same spark that I had yesterday. I could get used to this. It was easy to feel safe by his side as we made our way through the hospital.

"The car is right outside," he said as he stopped before the exit. His hand fell from mine and I instantly felt cold.

"Aren't you coming?"

"Yeah, I'll be right there." He looked down at his watch like he was studying something.

"Is everything okay?"

He smiled and looked back up at me. "Everything's fine, Penny. I just forgot something from your room. I'll be right back down."

"I'll see you at the car then." I made my way out the doors even though I had no idea what our car looked like. I glanced over my shoulder before the doors closed. James had his hand pressed against the wall and was hunched over slightly. Maybe he wasn't as broken as I originally thought. Maybe the dark circles under his eyes weren't caused by me. Maybe it was something else entirely. He looked...ill.

I was about to walk back into the hospital when someone called my name. I turned around just in time to see the man before he threw his arms around me.

"I knew you needed me back," he said. "Despite what Jen thinks, this is the best position I've ever had, and I'm not going anywhere this time."

Who the hell was this? And who the hell was Jen? "Oh, okay," I said without hugging him back.

He pulled away. "Sorry. I...let me start over. I'm Ian." He held out his hand for me to shake. "I'm engaged to James' sister, Jen. You know...your sister-in-law."

"Ah, got you." I had met Jen the other day. *I think.* "So you're my soon to be brother-in-law."

"Also the head of your security detail."

"Security detail? Why on earth do we need a security detail?"

"Well, for starters because it seems like everyone's out to get you."

I laughed. "Who? I don't think I have any enemies. I barely talk enough for someone to realize if they hate me or not."

"Just trust me when I say that you need us."

"There's more than just you?"

"Four of us in total. You had three and then you hired me back."

"Me?" I thought three security guards wasn't enough? What kind of paranoid weirdo had I become?

"Yes, you," James said as he rejoined me, slipping his arm around my waist. He did it like it was the most normal thing in the world. Like he didn't realize how much his touch accelerated my heartbeat. "Let's get you home."

Ian opened up the back door of the car in front of us. A sleek black sedan that probably cost more than my college tuition.

"So we have a security detail?" I asked as I slid into the back seat. *And a fancy car that we don't drive ourselves.* I stared at James as he sat down next to me.

"To keep us safe," he said as he buckled his seatbelt.

"From who?"

"When you're in the limelight like us, you'd be surprised by how many people are a threat."

"And why are we in the limelight? Are you like a famous actor or something?" It seemed like the most logical conclusion. He was beautiful. There was no doubt about that. His dark brown eyes and sharp jaw line would make anyone in their right mind weak in the knees. And it really seemed like he was part of some elaborate scheme to make me feel insane. But if that was the case, he probably wasn't an A-list actor. Maybe he was just starting out in showbiz.

He sighed. "A lot of reasons."

"Like?"

"I sold my first company for a large sum." He shrugged. "We donate to a lot of great charities. The way we met didn't exactly pull me out of the limelight either. It just thrust you into it."

"You avoided my question about how we met before. Are you going to answer it now?"

"I fell in love with you the moment I saw you."

His words reverberated through me. I could feel that he was telling the truth. It made our make-believe relationship feel real. "And how did you meet me?"

He smiled. "We bumped into each other in a coffee shop."

"That hardly sounds like something that would make us need a security detail."

He lowered both his eyebrows. "Well you weren't just some woman who stole my affection." He paused, catching my gaze. There were so many secrets swirling in his dark irises. I wanted to know everything he was holding back.

"I wasn't?"

"No." He reached out and cupped the side of my face in his large hand. "As much as I wished that you were, that wasn't the case."

"Because I'm only 19? Er...*was* only 19."

He lowered both eyebrows. "Yes. But more so because you were my student."

I started laughing.

His expression didn't change.

I started laughing harder. And I couldn't seem to stop. So he wasn't an actor after all. But he was most definitely a comedian.

CHAPTER 7
Thursday

James hadn't taken his eyes off of me since I laughed at our apparent meet cute. A coffee shop? Too cliché to have really happened, but a dream was supposed to be cliché, right? But him being my professor on top of that? Ludicrous. Hilarious. Absurd. So why wasn't he laughing?

It wasn't worth dwelling on. This man sitting next to me wasn't real. And he certainly wasn't a professor. No chance. I knew professors. They were usually in their fifties, had comb-overs, and carried their weight all wrong. James was the complete opposite. He was older than me, but he was still young. And fit. I wouldn't be surprised if he had abs of steel under his dress shirt. And why wouldn't he? It was my dream. I had plenty of dreams of hot men falling head over heels for me. Didn't everyone?

He closed his eyes and pressed his lips together like he was holding back a sigh. I stared at the dark circles under his eyes again. Or maybe he was holding back a grimace. He truly did look like he was in pain. Before I could ask, he opened his eyes again and ran his fingers through his hair.

More proof that he wasn't a professor – he had a head full of dark hair that just begged for me to run my fingers through it. Now I was the one pressing my lips together. Where on earth had that thought come from? I was being sucked into this fantasy. It happened to me a lot. Whenever I read, I always pretended I was the main character. I had traveled the world through books. Fought monsters. Fallen in love. I had done more make-believe than actual living. And this felt like some weird combination of the two. I tried to shake the thought away. *This. Isn't. Real.*

I'd wake up soon enough and Melissa and I could laugh about this dream together. I could already hear her analyzing my dream in her head. She'd probably say something like, "Clearly you need to move on from Austin and you're dying to go to this party with me tonight!" Or something equally unhelpful. Just the thought made me smile.

I glanced at James again. Even though I desperately wanted to wake up, it didn't mean I couldn't enjoy this dream. I had told the doctor I'd play along. And that's what I was going to do.

The car slowed down to a stop in front of a towering building.

"Here we are," Ian said from the front seat.

"What's here?" I asked. Was he taking me to work or something? Was it take your imaginary wife to work day? This certainly didn't look like a college. *I knew he wasn't a professor!*

James unbuckled his seatbelt. "We're home."

"Home?" I looked out the car window at the building. "It looks so…un-homey."

James laughed. "When we first moved to New York, you said every apartment looked cold. But trust me, you love it here." He reached over and unbuckled my seatbelt.

How could I possibly love living in this building? I loved grass and trees and fresh air. You probably couldn't even open a window in that building. What kind of life was that? I looked over at him, and he was staring at me so intently. And I found myself wanting to trust him. What was the harm in that for now?

"Okay, husband, show me the way."

He smiled. "As you wish, wife."

I laughed. "Oh, I love that movie."

"What movie?"

"The Princess Bride. Westley always says, 'As you wish,' to Buttercup but really he means 'I love you, I love you, I love you!' And it took her so long to realize it."

He just stared at me. "I've never seen it."

"What do you mean you've never seen it? It's my favorite movie. You're my husband, of course you've seen it."

"You never told me."

I never told him? What kind of sham of a marriage was this? Did we rarely ever talk? Was it a marriage of convenience somehow? It didn't matter. It wasn't real anyway. "Well, come on then. Let's go watch it right now." I opened up the door and stepped out onto the city street.

A wave of hot air hit me. And the stench of trash. I scrunched up my nose. *Welcome home to me.*

Ian was standing there like he had been about to open the door for me. He said he was a security guard, not a driver. Did he usually open the door? He looked upset. Had I done something to offend him?

He gave me an odd look, his hand still awkwardly outstretched.

"Thank you so much for the ride." I thrust my hand into his and shook it.

"Penny, get back into the car," he said, his voice much more serious than it had been when we first met.

"Um…isn't this my home? I'd like to go see it." *This should be fun.*

Ian put his hand on my shoulder and tried to push me back into the car with too much force.

"Don't touch me," I hissed and tried to shove his hand away. When he tried to push me again, I yelled, "Don't touch me!"

"Jesus." James climbed out of the car and grabbed my hand with a harsh tug. "Come on."

I pulled my hand out of his. I wasn't going anywhere with him. Not when he looked like he was about to kill someone. I was wrong before, I didn't want to trust him. He didn't seem like someone I could ever rely on. He seemed angry and irrational and unkind.

He grabbed my forearm, this time his fingers dug into my skin. "Penny, we need to get back in the car."

"Stop." I tried to pull away, but he gripped my arm even tighter.

A swarm of people surrounded us, microphones were thrust into my face, cameras flashed.

"Mrs. Hunter, are you alright?"

"Is the baby okay?"

"Penny, where is the baby?"

Baby? What baby? I thought about the little redheaded girl from my dream. A figment of my imagination of myself as a child. The one that had run toward me instead of toward my mother. That had been a dream, right? God, it was too hard to keep everything straight. My head started to swirl.

"Back away before I called the cops," Ian said, trying to keep the microphones out of my face.

I felt my body start shaking. My heart raced. Why did all these reporters care about me? I tried to back away from them and ran into James' hard chest.

"Jesus, you're shaking."

How did I find comfort in his voice when I barely knew him?

He wrapped his arms around me, sending warmth I didn't know I needed through my body.

A microphone was held out a few inches from my lips.

"Penny, have you and James fully recovered?"

James' strong arms tensed around me.

Had he been hurt too? What had happened to him? He was the one thing in this crazy fantasy that was able to calm me down. I didn't want to lose him. Although he did freak me out at the same time. But facing all of this newness on my own didn't sound very appealing. Why wasn't I just allowed to go home with my parents?

"I need to get out of here," I whispered.

The man with the microphone gave me an odd look.

"Get me out of here. I want to go home. Please take me home." I tried to swallow down the lump in my throat, but it wouldn't go away.

"Back up!" Ian yelled, but more people were swarming us. Flashes. Voices. He knocked the mic out of my face.

I closed my eyes. I felt like I was going to faint. "Please."

And then I was being lifted up and over James' shoulder. My eyes flew open and I was staring down at his ass. His very perfect looking ass. But its perfection didn't distract me from wondering what he was doing. I hadn't been asked to be lifted like a child. I was about to protest, but he pushed through the front doors of the building and the blast of air-conditioning and silence of the lobby made my breath come back. I felt myself sink into him.

"It's okay," he said gently. "You're safe."

I had asked to go home. But in my dream, this was my home. *Try to embrace it.*

James' breathing sounded labored.

"You can put me down," I said. I thought about my strange beer belly. It was probably hard to lift me. "I know I'm a little heavy."

He laughed, but slowly set me down on my feet. "You're not heavy, Penny." But his face looked ghostly pale. And his breathing still didn't sound normal.

I stayed pressed against him, staring up into his eyes. "You were hurt too."

"Penny, I'm fine."

"You don't look fine. Whatever hurt me also got you too, didn't it?"

He touched the side of my cheek ever so slightly.

I tried not to wince or step back. I continued to stare at him. What was he hiding from me?

"Truly, I'm fine." He ran the pad of his thumb along my cheek. "Let's get you home, okay?"

Whatever had happened to him, he didn't want to talk about it with me. I wondered if he usually would. Maybe he didn't recognize me as much as I didn't recognize me. I stepped back, not able to keep staring into his eyes so intently. "So that's what being badgered by paparazzi feels like? No wonder so many celebrities punch them in the face and wind up in rehab."

James laughed.

I smiled at him. I liked when he laughed. "Heck, I'd probably start drinking too if they followed me around all the time. I'd be one of those crazy people in rehab." I laughed at my own joke. "How do we usually deal with them?"

He lowered both his eyebrows and the smile on his face vanished.

What had I done wrong now? James' smiles seemed so rare. I wanted them to be permanently affixed to his face. He was too serious. Way too serious for me.

"I'm sorry if I did something to offend you," I said. "I'm new to all this. I mean…" I awkwardly cleared my throat. *Just keep pretending.* "Let's just go home, okay?" I instinctively walked back toward the exit.

"Our place is upstairs," James said.

I turned around. *Of course.* "Right. We're on floor…"

"Let me just show you," he said and lightly touched my lower back to guide me toward the elevators.

It seemed like he wanted some kind of expression from me as we walked through the luxurious lobby of the apartment building. But it all made sense to me. In my fantasy, this is what I had. And I was having an easy time pretending it was real now. How wonderful would it be if it was reality? I mean, it was enough to make anyone swoon. But I knew it wasn't real.

We were rich in my make-believe world. Even the elevators were decadent. The music that was playing through the speakers was straight from a 1950's movie. It was all elaborately overdone. I had an overactive imagination.

And to think in my dream world I'd had a scandalous affair with my super hot professor. Who just so happened to be rich? Yeah, right. Never could have happened. First of all, I never would have dated my professor. Second of all, professors weren't rich. Tenure didn't make you wealthy and he was too young for it anyway. I laughed out loud.

"Something amusing?" James asked as the elevators dinged open on our floor.

"Nope. This all seems...normal enough for a fantasy. But seriously, James, how did we meet? We both know you couldn't afford any of this as a professor."

"I was serious when I said I sold my first company for a large sum."

"How large?"

He didn't respond. He just guided me down the hall to a door. *Our door.* He unlocked it and turned the knob. I didn't even care that he hadn't answered my question. Because I wouldn't have been able to listen anyway. It felt like all the air had been knocked out of my lungs. I took a step into the immaculate foyer. This was an apartment, right?

I looked through the kitchen to the right at the ornate, winding staircase. Did apartments have two floors? I had never seen anything like it in movies.

I turned my attention back to the foyer and saw that there was natural light streaming in. I walked through the foyer into a huge living room that was open to a dining area as well. But my eyes weren't on the room itself or the furniture. I walked toward the far wall. Although, it wasn't really a wall at all. The whole side of the apartment was glass.

I could see Central Park from the window. Cars still swerved and honked below, but it was easy to focus on all the greenery. It was breathtakingly beautiful.

"Do you like the view?" James asked.

I jumped at the sound of his voice. I had almost forgotten he was there. I laughed and folded my arms across my chest so I wouldn't be tempted to put my hands on the glass. "The city's actually kind of pretty from up here." I nodded toward the window.

"Being close to Central Park was one of the reasons why you agreed to move here."

"Yeah?" That made sense.

"And you can even see where we got married from here." He pointed to a large tree in the distance. It looked like a restaurant was beside it. There were tables beneath the tree and happy couples dining.

"It's pretty." I didn't know what else to say. I couldn't remember our wedding. Had it really happened? Was I even standing here right now? I glanced over at James.

He was staring at me in that way again. Like he could read my soul. Like he knew every secret I possessed. Like he knew me better than I knew myself.

CHAPTER 8
Thursday

I wasn't sure I had ever felt so awkward in my life. Looking at our wedding spot in the distance, standing by a man I didn't know, and feeling so lost. I didn't know how to clear the tension in the air. And as soon as I thought about the awkwardness, I realized I was missing a whole element of it. On top of everything else, I was alone with a man I didn't know. All alone. In this huge apartment. What did he want me to do?

"So where do I sleep?" I asked. *Really? You're jumping right to the sleeping arrangements? What is wrong with you?* I could feel my face turning red.

He smiled down at me.

God, his smile made me nervous. "Forget that last question. Is it okay if I go for a run? I think I just need some fresh air." The park across the street was calling to me. Maybe if I got in the very middle of it, I'd forget I was in the city. *Unlikely.*

"You don't like to run," he said.

I shrugged. "Usually I don't. But I feel like it today."

"No, I mean you really don't like to run. You hate running. Trust me."

I think I know myself better than you do. I bit the inside of my lip. *I think.* "So you know that but you don't know my favorite movie? Interesting." I tried to give him what I hoped was a playful smile and not a horrified one.

"Have you ever considered that when we met, that was no longer your favorite movie?"

No. Why would it change? "So what do you think it is?"

"You don't have one. You've always claimed that you don't. You're adamant about it really."

"And yet, I know my favorite movie. You're the one that doesn't."

He laughed, but it sounded exasperated. "I don't know what you want me to say."

"I want you to tell me anything that makes sense. It doesn't seem like you know me at all."

"You've changed a lot in seven years."

"So much so that I've lost myself?" I didn't mean for the words to spill out, but they did. And now it was too late. I hated that he looked hurt because of me.

"Some stupid movie doesn't define you, Penny."

"I'm not saying it does." My breathing was growing uneven. I should have been backtracking, going back to make-believe, but I couldn't stop myself. "And I'm not even talking about the movie. I mean all of this." I gestured to the enormous living room. "This isn't me. I like simple things. Homey things."

"I know. It's one of the many reasons why I love you."

"Then why do we live here? What happened to me to make me say all of this was okay?"

He ran his fingers through his hair, and I had the oddest sensation that if he hadn't, his fist would have gone through one of the walls.

"You fell in love with me," he said. "We fell in love. And we made all these decisions together. You love it here. All our family and friends are here."

"Oh, my parents live in New York?" I couldn't imagine them leaving their jobs in Wilmington. They loved them. *How strange.*

"I meant everyone besides your parents."

"I see." This conversation was pointless. I never should have started it. "I think what you meant was that your family and friends are here. Not mine."

"They're yours too."

I wanted to yell at him. I wanted to throw all the stupid decorative pillows off the couch. But I heard my doctor's voice in the back of my head. I was supposed to play along. Would me agreeing with James take away the worry line on his forehead? Would it really make everything smoother? Because it didn't feel like it would for me. I took a deep breath. Pretending made it easier for everyone but me.

"Penny." He stepped closer to me. Too close. His cologne was polluting my air supply.

"It's fine," I said. "I'm sorry I freaked out. I don't have any of my own friends. Got it. What about Melissa, though? Did we lose touch?" The thought made me want to cry. I had been holding out hope to talk to her. It felt like she was the only one that could help me.

"Baby, my friends are your friends. That's what I'm trying to tell you. Honestly, they probably like you more than they like me."

Did he expect me to laugh at that? "Awesome." I tried to keep my voice light and upbeat.

It just made him sigh. "And you and Melissa are still friends. She was planning on coming to town when the..." his voice trailed off. "I mean, she'll be here tomorrow. It was the earliest she could get off work."

"Melissa's coming?" I didn't even have to pretend to be excited at that news. "That's wonderful. She'll stay with us, right?"

"We usually offer to put guests up in that the hotel down the street while they visit."

"Why? This place seems big enough. Don't we have any guest rooms?"

"Two actually. But we prefer our privacy."

"Privacy for what? I'll text her and let her know she can stay here." I looked down at my shoulder and realized I didn't have a backpack. Or a purse. Or any of my things. I turned in a circle. "Where's my phone?"

"I want to be able to focus on just us for a little bit. I want to try to get you used to our lives. Together."

Was he keeping me hostage here? I thought about how he said I couldn't go for a run earlier. How he wouldn't let anyone stay here with us. How he had taken away my phone. I stared at him. There were a lot of red flags. But what could it hurt to let this weird fantasy play out? Maybe if I let it, I'd be able to wake up. I'd be able to go back to a time where I didn't know this man. "Okay."

He lowered both his eyebrows as he stared at me.

The action made me swallow hard. I wasn't sure I had ever seen anything so sexy in my entire life.

"Okay?" he asked. "That's it? I'm used to you putting up a little more of a fight."

I laughed. Finally something that sounded like me. "Sure. So what exactly did you want to do in this huge apartment all alone?"

This time he was the one that swallowed hard. I could tell because I had the pleasure of watching his Adam's apple rise and fall. Maybe I was wrong before, because this was the new sexiest thing I had ever seen.

"How about we start with a tour?" he asked as he stepped closer to me.

"Mhm." My voice came out weird and high-pitched. Had he seen me staring at him? I backed up and my butt collided with the couch behind me. "Okay, so…the living room."

"You've always been very intelligent," he said.

I laughed and folded my arms across my chest as I looked around the room. My eyes landed on a framed piece of artwork above the fireplace. It looked like it was taken from the boardwalk of Rehoboth Beach. I used to love going there with my parents. I smiled, picturing myself walking along the boardwalk. I had always wished that I had someone to hold hands with. It always felt like I was the only single person in existence on those lazy summer nights. But I wasn't alone right now. I wondered if I had told him that story.

"That painting is nice," I said. "It reminds me of summer trips with my parents to the beach."

"One of our first dates was a day trip to Rehoboth. We picked out this painting because it reminded us of that."

I smiled. "You know, I always wished I had a boyfriend to walk along the boardwalk with."

"I know."

He knew? I glanced at him out of the corner of my eye. He was staring at the painting like it was a distant memory. I had a million questions. Had we only ever been once? Did he like to play in the water or was he scared of sharks? And speaking of sharks, did he even like Shark Tank? Did we have the same hobbies? Did he truly love me?

"And now you have a husband to accompany you on the boardwalk."

I laughed. "Accompany? That's such a serious way to put it. It's more of a skipping, dancing, twirling in the ocean breeze kind of boardwalk experience in my mind. I'm starting to think you don't know how to have any fun."

"Trust me, I know how to have a good time. Especially at the beach."

"Why *especially* at the beach?"

"The first time we went together, we went skinny-dipping and some stupid kids stole your bikini."

I laughed. "I strongly doubt I did something so reckless." No favorite movie *and* skinny-dipping? Who the hell was this Penny Hunter person?

"Well, then maybe you're the one that doesn't know how to have any fun." He raised his left eyebrow like he was challenging me.

I rolled my eyes. "You can have fun without public indecency."

"But the best kind of fun is public indecency."

"If you want to wind up behind bars. Thanks, but no thanks. I don't want to end up in jail. My parents would kill me."

"Your parents can't exactly ground you anymore, Penny. You're 26 years old."

"Right." *Right! God, I'm 26 in this alternate reality!* I could legally drink alcohol. Now that was something that would make this fantasy easier to digest. "Speaking of being old, we should like...make a toast or something. To...being married."

James smiled. "Penny, you just stopped taking morphine yesterday. We should probably give it more time to flush out of your system."

"But I feel fine."

"That's probably the morphine talking."

"Oh come on. I'm a skinny-dipping jailbird. I'm sure I can handle my alcohol." I wandered into the kitchen and was happy that he didn't stop me. I opened up the stainless steel refrigerator and stared at the contents inside. Fresh fruits and vegetables jumped out from everywhere. I had never seen such a well-stocked fridge. And nothing was premade, it was all fresh ingredients. In the back corner I saw a bottle of white wine that was half empty. I grabbed it and opened up one of the cupboards. Only plates. Tons and tons of plates. Who had so many plates and what on earth were they all for?

"Next one over," James said.

I opened up the next cabinet and pulled out two wine glasses.

"None for me," he said from behind me.

Party for one then. I poured myself a glass and lifted it into the air as I turned to face him. "Here's to being in love." That was everything I'd ever wanted. And I had it. I could tell I did by the way he stared at me as I took my first sip. By the way his eyes lingered on my lips. By the way he so desperately wanted me to remember him.

I had never been in love before. I didn't know what I was supposed to feel. Or what I should suspect. All I knew was that his gaze made me nervous. And when he touched me I felt like I had been zapped by a bug zapper. I took a huge gulp of my wine. "This is great."

"I'm pretty sure that bottle has been open for weeks."

"I wouldn't be able to tell the difference. This is actually my first glass of wine." I swirled it in my glass as I looked down at the amber liquid. "So, we opened it before my accident? I mean…is that what it was? An accident? No one's told me what happened."

"It's a conversation for another day. When you're able to remember."

"But what if I never remember?"

He shook his head. "You will." But his tone screamed, "you have to."

I took another sip of my wine. "It must have been something serious. I have scars on my stomach. And I'm…fat."

"Baby, you are not fat."

The way he said "baby" made goosebumps rise on my skin. Did he often call me that? I liked the way it sounded. "Baby." I smiled. "No one's ever called me that." I awkwardly cleared my throat. "Besides you, I mean. You call me that."

"I do."

I smiled at him. "I like it." And I really did. It made me feel special. Safe. Warm. I tucked a loose strand of hair behind my ear. "So how about that tour?" I grabbed the bottle of wine to bring with me. I told myself that it was because I'd need to refill my glass again soon. But maybe a small piece of me was worried that I wouldn't keep my hands to myself. And I needed to keep my hands to myself. Fantasy or not, I didn't know this man. My reaction to him didn't make any sense. Technically I was kind of sort of still dating Austin. And I wasn't a cheater. That was Austin's job. *I really should break up with that prick.*

Maybe this was all a dream to motivate me to move on. A dream to show me that there was someone out there for me that was better than Austin. I followed James out of the kitchen and tried not to sigh at the sight of him. Hopefully that someone that was out there for me would be as sexy as my fake husband.

CHAPTER 9

Thursday

Most parts of this life would be easy to adjust to. A penthouse apartment that overlooked Central Park made the idea of being stuck in a city I hated a little more appealing. And my closet? I stared at the organized rows of dresses. I had never seen so many designer clothes. Everything in this apartment, even the closets, was over the top lavish.

But there were also secrets. A couple locked doors. Nails in the walls that held nothing at all. Like something important had been removed from existence. It was unnerving that I had no idea what it was.

And then there was James. He was the epitome of unnerving. In a lot of ways, he wasn't even my type. Or maybe he was, but he was just a little too old for me to realize it. He didn't exactly look that old, but he certainly acted older than me. He even refused to drink with me. I had to finish the bottle of wine alone. It kind of seemed like he had a stick up his perfect butt. Every time I looked at him, he was studying me seriously instead of smiling. His smiles were short. His laughter shorter.

I took one more glance at the contents of the closet. There were more shoes than I could even count. Mostly high heels. Everything looked amazing, but honestly, all I wanted to do was change out of this stiff dress into something actually comfortable. Were there any unsophisticated clothes in here? Leggings? Tank tops? Anything that would cover me from head to foot so I felt safe around James tonight?

I knew I was dilly-dallying. But as soon as I found something to wear to sleep, I'd actually have to crawl into bed with a stranger. My attempts at suggesting I stay in a guest room were all immediately thwarted. And he didn't seem to take the hint that maybe he should sleep in one of them. It was his house. I couldn't force him. I bit the inside of my lip. Where were the freaking sweatpants?

"Your nightgowns are in the second drawer from the top," James said from the master bedroom.

Nightgowns? What was I, 80 years old? *I'll wear a pair of pajamas to bed, thank you very much.* I opened up the drawer and looked down at the silk and lace scraps of material. These weren't big enough to be nightgowns. I was pretty sure the last nightgown I owned had been flannel and floor length. I could picture myself wearing it on Christmas morning. No way in hell was I wearing one of these skimpy things.

"Where are all my favorite pajamas?" I asked and turned around.

James was leaning against the doorjamb with his arms folded across his chest. Staring. Always staring. "You don't own any pajamas."

"What about my favorite ones with the little panda bears all over them?"

He just stared at me. "I've never seen them."

"What about a pair of sweatpants?" I was capable of compromise.

"You don't own any of those either."

"Seriously? They're like my go-to thing to comfort me after a bad day. Well, that and ice cream."

"The ice cream I know. But usually you come to me to be comforted. The sweatpants probably just aren't necessary anymore."

Oh. That was sweet. However, it didn't take away from the fact that I was sweatpants-less in a time of crisis.

"I'll let you change." He left me alone in the huge closet.

I turned back around. What kind of uptight woman had I become? No sweatpants or comfy pajamas. The horror of it all. I lifted up one of the silky nightgowns. It looked like something a porn star would wear. The t-shirts on James' side of the closet were calling to me. At least they'd be long enough to cover my ass. I grabbed a black one off the hanger and quickly changed.

I studied my reflection in the mirror. Simple. Unsexy. I smiled to myself. I had always loved in romantic comedies when the female lead wore the hero's shirt to bed. It seemed chic and sexy…my thoughts came to a halt. I didn't want to be sexy. I wanted to be the opposite of sexy. I wanted to be frumpy.

My eyes scanned the closet once more but I didn't see a better alternative. *God, please already be asleep.* I stepped out of the closet, tugging at the hem of the shirt, hoping to lower it even more.

James was sitting on the edge of the bed, leaning forward with his elbows on his knees. He looked exhausted. But his eyes lit up when he saw me. Like I had done something to make him happy, even though all I had done was stolen one of his t-shirts.

"I'm sorry, I should have asked." I stopped pulling on the fabric. "It just seemed more comfortable than those…nightgowns." I had almost lost my words because he had chosen that moment to sit up straight. He had lost his shirt and was only wearing a pair of boxers. And he was perfect. Every cut of muscle on his stomach made him look like a Greek God. His arms were lean and strong. His skin was even perfectly tanned.

"It's fine. Really." He smiled at me staring at him. And this smile didn't look concerned or tinged with sadness. He looked genuinely happy.

"Alright. So…" my voice trailed off. "I guess that's my side." I pointed to the opposite side of the bed that he was sitting, trying my best not to keep ogling him.

"Unless you'd prefer here," he said.

"No, that's okay." I walked over to my side of the bed and pushed back the sheets. I figured once he fell asleep, I'd slip out of bed and go sleep on the couch downstairs. Or maybe I'd take the time to figure out how to unlock one of the doors down the hall. Or find some of the pictures that had been removed from the walls.

I slid into bed and pulled the covers up to my chin. I felt him staring at me before he switched off the lights. The bed sagged slightly when he climbed in, but he didn't try to come on my side.

I kept my eyes open, waiting for them to adjust to the darkness. Hints of his cologne swirled around me. I'd had too much to drink tonight. Or maybe it was his cologne intoxicating me. But words spilled out of me to fill the silence. "I'm glad I married you," I said. *And not Austin.* What a nightmare that would have been.

"Me too." His words sounded harsh and broken, like maybe he was holding back tears.

The sound made tears well in my own eyes. "I'm trying. To remember." I wasn't sure if that was true. But it would be tomorrow. I needed to do a better job pretending. I didn't want to break him any more than he was broken.

"This is hard for me too," he said into the darkness.

"I know." My voice was quiet. I remembered waking up in my hospital bed with his arms wrapped around me. I had thought he was Austin. But if I was being honest, I had never felt that content in Austin's arms. It was like my body knew it belonged to this man, but my heart and head didn't understand. But I wanted to feel comforted again. And I didn't have any sweatpants in this apartment. I slid my hand into the middle of the bed.

Even though the act had been silent, it was like James could tell I was reaching for him. His hand slid toward mine. Just the tips of our fingers touched. But it felt momentous to me.

CHAPTER 10

Friday

I half expected to wake up in the cocoon of warmth that only James' arms seemed to provide. But I wasn't tucked into his side when I opened my eyes. His smell was still all around me though. I sighed. So I was still stuck in this alternate reality. I took a deep breath. Why was I comforted by the smell of him?

"Morning, hot stuff," said a deep, unfamiliar voice.

I screamed at the top of my lungs as I fell off the bed in a pathetic attempt to get away.

"Shit. You okay?"

I looked up at the face staring down at me. It was the man that looked similar to James. His brother. I couldn't remember his name. "What are you doing in my bed?" Was this a brother thing? Them showing up in inappropriate places?

"I promised James I'd watch you. And when I got here last night you were already sleeping." He climbed off the bed and stuck his hand out for me to help me to my feet.

I ignored his outstretched hand and scrambled to my feet by myself. "That doesn't answer my question. Why were you sleeping next to me instead of James?"

"Because I was tired." He pushed his hair away from his eyes. "Geez, lighten up, will you? It's not like we banged. Even though I'm sure you wanted it." He winked at me.

"Excuse me?"

"Don't get your panties in a bunch, Penny. You're acting like we've never joked around like this before."

"Because we haven't joked around like this before. Wait, do we usually?"

"Always."

"Oh my God, am I cheating on James with you?"

"What?" He laughed and stared at me like I was a lunatic. "Of course not. We're both happily married. To other people. But don't look so shocked. I would have thought we'd have ended up together too." He winked again.

"Stop winking at me."

He proceeded to wink a third time.

"You're juvenile."

"Me? I'm not the one strutting around here pretending to be 19 years old."

"I haven't been strutting. And I *am* 19 years old. Everyone around me has lost their freaking minds."

"Cut it out." He started walking away from me like he was frustrated.

It was my job to be frustrated, not his. "Cut what out?"

"This whole woe-is-me thing you've got going on. It's like you're not even trying to remember. And stop attempting to distract me from how annoyed I am by not putting pants on."

I knew my cheeks were turning bright red. I tugged on the hem of James' shirt. "I'm not even convinced that there is anything to remember. As far as I know this is all just a really awful dream."

"Exactly. You're not trying. Meanwhile, James needs you. You're the only one that can fix this."

"I don't know how to fix anything. He's an adult. I'm sure he's fine."

"Earth to Penny. You're an adult too."

I'm a teenager. My fingers abandoned the hem of the shirt. "Why are you so angry with me?" All of this was hard on me too. At least he had all his memories intact.

"I'm..." his voice trailed off. "I'm not mad at you." He lowered both his eyebrows just like James frequently did. "You just freaked me out, Penny. I thought I lost you." He stepped forward and wrapped his arms around me. "I thought I lost you," he mumbled into my hair.

This seemed...intimate. I could tell that we were close. Maybe he'd fill me in on the details I was missing. He thought he lost me. So whatever had happened to me was really bad. "Did I almost die or something?"

He squeezed me one last time before releasing me from his embrace. "I'm under strict instructions to only talk about positive memories. Things from early on in your relationship with James to help jog your memories." He tapped the side of my head. "You hungry?"

I shied away from his outstretched hand. "I could eat."

"That's the spirit." His eyes traveled down my body, reminding me I was just in a t-shirt. "Pants. Now. You're killing me, woman."

I laughed and stepped back from him. "Aren't you married?"

"Aren't you? Stop flirting with me, it's inappropriate."

"I'm not flirting with you. If anything, you're flirting with me."

"Sure." He winked at me. "I'll be downstairs. Put on a bra too."

Before I could respond, he was out the door.

What a weirdo. But I liked him. He was fun and carefree. The complete opposite of James.

***

"What's your name again?" I asked as I scooted into the seat across from him at the table.

He laughed. But when he realized I wasn't kidding, his smile vanished. "You're shitting me."

"I know we met the other day. I just...I met so many people and I..."

"Rob." He cleared his throat. "Robert if you're being an ass."

"Okay, Robert."

He laughed. "What have I done to earn that?"

"Nothing, I just wanted to see your reaction. Did you make this?" I lifted up the fork that was sitting next to my plate. Delicious looking pancakes, fresh fruit, hash browns...I practically started drooling before I got a bite into my mouth. *So freaking good.* It was like Rob knew all my favorite things.

"No, Ellen did."

"Who's Ellen?"

"James' other wife."

My fork clattered down onto my plate. "What? Are you serious? I'm in some sort of polygamy nightmare? I knew it.

I knew all of this was too good to be true." I waved my arm around the fancy room and then lowered my voice. "How many women is he married to?"

Rob had started laughing halfway through my rant and by the time I was finished he was doubled over laughing.

"Rob!"

"You're still as gullible as ever," he said through fits of laughter. "Geez, you should have seen your face."

"It's not funny." I reached across the table and slapped his arm. "Does that mean it isn't true?"

"James is head over heels in love with you and only you. I swear."

"Good." *Good?* I didn't even know the man. Why was that a good thing?

Rob smiled. "Good."

I took another bite of my pancakes. They really were delicious. "Wait, so who is Ellen?"

"Your housekeeper slash chef slash personal shopper slash whatever."

"You mean I don't have to cook or clean or…"

"Yup. You've got it made."

"Huh."

He finished chewing as he stared at me. "What?"

"Nothing. I just…" I let my voice trail off. "I kind of like cleaning. And cooking. I've never pictured myself having a housekeeper."

"Trust me, you love Ellen."

"Where is she?"

"She cooked and ran. James is trying to make sure you're not too overly stimulated."

"So waking up to you in my bed wasn't supposed to be jarring?"

"You tell me."

I laughed. "It was."

"In a good way?" He flashed me his charming smile.

"Oh yeah, in a great way." Honestly, it hadn't been so bad. He was much more fun to hang out with than James. "So I was thinking maybe I'd go for a run this morning."

"Nah, you don't want to do that. How about you do some yoga or something?"

I glared at him. "No, I want to go for a run. I'm craving the wind through my hair."

"I think you're supposed to be taking it easy for a few more weeks."

"I need to get rid of all this fat." I gestured toward my stomach and laughed awkwardly. *Seriously, where did this belly come from?* "I'm going to go try to find a pair of sneakers." I stood up and started walking toward the stairs. I couldn't wait to get some fresh air.

"Penny?"

"I'll be right back." I grabbed the railing.

"Wait."

"It'll just take a second…"

"You're not allowed to leave the apartment."

I froze on the first step. *I'm not allowed?* I thought about last night when it seemed like James was keeping me prisoner. Part of me wanted to believe it was the wine giving me an overactive imagination. But apparently my memory was perfectly intact from at least one day ago. I walked back over to the table. "What do you mean I'm *not allowed?*"

"You know what I mean…psh." He was trying to backtrack. But he wasn't getting off that easily.

"Honestly, I have no idea what you mean. Are you saying that I'm actually not allowed to go outside?"

He looked so sheepish. "Technically you are. I guess. I mean, of course. But James would prefer if you didn't leave. And if you do…it should be with him."

"Seriously? Why?"

He just stared at me.

"Why, *Robert*?" I emphasized his name as I glared at him.

"Please don't call me that." He scrunched his mouth to the side like the name Robert disgusted him.

"Look, I'm pretty sure I can ignore a few harmless paparazzi." *I hope.* Yesterday had been stressful. The blinding camera flashes. The questions I didn't know how to answer. "It's not a big deal. I'll be back in half an hour. I'm clearly out of shape."

I turned to start walking back up the steps.

"It's not the paparazzi we're worried about."

"Then what is it?"

"I should probably call James."

"Rob, just tell me. What possible reason does James have for locking me up in here?" I felt like I was Rapunzel, locked in a tower. Except I was in a sky rise in the middle of the worst city ever. And my hair wasn't blonde. *Minor details.*

"I'm going to call him real quick."

"You do that. I'll be looking for sneakers." I jogged up the stairs. *Ow.* I touched the side of my stomach. When was the last time I exercised? I couldn't possibly already have a cramp.

I ignored the pain as I rummaged through the closet. It had taken me awhile to find the spandex shorts, sports bra, and tank top I was currently wearing. But sneakers were easier. They were on the bottom row of the shoe rack. I lifted up one of the pairs. They were as light as a feather. Why wasn't I in better shape when I had such amazing workout gear? I quickly laced them up and headed back downstairs.

"James is on his way home," Rob said.

"Cool. I'll catch him when I get back."

"Please don't leave. You're going to get me in so much trouble."

"Then tell me why I'm supposed to stay," I said.

"God I hate you sometimes."

"Ditto."

He laughed. The sound reminded me of James' laughter. Albeit, much more frequent. "Fine. You win. You can't leave because you're in mortal danger."

"What is this, an episode of Power Rangers?"

"Well now you're acting like you're 10 instead of 19."

I wanted to tell him off. But every rebuttal I thought of did make me sound like a child. *Damn it.* "You're the 10 year old." Really? That was the response I chose?

He laughed. "Penny, just trust me, okay?"

"Not unless you tell me why I'm in mortal danger." I put 'mortal danger' in air quotes.

"That's something James wants to discuss with you."

"Great. And I'll see him when he gets back." I walked toward the front door.

"Penny, you can't go."

I ignored him and threw the door open.

Two men were standing in the hall facing me. Their arms were folded in front of their chests and their large frames blocked my path.

"Excuse me," I said and tried to sidestep them.

But neither of them moved.

"Mrs. Hunter, we have strict instructions to not let you leave the premises."

"Please don't call me that. My name is Penny." I tried to sidestep them again.

"Ma'am, if you'll please make your way back inside."

"This is ridiculous."

"Please step back inside. Penny," one of them added. The kind gesture of using my name was a little small considering they were keeping me locked up.

But I didn't exactly have a choice. It wasn't like I could bulldoze my way past these two huge men. It was possible that I could slide underneath their legs. But then I'd have to outrun them. And I had gotten a cramp by jogging up the stairs. I went back into the apartment and slammed the door. *Back to my 10 year old ways.*

Rob was standing there with a pained look on his face. "It's just for a little while."

"Until my memory is back?" *What if I never remember?*

"Until it's safe."

I thought about the scars on my stomach. "Did someone try to hurt me?"

He didn't respond.

"And where is James, huh? You said he loves me, but he left in the middle of the night? If someone's trying to hurt me, where is he? And where the hell is my phone? I want to talk to my parents. I…"

"Penny."

"You can't just stand there and tell me nothing. Am I in trouble?" My voice cracked. "Did I do something wrong?"

He stepped forward and wrapped his arms around me. "You didn't do anything wrong."

I melted into him. I felt more comfortable in his arms than James'. Maybe it was because I was lonely in this new world. Or maybe it was because he was closer to my age. Or maybe it was because he was the one that was actually here with me, trying to calm me down.

I shifted my head so that it was pressed against his chest. "When we were upstairs, you mentioned that you would have thought we'd have ended up together. Why didn't we?"

"Bro-code. My brother met you first."

"That's the only reason?"

"You're his person."

He didn't say I wasn't his. "You seem like so much more fun than James. I always thought I'd end up with someone more like you. James is so serious."

Rob laughed and squeezed me tighter for a moment before releasing me from his embrace. "He is serious. You should have seen him before he started dating you. It was like he always had a huge stick…"

"…up his ass," I finished for him. "He still does."

Rob smiled. "He has a lot going on. He's just worried about you."

"Can I ask you something else?"

"Anything."

"You said he loves me. But do I love him? I mean, do you think that I did? Before all of this?"

"He hasn't given you the book?" he asked.

"What book?"

He shook his head like it was nothing. "Never mind, it's not important. But yeah, Penny, I think you loved him back. You transferred out of the University of New Castle for him. You moved your whole life here."

"Why did I give up so much?"

"It was a two-way street. He had to resign from teaching. You two had a rough start but you're both happy now. I don't just think it, I know it."

We were really close. Geez, was this man my best friend? How was that possible? It wasn't like I could share intimate details about his brother to him. I stared at him. "I thought James was joking when he said he was my professor. This apartment doesn't exactly scream a professor's salary."

"When he gets home, ask him about the book I mentioned earlier. I think you should read it."

"What's it about?"

"You'll just have to read it. Come on," he said and grabbed my arm to pull me into the kitchen. "We're going to spend the rest of the morning eating ice cream and watching TV."

In just that one sentence I realized how right I was before. He was a much better match for me than James was.

CHAPTER 11
Friday

It took me awhile to completely relax around Rob. But his inappropriate sexual comments and the fact that I barely knew him went out the window when we found a show we both loved. Now my feet were propped up on his lap and we were laughing at a re-run of Shark Tank that didn't feel like a re-run to me.

"I bet Kevin's going to offer him a terrible royalty deal," Rob said.

"Are you saying that because Kevin always offers royalty deals or because you've seen this episode before?"

Rob laughed. "Both. I've missed this," he said and looked over at me.

"Missed what?" I asked through a mouthful of Ben & Jerry's Chunky Monkey ice cream.

"Hanging out just the two of us. We used to do this all the time."

I set my ice cream down on the coffee table. "What changed?"

He shrugged. "Marriage. Kids. Work."

"You have children?" I smiled at the thought. He was probably such a good father. He was so fun. Any kid would be lucky to call him Dad.

"Two. Well, one with another on the way. My daughter Sophie is three and a half. And my son will be born next month as long as everything goes smoothly."

"I'm sure everything will go smoothly," I said. "If there weren't any complications with the first delivery, there probably won't be with the second, right?"

"Yeah. I guess." But he didn't sound all that convinced. It was charming that he was worried about his wife and child.

"If I ever have kids, I don't want to know the sex. The surprise is half the fun."

He pressed his lips together, like he was holding something back.

"What?"

He shook his head. "Nothing."

I looked back at the screen, but I was having trouble focusing on the show anymore. Rob had been so carefree moments ago, and now it seemed like he had the weight of the world on his shoulders. I didn't want to press him, but I still had so many questions. Mostly about James and my life here. What we were like as a couple. What a normal day for us looked like.

"Where's James?" I asked as nonchalantly as possible.

Rob kept his eyes on the TV. "Um…he had a class."

That pause was a little suspicious. "He teaches during summer session?" I pulled my feet off of Rob's lap.

"Yup. He's teaching two classes until fall when he'll have a normal schedule again." It was like his eyes were glued to the TV.

"And one of those classes takes place in the middle of the night?"

He took another bite of ice cream, clearly buying time for whatever lie he was about to tell. "He has more on his plate than just teaching."

Like what, a mistress? I ignored the comment that wanted to spill out of my mouth. "Do you have work?" I asked instead. "It's Friday morning. Surely you have something better to do than babysit me?"

He finally pulled his gaze away from the screen and smiled at me. "There's nowhere I need to be right now."

"The two bulldogs keeping watch outside aren't exactly going to let me out. An inside man isn't really necessary. Two watchdogs is plenty."

"I'm sure Briggs and Porter will appreciate their new nicknames. And actually, you have four members in your security detail."

"Yeah, I heard about that. It seems a little obsessive."

"Apparently not obsessive enough. James called me in as backup. I'm lucky number five."

I pulled my knees into my chest, hugging my legs close. "Why exactly do I need five security guards today?"

"I've already told you, you're going to have to talk to James."

"Pictures are missing from all over the apartment." I looked over at one of the empty hooks on the walls. "Who were they of?"

"Penny, you know I can't tell you."

I looked up the stairs. I couldn't see the locked rooms from my seat on the couch, but I knew they were there. I knew there were secrets that I wouldn't understand all over this house. But I wanted to try to understand. "There are two rooms upstairs that are locked. Why? What doesn't James want me to see?"

Rob lifted the remote and turned up the volume.

I should have laughed the action off, but it made me angry. "You're keeping secrets for him." I practically had to shout. "Why?"

He ignored me.

"Rob! You can't expect me to sit here all day with all these questions running through my head. I'm sorry if this is stressful for you, but..."

He reached over and started tickling me.

"What are you doing? Stop!" I gasped for air as I started laughing. "Get off of me." I tried to push his hands away as I laughed hysterically. "Rob!"

When he started laughing at my pain, I took the opportunity to retaliate. "Oh, it's so on!" I said and tickled his side.

He barely even flinched. It was like he was a tickling aficionado. He climbed on top of me and grabbed my arms to pin them down.

"Stop!" I yelled through a bout of laughter as he tickled me with his free hand. "I can't breathe." I tried to squirm away from him, but I was trapped underneath of him. "I surrender!" I said through a giggle. But I didn't actually want him to stop. I couldn't even remember the last time I had laughed so hard. Probably before meeting Austin. And I'd be lying if I said I didn't like his hands on me. Or him on top of me. God, did I have the hots for my husband's brother?

Suddenly the sound from the TV disappeared. The living room was quiet except for the sound of my incessant laughter.

"What the fuck are you doing?" James said.

Rob's hand froze on the side of my ribcage. His smile immediately disappeared as he looked up at James. "Okay…so this looks…bad. But she started it." He tried to stifle another laugh as I squirmed beneath him.

"I did not, Robert," I protested. "And I said I surrendered. You can let me go now." I was very aware of his body pressed against mine. But I was also aware of the edge in James' voice. He was clearly pissed about this. Couldn't Rob sense that? I avoided looking at James. Could he tell how much I liked this? Could he see through me?

"Ugh, back to Robert, huh? Don't make me tickle you again."

I laughed. I couldn't help it. He was funny.

"Get the fuck off of my wife. And out of my house."

Rob slowly climbed off of me. "Lighten up, man. She was upset. I made her laugh."

"If I ever see you touch her like that again…"

"We were just messing around, James. Chill."

"I don't care what you said were doing. I asked you to leave." James stepped to the side to let Rob pass.

But Rob didn't move. "Yeah, I'm not leaving right now. She's scared enough without you acting like this. Can't you see that?"

"I think I know her better than you. And all I could see was you taking advantage of her because she doesn't remember…"

"Oh my God, stop." I stood up. "Both of you. Don't talk about me like I'm not in the room. What is wrong with you?"

"Penny." James stepped toward me but I put my hand up for him to stop.

"Honestly, I'm not interested in talking to you right now."

Rob laughed.

"Either of you," I added and glared at him. "You're treating me like I'm some delicate damsel in distress. So clearly neither of you know me at all. I can take care of my freaking self. So you two pussyfooting around by not telling me the truth isn't helping me at all."

"Pussyfooting?" Rob laughed.

"Laugh at me all you want. But I'm not talking to either of you until you're ready to tell me what happened to me. I need to know why I'm not allowed to leave this apartment. And what pictures were removed from the walls. And why there are locked doors upstairs. And why I freaking look like I'm pregnant."

James placed his hand on the armrest of the couch. He looked exhausted. But I didn't really care. How was I supposed to help him if he didn't let me in? How was I supposed to remember anything if pieces of my life were being hidden away?

"So, if you'll excuse me," I said and walked out of the room. I wasn't sure where I was planning on going. I couldn't storm out of the apartment. Running upstairs to my room was the best option. I just hated that it was James' room too.

CHAPTER 12

Friday

"Why haven't you shown her the book yet?" Rob asked. "It'll jog her memory."

I didn't even have to eavesdrop. Rob and James' heated discussion easily drifted upstairs. But I still climbed off the bed and settled by the side of the door to hear them a little more clearly.

"I want *her* to remember. I don't want her to be told what and how to remember it."

"They're her words. She has a unique opportunity to hear about her life through her own eyes. Not many people with amnesia get that."

"But it's a work of fiction. The memories are blurred. It's not like experiencing it for the first time."

"It's not that much fiction."

Did I write something? The thought made me smile. I loved reading. I always wished that I could articulate a story that was as good as the ones I read. Was that my job? Was I an author?

"James, I get that some of it is hard for you to think about, but she needs to remember it. The good and the bad. This is the easiest way."

"Haven't we had enough bad?"

"You can't expect her to remember anything if you're hiding pieces of your lives from her."

"I just...I don't want her to read about loving me. I want her to fall in love with me all over again."

"Why? When all she has to do is remember how much she loved you in the first place..."

"Because we were broken! I have an opportunity to fix it."

"You weren't broken."

"She thought I cheated on her, Rob. The fact that she thought that means something wasn't right. And it's more than just that. I'd catch her crying and she'd wipe away the tears and pretend she hadn't been. Her frowns killed me. She wasn't happy."

"You don't know that."

"Of course I do. You think I can't tell when she's hurting? That look she gave me a few minutes ago...that wasn't the first time I've seen that. I feel like all I ever do is upset her."

"You're being a little hard on yourself."

"Am I? Right now she doesn't really know either of us. But when I touch her she cringes. Yet when I walk in and you're on top of her tickling her, her whole face is lit up."

"Because I was tickling her. She didn't have much of a choice."

"It's more than that. It's pretty clear she doesn't like me. She's disappointed in her life. Disappointed in her choice of husband. It's all over her face."

"She couldn't possibly be. Look at everything you've given her."

"It was never about expensive things with her. She doesn't care about any of this. She never did. It's one of the many reasons I fell for her in the first place."

I let my head rest against the doorjamb. Maybe he knew me better than I realized. I bit the inside of my lip. So had I been unhappy? Had I hated this life?

"So what's the game plan then?" Rob asked. "Try to swoop her off her feet? Again?"

"That's the problem. I don't really think I swooped her off her feet to begin with. I'm pretty sure she swooped me off mine."

Rob laughed. "She was your knight in shining armor." Even though he just laughed, he said the words seriously.

"And now I have a chance to save her. I need this. I think we both need it."

I wiped away a tear that had fallen down my cheek. The first thing I realized about James was that he was broken. Why was that? What had I saved him from? I closed my eyes. I wanted to wake back up in my dorm. I wanted everything to go back to normal. Listening to their conversation wasn't helping at all. It was just twisting my stomach further into knots.

I slowly stood up and started pacing back and forth. James wanted me to fall in love with him again. But I wasn't sure I knew how. I had never been in love. I couldn't just turn a switch in my heart and make myself understand that I needed him. And what if I had been unhappy as his wife? Why would I want to trick myself back into being miserable for eternity?

What I needed was to get out of this apartment. I needed to find some cash and get as far away from New

York City as possible. My gut told me to go to my parents. But they seemed mixed up in all of this too. I needed to get away from everyone and clear my head. *Yes.* That's what I had to do. Maybe one day I'd remember, or maybe I wouldn't. But it would all be on my own terms. And then I could decide if I wanted this life or if I needed to make a new one for myself.

I ran over to the closet and searched around for a backpack. I knew I couldn't run right now, but I could prepare for whenever I had the opportunity. After rummaging through the drawers, I found a small duffel bag shoved in the back of the closet. *This will have to do.* I stuffed it full of workout clothes like I'd actually be running the whole time I was running away. I even found a spare toothbrush to throw in. And then I hid it behind my extravagant shoe collection.

I took a deep breath. A go-bag. I felt like a criminal when I walked back out of the closet. But I wasn't sure why. Everything in the bag was mine. *I think.*

***

"Do you want to go for that walk?" James asked.

I closed the nightstand drawer I had been searching through. Where did he keep all the loose cash? I couldn't exactly leave without any money. Identification would be nice too, but James had definitely hidden my purse from me. Probably the same place he hid my phone. "Um. Sure." I stood up.

"Everything okay?" he asked.

"You mean before or after the fighting match downstairs?"

He shoved his hands into his pockets. "I tend to be a little possessive."

"Why don't you trust your brother though? He's married. And you know...*your brother*. I doubt he'd ever do anything to purposely hurt you."

"He may have used to have a thing for you."

"Well, now I'm fat and old. I don't think you have anything to worry about." I smiled at him.

"You're young. And beautiful. And not at all fat."

I looked down at my stomach. "Then you're blind."

He laughed. It wasn't as carefree as his brother's laughter, but it still made me smile.

I stared at him. "Are you going to answer all of my questions?"

"I am," he said. But he didn't add anything else.

"So...what happened to me?"

"I want to show you something first. I think it might help jog your memory." He put his hand out for me.

"We're leaving the apartment?"

"We are." He kept his hand outstretched.

What's the worst that could happen if I take it? I slid my hand into his and let him lead me out of the bedroom. He was wrong when he told Rob that I cringed at his touch. I wasn't cringing. I was scared of the energy I felt when I touched him. I wasn't repulsed at all. I was terrified.

CHAPTER 13

Friday

I looked over my shoulder to see the two security guards following us through the winding paths of Central Park. "Do they always accompany us when we leave the apartment?" I asked.

He nodded.

"So we're always in danger of something? Or someone?"

"Not necessarily. I may be a little overprotective of you. And especially when we're apart, I worry." He squeezed my hand.

I think he meant the action to be comforting. But his words made him seem overbearing. I hadn't been allowed to leave the house today without him. What else wasn't I allowed to do without his permission?

"But are we in danger now?" I asked.

He sighed. It sounded so heavy, like he had been holding it back for years. "I honestly don't know anymore."

"You promised you'd answer my questions, James."

"And I will. Are you hungry?" He had stopped in front of the restaurant he'd pointed out yesterday. The one with the huge tree that we apparently got married under.

It really was breathtakingly beautiful. There were a few wedding pictures in our apartment and I truly had looked happy. Painfully happy. That was the only way to describe it. I had been smiling so much it looked like my face probably hurt for days. And it was painful now to look at, because I couldn't remember a single second of it. Weddings were known to be one of the best days of a person's life. My best day was still when I got my acceptance to The University of New Castle. I had never been so excited. Did my wedding day top that? Was it as perfect as everyone claimed it would be?

"No, I'm good," I said. I didn't want to sit under that tree and eat lunch with him. Not just because not remembering made me uncomfortable. But because it would be hard for him. I got why he brought me here. I understood what he was doing. Even if I hadn't overheard his conversation with Rob, I would have known he was trying to trigger my memories. But I had no memories of him. I just…didn't.

He looked pained that I wasn't trying. Or maybe he was just in pain.

"What happened to us, James?" The expression on his face made me want to cry. I wanted to hug him and fight away all his demons. I wished that everything that came out of my mouth didn't hurt him so much.

He pulled me over to a bench outside of the restaurant and we both sat down. He grabbed my hands, cradling them between his, like he was worried I'd try to flee if he let go. I thought about my go-bag hidden in the back of his closet. Would it crush him when I left? Would he eventually heal?

James ran his thumb along the back of my hand. I found it oddly comforting. It pulled me out of my thoughts. I stared into his eyes, willing myself to remember a past I wasn't sure I even believed was real.

"We were happy, Penny."

That wasn't what he had said to his brother. He said he caught me crying all the time. It sounded to me like I had been depressed. "You used the past tense. Is that because you're not happy now? Or does it go further back than that?"

He glanced over at the tree. I could tell that memories were flashing through his mind. Glimpses of us.

I felt like he was lulling me into a false sense of security. He was making me feel safe. But I felt like whatever he was about to say was going to terrify me. "James."

He pulled himself out of his memories and looked back at me. "I'm going to start at the beginning." He continued to rub his thumb along the back of my hand. "We met outside of class. You literally fell into my arms."

I laughed. "I'm not the most graceful person."

"I don't think it had anything to do with that. I think we were meant to run into each other that day. I needed you in my life. And I like to think that you needed me too."

His words made my chest hurt. I had never heard anything so romantic in my life. "You're a believer in fate?"

"I wasn't. But then I met you. You changed everything, Penny." His Adam's apple rose and fell. "Every single thing."

"How?"

"I…" He leaned forward slightly. "I wasn't whole before I met you."

Everything he was saying was romantic. Yet vague. And rather cliché. I wanted to hear him out, but he wasn't giving me any details. "So…you were a single professor looking for love on campus?"

"No." He looked like I had slapped him. He let his hands fall from mine. "It wasn't like that."

"Because we met outside of class? After you found out you were my professor, shouldn't you have forgotten about me?"

"You made that impossible."

"Me? I find that hard to believe."

"We kept running into each other outside of class. And when we were in class, you flirted with me. You showed up at my office hours unannounced. You ingrained yourself in my mind and wouldn't leave."

"You're saying that it's *my* fault? You were the adult in the situation."

"I'm not saying it was your fault. This is coming out wrong." He grabbed my hands again. "Penny, I tried to do the right thing. But I couldn't stop thinking about you. You completely possessed me. It was hard enough keeping you out of my thoughts during the day, but then at night I'd dream of you in my bed with me. I couldn't control it. And I didn't just want you. It felt like I needed you in my life. Like you were the answer to all my problems. It wasn't your fault at all. It was mine. I could have squashed your flirtations. I could have ignored you. I could have not flirted back. But I didn't. I wanted you to want me despite how wrong it was. And I still have a hard time thinking about what I did. I know it was wrong. But I don't regret it either because I don't know how to live without you."

I didn't have the heart to tell him he *should* regret it. That he tore me away from the school I loved. From the town I loved. From everything I knew. "If you loved me as much as you say, why didn't we just wait? I could have finished school there."

"We were going to. But it got complicated rather quickly. I was going through a divorce and…"

"You've been married before?" I never in my life thought I'd be someone's second choice in the end. I had been second my whole life. The thought of Austin blowing me off made me want to cry. I'd gone from one jerk to the next.

"I never loved her. It wasn't like our relationship at all."

"If you didn't love her then why did you marry her?" I didn't know why I was jealous. I didn't even like James. But my mind was already running a million miles a second. Was she prettier than me? Skinnier? Did she still have all her memories intact?

"My parents were very controlling. And I…" he let his voice trail off. "I was numb to the world. I had given up on happiness at a pretty early age. My life was laid out for me. And I didn't fight it like I should have."

"Why were you numb to the world?"

"Penny, I wanted to talk about how in love we are and how perfect we are for each other. I brought you here to try and help remind you…"

"I don't want to be given some lies about how our life was a fairytale, James. I overheard you talking to Rob. You said I wasn't happy. I don't want to hear some dream you made up…"

"I didn't make any of this up. We were happy. Baby, we were so happy."

"Then why were you numb to the world?"

"That was before I met you…"

"But it's still a part of who you are. You can't tell me the good and keep away the bad. You said you'd be honest with me. And I want to know about this."

"I was depressed, okay?" He stood up, like the idea of being so close to me made it hard for him to breathe. "Before I became a professor, I was working at a job I hated with a wife I loathed. I contemplated ending my miserable life."

I looked up at him. "So what changed?" *Don't say me. Don't say I saved you.* His conversation with Rob tumbled through my head. *Don't put it all on me.*

"I turned to teaching because it was something I was actually passionate about."

I breathed a sigh of relief.

"But I gave it up for you. Because you're the only thing I love in this world more."

Damn it.

"I swear to you, Penny, we were so happy."

"So why'd we stop being happy?"

"Because you're everything to me. But I'm not enough for you." He ran his fingers through his hair as he looked over at the tree. "I was broken when I met you. I've had issues with substance abuse and depression. My life was a series of bad events until you fell into my arms."

I'm married to a divorced addict? God. Had I known about his issues all along? Or had he hidden them from me like he had been trying to do now? I watched a tear slide down his cheek before he quickly brushed it away. And suddenly my questions didn't matter.

"You've always been the light to my darkness, Penny." He continued to stare at the tree instead of me. "And I think you finally realized that you deserved more light in your life than a man like me could possibly give you."

My heart shattered. I didn't even know him, but his words broke me. I felt big, fat tears roll down my cheeks. "You know...I think I could eat. If you still want to." I wiped the tears away before he turned back toward me.

He smiled like I was giving him hope. And I'm pretty sure he pieced my heart back together just as quickly as he shattered it.

In that moment, I knew I was in trouble with this man. Because my heart seemed to know it belonged to him, even though my mind didn't remember. He killed me and brought me back to life in a matter of seconds. And I was even more terrified of him than before.

CHAPTER 14

Friday

I listened to our story from his point of view. The good, the bad, and the in-between. But it was mostly good as far as I could tell. I laughed at his retelling of the first time he met my parents. And I was entranced by how strong I seemed to be when our affair blew up in our faces. I understood why we left Newark. All of it made sense if we loved each other as much as he said. And how could I not believe him when he stared at me with such intensity? I was like putty in his hands.

"You thought I was unhappy because I wanted to have a career? It doesn't sound like that had anything to do with you not being enough for me. It sounds like I wanted to...I don't know..." I let my voice trail off. "You've given me the whole world. I probably felt like I didn't deserve it."

A smile spread across his face. "You always say that."

"I do?"

"You do." He reached across the table and grabbed my hand. This time he ran his thumb along my palm.

I thought him running his thumb along the back of my hand was calming. But this? I closed my eyes. It was like he could take away all my stress with one touch.

"Are you okay?" he asked.

I opened my eyes. "Yes, I just…" I stifled a sigh and glanced down at our hands. "I really like when you do that."

"I know."

I felt the color rise to my cheeks. What else did he know about my likes and dislikes? I looked back up at him. The heat in his gaze was palpable. I had this all-consuming feeling that he knew every single thing that I liked. Probably better than I knew myself. I swallowed hard. "I think it sounds like I was still madly in love with you."

"I hope you're right."

I hope so too. I was surprised by my own thought. For the first time, I found myself wanting to fit into this life. I wanted him to exist. I wanted someone to truly love me as much as he seemed to.

"If you want, we can go home and I can give you a copy of the book you wrote. You can read all about your version of us."

I shook my head. "I kind of like your version."

He smiled. "I wanted to shelter you from the bad so that you had a chance to remember the good instead. But it was better that you heard about everything."

"I get it. My amnesia is basically a fresh start for us."

"But I was wrong, we don't need a fresh start. I wouldn't change a thing about our past because it brought us here." He pressed his lips together. "I mean…I'd rather this hadn't happened to us. I'd prefer if you knew me."

He was older than me. Richer than me. Certainly more charming than me. I knew he was trying to make me fall for him all over again. I had overheard his plan to do just that. But it was still working. I didn't have the urge to run. At least, not as strong of an urge. There were still things he hadn't told me, though. I wasn't sure how many times I had asked what happened to me, and he always skirted around the question. I was about to ask him again, but he started talking before I opened my mouth.

"You've barely touched your food," he said.

Instead of focusing on the delicious meal that was placed in front of me, I had been listening to his stories. The meal was good, but I wasn't really hungry. "I'm officially on a diet," I said and pushed the plate aside. "Besides, I may have eaten quite a bit of ice cream earlier today."

"You were upset?"

It was unnerving how he knew me so well. "I woke up to your brother in my bed. I tried to leave the apartment and was stopped by two security guards. And Rob wouldn't tell me anything that was going on. I wasn't just upset, I was frustrated and scared and…"

"I'm sorry."

"Where were you?"

"As much as I wish it could, my life can't just stop because you forgot who you are. I have a lot of obligations. Trust me, I wish I could have woken up next to you."

I looked at the dark circles under his eyes. "Did you even sleep?"

"I haven't been sleeping well since you've been in the hospital."

"But I'm back now."

"Not completely. It's easy to forget when we're like this. You look and sound and act like my Penny. But I can see the difference in your eyes. There's no love there. What's the point of sleeping when it already feels like I'm in a nightmare I can't wake up from?"

That's what I had been thinking this was. A terrible nightmare I was stuck in. I didn't have the heart to tell him I felt the same way for the opposite reasons. My lack of love toward him terrified him. And his love for me terrified me. "I'm sorry."

"I'm not asking for you to apologize. This isn't your fault. I just…I never thought I could miss you so much when you were sitting across from me. You really don't remember anything? Nothing I told you jogged your memory?"

"I'm sorry."

He cringed at my apology. "Please stop apologizing. You've done nothing wrong."

"I'm sorry…geez. I can't seem to stop," I said with a laugh. "I always apologize for everything."

"Yeah." He squeezed my hand. "You did that a lot when we first met."

"I did?"

He nodded. "Not so much since. It must have been a 19-year-old thing."

I laughed. "Probably because any time anyone gave me attention it felt like I was in trouble. I've spent most of my life being invisible. I'm pretty sure I'm the only person that is capable of feeling alone in a crowded room."

"But you're never alone. You have me."

My heart felt like it stopped beating as I stared into his eyes.

"I've always seen you, Penny. The only time I'm happy is when you're in a room with me."

God was he handsome. When he looked at me like that if made me want to melt into my chair. My whole body felt like it was on fire. And I had the strangest urge to lean across the table and kiss him. "What time is Melissa coming today?" I blurted out. I wanted to punch myself in the face as soon as the words spilled out of my mouth. Why had I felt so compelled to take that beautiful moment and ruin it? *What is wrong with me?* Love was staring me in the face and I had just pissed all over it for no reason at all.

He let go of my hand and straightened in his seat. "Not until 8:30." He glanced down at his watch. "I didn't realize how late it had gotten. We should probably get going."

"You told me everything except what happened to me." I felt like there was more he was holding back. There were holes in his story that I was only just starting to realize. I was dying to get my phone back so I could research his ex-wife and see what she was up to. And to see what she looked like. *Stop it.*

"I'll tell you when I get home tonight." He slowly stood up, pressing his hand against the table as if he needed the support. He looked so unbelievably tired. "I'm already running late."

"You're not coming back to the apartment with me?" I walked with him out of the restaurant.

"I have some errands I have to run."

Hadn't he just said he was late? Like for an appointment? Errands and an appointment weren't the same thing. *You're hiding something from me.* Hell, he was probably hiding a ton from me. But whatever he was doing, I was pretty certain it wasn't a class. Rob's cover for him was flimsy at best. Besides, if James had been going to teach a class, he would have just said that. Instead, he was acting all mysterious about running secret errands. I tried not to let it bother me, but it did. His lies stung after our nice evening.

"I…" my voice trailed off as we stepped back into Central Park. "James, I'm not sure I know how to get back." I was all turned around. Had we turned right or left on the path to get here? And hadn't Rob said I was in danger? I felt a chill run down my spine. As soon as I thought about being in danger, it was like I could feel someone watching me. I looked over my shoulder at the restaurant we had just been in. No one was looking at me. Everyone was eating and talking and having fun. I tried to shake the thought away as I turned back to James.

"Briggs and Porter are going to walk you home."

It was like they materialized out of thin air before me. "Where did you guys just come from?" I asked.

"The bench over there," the taller one said.

I glanced at the bench he pointed at. They must have been blending into it because I swear I had just seen that bench empty a moment ago. It was probably them watching me though. I took a deep breath, trying to calm the unsettled feeling in the pit of my stomach.

"Can't I come with you?" I asked James. I didn't want to be left alone with the strange men. I was just starting to get used to him. Why was he leaving me again?

James shook his head. "You should be there to greet Melissa. I told her she could stay at the apartment, like you requested."

"Thank you." Our conversation had flowed so easily before, but now it was stiff and formal. I was tempted to shake his hand and wish him a nice night like I was never going to see him again.

He stepped forward and kissed my temple. "I'll catch you up on everything tonight. I promise," he said.

I was pretty sure Melissa would fill me in on everything as soon as I saw her. Or better yet, she'd tell me I had been kidnapped and everyone around me was a psychopath. And she'd rescue me and take me back to college where I belonged.

"What time will you be back?" If I was going to escape, I needed to know how long I had.

He glanced at his watch again. "As soon as I can. If it gets too late, you don't have to wait up for me. We can always talk tomorrow."

I felt guilty thinking about leaving. And I wondered if he felt guilty for all the secrets he was keeping from me. Our dinner had been lovely. It was like I was transported into another reality that was starting to feel like home. But standing here now? I knew James and I would never work. We were too different. "Okay."

"Okay." He gave me a forced smile. "I'll see you tonight. Briggs, Porter," he nodded at them. "Call me if you need anything." He turned around without another word and walked in the opposite direction of the way we had come. As soon as he was out of earshot, he pulled out his cell phone and pressed it to his ear. And he never looked back.

"Where is he going?" I asked no one in particular.

One of the security guards cleared his throat. "Ma'am, we should probably get you home."

I turned around to see them both staring at me. "Who do you think he was calling?" *His ex-wife?* I wasn't sure where the thought came from. I squashed it down and tried to bury it in my mind. What did it matter? He needed to rely on someone and I wasn't that person.

One of the security guards glanced over his shoulder, like he could feel someone watching him too. When he turned back around he was frowning. "Trench coat at 7 o'clock. I'm going to call William to bring a car around and I'll wait with Mrs. Hunter in the restaurant." He grabbed my elbow and pulled me back toward the restaurant before I could even try to see who he was talking about.

"What's going on?"

He ignored my question as we hurried toward the restaurant. He let go of my arm as soon as we were inside and started scratching the side of his neck. It seemed like a nervous tick, and it made me nervous to watch him.

"Is everything okay?" I asked.

"Yeah...I'm sure it's nothing. This place just always makes me unsettled after everything that happened here."

"You mean...at our wedding?" I couldn't think of what else he would be talking about that happened here. Was he not invited to the wedding or something? That seemed harsh. God, was I a bitch in this world? Or maybe he didn't have a fun time.

"Yeah. I can't believe I didn't see the shooter that night. I'll never forgive myself for James getting shot."

What? It felt like I couldn't breathe. I knew Rob said I was in danger, but I didn't know if he was being serious or not. He seemed to joke around about everything.

"Not that the guy outside is a sniper, but who wears a trench coat on a clear night in the middle of summer? It's like a thousand degrees out." He loosened his tie.

"James got shot?" I thought about how every now and then he seemed out of breath. Or needed something to lean on. But our wedding was supposedly years ago. Was he still hurting from that? Again I got the unsettling feeling that someone was watching me.

"Oh, shit." The security guard said. "He told me he was going to tell you everything. You didn't get to your wedding yet?"

"No, we did. He just failed to mention the part where he almost died." God, this really was a nightmare. It was like I was in a horror movie. Rob was right. I was in mortal danger. "What happened?"

"It's not my place to say…" his voice trailed off.

"If my life is in danger I think I have a right to know."

"Mrs. Hunter…"

"My name is Penny Taylor. Taylor, not Hunter." I wanted to unleash hell on everyone around me. James had sat there and lied to my face about our perfect life, leaving off the fact that he almost died and that I probably had too. "Am I in danger?"

"Briggs and I would never let anything happen to you."

"But am I in danger?" I asked again.

He pressed his lips together.

"I need to know. I need to be able to protect myself. Is someone trying to hurt me?"

He hesitated, but only for a moment. "Yes. But we won't let him get to you again."

Again? Who? I didn't have to think about it any longer. I needed to get the hell out of New York before my fake lying husband got me killed.

CHAPTER 15

Friday

I tossed the duffel bag on my bed and unzipped it. The zipper snagged on one of the articles of clothing inside. *Come on, not now.* I pulled harder, but it just made it worse. My mom was an expert at getting zippers unstuck. But me? I didn't have the patience for it. I tried to pull the zipper back in the opposite direction, but it wouldn't budge. *Come on, you stupid piece of crap.* I abandoned the zipper and slammed my fist down on the duffel bag.

I wasn't even frustrated with the zipper. I was upset because I had searched the whole freaking apartment and I hadn't found any cash, my phone, my ID, or anything that belonged to me. How was I supposed to make a run for it without my stuff?

The zipper could wait until I got wherever I was going. I slid the expensive looking watch I had swiped from the closet into the small opening of the duffel bag. I could sell it at a pawn shop for cash. And I didn't really need a phone, I had no one to call. As for the ID, I just wouldn't try to get on a plane. There were a row of car keys hanging downstairs. If he had that many cars, he probably wouldn't miss one. And I'd drive slowly to avoid being pulled over. Or I could always try to flirt my way out of a ticket. I'd never done it before, but I could try. It wasn't like I had a wedding ring on my finger to prevent me from trying.

I looked down at the tan lines on my finger. *Those rings would have made it easier to get cash.* Where were they? Was James hiding them for some reason? *Maybe he doesn't trust you with them.* That would be fair enough. He didn't trust me and I certainly didn't trust him.

God, I was so pissed at him. He went on and on about our wedding and how I cried when he said his vows. He said it was perfect. How was getting shot on our wedding day perfect?

I tried the zipper once more to no avail. *Screw it.* I pulled the bag over my shoulder. It was time to make a run for it.

A knock on the door downstairs made me freeze. Who the hell was that? I set the bag back down, abandoning it on my bed, and tiptoed down the stairs. *Please don't be James.* If he was back already, I'd have no chance to escape. And he'd know I was upset with him. He could read me like the back of his hand, which was totally unfair because I couldn't read him at all.

The knock sounded again as I tiptoed through the kitchen. It probably wasn't James, or he'd let himself in. Maybe it was Rob again. James liked to send people here to watch me. But Rob had also let himself in. Which meant it was most likely someone James didn't trust.

The thought made me pause. There was no way that I was going to die tonight. I grabbed a knife from the knife block on the kitchen counter before making my way into the foyer. I peered through the peephole in the door and all my fears melted away. Melissa was standing there with a suitcase and a huge smile on her face. I set down the knife.

"Penny!" Melissa screamed when I opened the door.

"Melissa!" I threw myself into her arms.

"I've missed you," she said.

"God, I've missed you too." I didn't want to let go. Someone was finally here to help me make sense of everything. I trusted her with my life. She'd help me get out of here. She'd help save me from this hell.

I pulled away from her embrace and held her at arm's length. "You have to help me. I need to get…" my voice trailed off when I saw Josh standing behind her. A much older looking Josh. I glanced back at my best friend. Her hair was longer than it had been a few days ago when we were studying for finals. And she was tanner and wearing way more eye makeup than she usually did. A small piece of me was holding out hope that she'd be from the life that I remembered. That she'd hold the key to my going back in time where I belonged. But she wasn't who I remembered either. She was different. Older. She wasn't the Melissa I knew anymore.

I felt tears forming in my eyes. "You're not 19." I wish it had come out as a question, but there was no reason to ask. She was definitely not 19. Just like when I looked in the mirror, I didn't see a 19 year old anymore either. Which meant this was real. This horrible nightmare was my new reality. My chest hurt. My lungs felt like they weren't taking in air.

The light in Melissa's eyes seemed to dim. "I was hoping your memory would be back before I got here. I'm sorry it took me so long, but it was hard to get off work. We came as soon as we could. We originally planned a whole vacation here a few weeks from now but…" her voice trailed off.

"The plans changed." She practically grimaced at her own words.

"Melissa…" I was having trouble breathing. "I want to wake up. Help me wake up. You have to help me."

She wrapped her arms around me again. "Penny, we're going to figure this out together, okay? I'm not going anywhere until we get your memory back. I promise."

I clung to her like she was the only thing keeping me from sinking to the floor. "I don't want it back. I just want to be me again. Before all this. This isn't my life, I know it's not. It couldn't possibly be. I wouldn't have done the things that brought me here. Help me go back."

I heard her try to stifle a sob. "I'm sorry, Penny. I'm so sorry."

I rested my head on her shoulder and let myself cry. I felt like I had been holding back tears for years. And now that I had started crying, I couldn't stop. "This can't be real." I wasn't sure if she could even understand me through my sobs.

"It's okay," she said in a soothing voice. "Everything's going to be okay."

But it wasn't. I was in hell and there was no escape.

***

"Here you go," Melissa said and set the cup of tea on the coffee table in front of me. "You think tea is a cure-all."

There was no denying anything now. Melissa was my last hope and she was sticking with everyone else's story. "That's nice," I said and lifted the cup. Having the warm cup between my hands was soothing. Maybe the new me had a point.

"So tell me what the last thing you remember is. James caught me up on the phone, but I'd like to hear it from you."

"I was studying for my sociology final. I thought I must have fallen asleep or something while I was reading through my notes." I shrugged my shoulders. "I feel the same as I did when I was 19. My heart even still feels broken from the last message I got from Austin…"

"What did he say in it?"

"That he thought we should maybe take a break over the summer and see how things go next semester."

"Oh. I remember that one. You were really upset."

I looked down into my teacup. "I *am* upset."

"Penny, that was seven years ago."

"It doesn't feel that way."

"Well, I'm going to give you a quick rundown, okay? You aced your Soci exam."

I smiled.

"And all your other exams, like always. And you went home and worked some dumb retail job over the summer. We talked all the time even though we were apart. You were still torn up over Austin. And then near the end of summer he said he was coming back to campus early and that he hoped to see you soon. So you went back early too. And he stopped texting you like the ass that he is."

"So I never heard from him again?" I looked up from my cup. That hurt. *He totally ghosted me.*

"Not exactly. I forced you to go out with him one more time. But it was only because you didn't tell me that you were dating your professor."

"I really did that? Why? I don't understand how I could risk everything for something so ridiculous."

"Love isn't ridiculous, Penny."

"Fine, but I couldn't have loved him right away. I risked everything for what? Lust? A teenage fantasy?"

"I don't think so. I think it was love at first sight."

I laughed.

"You're bitter because all you remember is Austin and how he treated you. But Penny, James is a great guy. He was this mysterious, uber sexy, older man that was completely and utterly unattainable. I can see why you lost all reason around him."

"But having sex with my professor?" My voice was hushed even though it was just the two of us. "I would never ever do that."

"I don't know what to tell you. You did."

"I like to follow rules, Melissa. And that's so against every rule in the book. Not to mention I hate upsetting my parents. I would never do something so reckless. People don't just change overnight."

"You did. You just…you met him and things changed. You both pushed each other's boundaries. And you both grew together."

"He didn't need to do any growing. He was already a grown up."

"You were almost 20 when you met. You were basically a grown up too."

I sighed. "I just… I don't understand how I could be so madly in love with him that I'd ruin the rest of my life. James and I have nothing in common. We're not exactly two pieces of the same puzzle. I'm not even sure I like him, let alone love him. We don't fit. He's not my person."

"You do fit. And your life wasn't ruined. Look around, Penny. Your life is amazing."

"I want to go back to Newark."

Melissa sighed. "James was right, you're not even trying."

"Whose side are you on here?"

"Yours. Of course yours. But the thing you're not understanding is that James is your world. He's what makes you happy. He means everything to you."

"I'm not even sure he's my type."

She laughed. "Then what is your type?"

"I don't know…blue eyes, dirty blonde hair."

Melissa's eyes bulged slightly. "You never told me that before."

I shrugged. "Well, if I'm thinking about it…that's my type. Like…lifeguard-esque. And funny and carefree. And you know…closer to my age." *All the opposite things as James.*

"That's extremely interesting, Penny."

"Why?"

She just stared at me and shook her head. "Well, how would you feel if I told you that you passed up that exact person you described in order to be with James? Would that convince you of how much you like him?"

"You mean I dated someone else before James? Someone just like that?"

"You did."

"Well, I'd say I don't believe you. Because obviously I would have chosen to be with him over James."

"Penny, everyone loves tall, dark, and handsome."

"I don't. I want young and fun and blonde."

"Shut up." Her words came out harsh, like she was pissed at me. "I'm sorry, I…" her voice trailed off. She set her cup down on the coffee table. "Penny, you dated them off and on at the same time. And it was always James. You even made a pro-con list and everything pointed to Tyler. But you chose James anyway. You're head over heels for him."

"Tyler." I said the name out loud, hoping it would trigger a memory. But his name meant nothing to me. "What happened to him?"

"This conversation isn't about Tyler. It's about James. Penny, you need to try to remember."

"I was just wondering." *Geez.* Melissa was never this serious. I was surprised she wasn't raiding my closet and making me wear slutty clothes out on the town. It was a Friday night after all.

She sighed and lifted her cup back up. "Tyler is one of your best friends now. He's happily married to another great friend of ours, and they have an adorable three and a half year old son together."

"Oh."

"Don't look so disappointed." Her smile was back. "You had your chance with him. As did I."

"You dated him too?"

"Well, you happen to be right. Young, fun, and blonde was appealing to me as well. But I wound up right back where I started with Josh. Tall, dark, and handsome always wins. See? It's a thing."

"Huh." I took a sip of my tea. "Rob's daughter is three and a half too. Do their kids hang out? Or I guess I mean…are they friends too? Or is Tyler just my friend? You do know Rob, right? James' brother?"

She rolled her eyes. "Yes, I know Rob. I had a fling with him too."

"Of course you did."

"And yeah, they're all friends. Axel and Sophie are adorable. Those are their children's names."

"Cute names."

"For cute kids."

"Well, if I had to end up with a Hunter brother, I don't know why I didn't choose Rob. He seems more like my type too."

"Stop saying stuff like that. It makes my chest hurt."

I pressed my lips together.

Melissa set her cup back down and leaned forward. "Penny, you trust me, right?"

She wasn't exactly the same Melissa that I remembered. But it seemed like we had remained close. I still felt comfortable around her. She still made me smile and laugh. "Of course I trust you."

"James was the most eligible bachelor in NYC before you scooped him up. He's handsome, and smart, and kind, and very very possessive. In a sexy way," she said quickly when she saw the expression on my face. "It's endearing, trust me. So just please do me a favor and try. Look at him when he gets home tonight. Really look at him and tell me you don't think he's sexy. And please do everyone a favor and don't say stuff like that about Rob and Tyler around him, okay? Please?"

"Fine." I bit the inside of my lip. "But I don't see why an addict would be the most eligible bachelor in NYC. I guess it makes sense though. This city sucks."

"What?"

"I've always hated New York. It's...dirty and loud here."

"I'm not talking about the city. I'm talking about what you just said about James. He's not an addict. Why would you think that?"

"Um…" I let my voice trail off. Maybe we weren't as close as I thought anymore. If we were still best friends, wouldn't she have known that? Surely I would have told her.

"Penny, it's one thing to say he's not your type. It's another to make up horrible lies about him. That's cruel. He's not an addict. Why would you jump to a wild conclusion like that? I've never known you to judge someone without getting to know them." She was looking at me like she didn't know who I was either.

"I'm not jumping to conclusions. He told me he had issues with substance abuse."

She shook her head.

"I swear, Melissa. We had dinner earlier and he told me his version of everything that happened. He brought up the drug thing. I'm not making stuff up about him."

"Penny, you never told me that before. I…" her voice trailed off. "Maybe it's a new thing? Since you got hurt? He's taken all of this really hard."

"No. He said he had those issues before he started teaching. He basically said his life was horrible before we met. I overheard a conversation between him and Rob earlier too. James said that I saved him. And after our talk, I think he meant from his life as an addict."

"If that's true, you kept it from me." She looked hurt, like it was my fault she had been kept out of the loop. I didn't even remember any of it. She couldn't be mad at me.

"I don't know why he'd lie," I said. "He was trying to woo me. It seems like a bad idea to mention something like that on a first date."

"Yeah."

"Still a catch, huh?"

"I mean...all I know is what you've told me. And you always seemed happy. He always seemed perfect. But maybe..." her voice trailed off.

"Maybe tall, dark, and handsome isn't all it's cut out to be? Especially when it's combined with serious, liar pants, druggie."

"I feel like this is just a misunderstanding."

"Well, it's possible he did lie. Because he sat there and told me all about our perfect wedding and failed to mention the part where he got shot. Did you know that?"

"Yeah, I was there. I was your maid of honor."

At least some things seemed like they were right in this world. "And have you looked around the apartment? There are pictures missing from the walls. And there are doors locked upstairs. There are so many secrets in this house. And it feels like someone is watching me all the time, I can't even explain it."

"Well, the last thing is easy to explain." She pointed to a device mounted in the corner of the living room. "You are being watched. James has cameras everywhere."

A chill ran down my spine. "Why?"

"Your security guards monitor everything to keep you guys safe."

"They're watching us right now? Are they listening to us too?" I looked over at the camera.

"I don't know. You get used to it though. I forgot the cameras were even there until you just mentioned it."

It was like I was living in one of those books that I had to read during one summer for a high school English class: 1984 and Brave New World. I don't know why they made us read them at the same time. Ever since then, I always got them confused. But I knew in one of them someone was always watching you. Or maybe it was both of them. Either way, those were terrible dystopian worlds. How had my life turned out so wrong?

"One of the security guards told me that I was in danger," I said, still looking at the camera. "That someone tried to hurt me. So despite them and all this fancy equipment, I still got hurt. Which means I'm still in danger."

"You're safe here. Trust me, if you leave, you're putting yourself at a much greater risk."

"Of what?" *Tell me. Someone fucking tell me what's going on.*

"I promised James I wouldn't say anything, but keeping you in the dark is clearly not helping anyone. Someone tried to kill you. We know who did it, and there's a warrant out for his arrest, but the police haven't caught him yet. Everyone's worried he's going to come after you again. That's why you have to stay here, where it's safe."

Safe? If I stayed here, I was a sitting duck. If I was a murderer, the first place I'd look for a victim was her home. How naïve was everyone?

"Trust me, Penny."

I stared at her. And suddenly all I saw were all the things that were different from the Melissa I remembered. She was a complete stranger. *Trust her?* I didn't know her.

CHAPTER 16
Friday

"There are a ton of cameras in this apartment," I said as I stared at one of the two that were mounted in the kitchen. I had walked around searching for them, despite Melissa trying to distract me. "How many do you think there are total?"

"I don't know," Melissa said. "I don't live here."

"But if you could guess. How many do you think are in each room?"

"At least one." She shrugged. "Maybe two or three depending on how big the room is and if there are any weird angles I guess."

"Are there more than just two in here?"

"Penny, I really have no idea. I only see two."

She was being very unhelpful. I wasn't trying to hang out with her right now. This was no time for a girls' night. I was in a life or death situation. Couldn't she see that? I was busy planning an escape, which now seemed impossible thanks to all these stupid cameras. "Do you think James watches me all the time? Like when he's at work and stuff?"

"No. I told you, they're for security reasons. I doubt he ever watches you. At least not without your permission." She winked at me.

Gross. "He just has other people look at me?" I lowered my voice. "There's a camera in my freaking bathroom. You can get arrested for shit like that."

"That's only if you put a camera in a public bathroom..."

"That's beside the point."

Melissa sighed. "If you tripped and fell in the bathroom, you'd be happy there were cameras so you wouldn't bleed out. Bathrooms can be very dangerous places. Just think of everything that could go wrong. Razor accidents, drowning, accidental choking by toothbrush." She laughed, but I was no longer paying attention to her.

I bit the inside of my lip. She was right. Bathrooms could be dangerous. And she had just given me a brilliant idea. Or an awful one. Really it was just brilliantly awful. An accident would definitely draw the two security guards away from the front door and give me time to escape. Their sole purpose was apparently to protect me. It was devious and perfect and...impossible. But now that the thought was in my head, it wouldn't go away.

I looked back up at the camera. I wasn't even really upset about the cameras monitoring me at all times. It wasn't like anyone was going to be watching me for much longer. I was upset because the cameras were an issue for my escape. The security guards were most likely watching me right now. I looked away from the camera.

My plan was already running wild in my mind. When I was little, I played an epic April Fool's Day prank on my dad. The toilet in the downstairs bathroom had an issue with overflowing. So I poured a cup of water on the floor outside of the bathroom and then locked myself inside. I screamed about the toilet overflowing and pretended to panic instead of letting my dad come in and fix it. He almost broke the door down. Needless to say, I never played a prank ever again because of how upset he got.

Melissa's idea about bleeding out in the bathroom had given me a similar idea. I could pretend to lock myself in the bathroom and cause some kind of distraction that would draw the security guards away from the front door. If I hid downstairs, maybe it would give me enough time to slip out undetected. There was just one issue. The stupid bathroom camera. And all the other cameras. They'd see me walking around prepping everything and they'd also know for a fact that I wasn't in the bathroom. *Unless...*

"I need to pee," I said.

"Um. Okay." Melissa gave me a weird look.

"I'll be right back!" My voice came out weird and high-pitched. *Stop it.* I practically ran out of the kitchen to avoid her scrutiny.

I glanced around the bathroom. It definitely seemed like there was only one camera. *This could work.* All I needed was to move the camera. And get some kind of disguise. *First things first.* I began humming and started to pull down my pants like I was about to use the toilet, but then paused and stared at the camera. I shook my head like I was truly disgusted that there were people watching my every move. Which was easy to do, because I didn't even have to pretend. I even gave the camera the middle finger for good measure. *Please believe I'm just pissed about you watching me.* I climbed on top of the sink and pushed the camera toward the wall so that it was no longer monitoring the bathroom.

I walked over to the tub. I didn't want to cause anyone distress, but I couldn't think of a better option. It wasn't like James would just let me walk away. There was an air of desperation around him. I felt bad for thinking it. I felt worse when I turned the faucet on in the bathtub and plugged the drain.

It probably wasn't the best idea, but it was the only one I could think of. I had been in here long enough. They'd be suspicious that I had irritable bowel syndrome if I took much longer. I slipped out of the bathroom and glanced around the master bedroom one last time. There were definitely no cameras pointed at the bathroom door. I locked the door from the inside, and closed it as quietly as I could.

I didn't know how much time I had, but it probably wasn't much. The tub would overflow soon. And I needed to hide. I walked as quickly as I could out of the room and down the stairs.

"Penny?" Melissa said from the kitchen. "Do you want to watch a movie or something?"

"Sure. You pick one. I'm going to ask Josh if he wants to watch too." *Smooth.* I ran to the guest room, knocked on the door, and opened it before he had time to answer.

"Um…hey, Penny," Josh said as he looked up from his laptop. He was sitting on the bed working. "I heard Melissa ask about watching a movie. I'll be out in a few minutes. Just gotta send one last email."

"It's freezing in here," I said.

He looked back up from his screen. "Yeah? It feels fine to me."

"Oh, good. Could I borrow your hoodie then?"

"My hoodie?" He looked at me like I had asked to borrow something much weirder than a sweatshirt.

It wasn't a big deal. It wasn't even the weirdest thing I was going to ask him for. *Give it to me*, I silently pleaded.

"I guess," he said. He pulled it off and tossed it at me.

I quickly pulled it on over my shirt. "That helped a little, but geez, it's still freezing. Our air conditioning must be broken in the way that it won't turn off. Can I borrow your pants too?"

This time he stared at me like I had asked to borrow his pants. Which made sense, because I had. I'd earned his stare this time.

"Um…no."

I laughed awkwardly. "Why? They're just pants."

"They wouldn't even fit you."

"I know. That's the point. They'll be big and comfy…"

"I pack light, Penny. I didn't bring a million outfits with me like Melissa did." He laughed. "I can't just give you my pants."

"Please?"

He just stared at me.

"I don't have any comfy clothes here. And I'm so freaking cold. And all I want in the entire world is a warm pair of sweatpants to make me feel normal again."

"If it seriously means that much to you, why don't you just borrow a pair of sweats from James?"

"I don't want his. I want nothing to do with him."

He pressed his lips together as he stared at me. And then he shook his head. "Fine. Turn around will you?"

I turned away from the bed. In a few seconds, I felt a rolled up ball of sweatpants hit my back. "Thank you!" I pulled them on over my workout leggings. "I'll let you get back to work."

"Eh, I'll just come watch the movie after I put on another pair of pants." He set his laptop to the side. "Work can wait until tomorrow."

"No."

"Why?"

"Your work is important." I literally had no idea what he did for a living. Hopefully it was important. "Plus, Melissa's going to be mad I stole your pants. Let me go explain everything to her. And I'll let you know when it's safe to come out."

He laughed. "You're probably right about her being mad about the pants. Okay, fine. I need a minute to change anyway." His bottom half was under the covers, but I knew for a fact that he was pants-less.

"Great. Just...stay here until I say you can come out."

There was that strange look again. "Okay."

I lifted the hood on the hoodie. "See you." I realized it was weird to say goodbye like that when I was supposed to see him again in a few minutes. But it was goodbye. And he had helped me tremendously in my escape. This was the perfect disguise. The security team would think I was still in the guest room and that Josh was the one trolloping around the house.

"Is Josh com..." Melissa's voice trailed off when she saw me. "What the hell are you wearing?"

"No, Josh isn't coming. He's working, remember? Don't bother him."

"It was your idea. Seriously, Penny, why are you wearing his clothes?"

"I suddenly got really cold."

"So you thought it was appropriate to borrow my boy-friend's pants? What is wrong with you?"

A big part of my plan's chance at success was mass con-fusion. It seemed to be working. I just had no idea why she was so upset about this. Did I make a habit of borrowing her boyfriend's pants? I doubted it. "Chill."

She glared at me like I was the devil. "You want me to chill? How about you take his pants off?"

"No. He gave them to me. And I'm cold. Actually, I'm so cold that I'm just going to go take a bath to try to warm up. I'll leave his pants outside the bathroom door for you, psycho."

"I'm not a psycho for not wanting you in my boy-friend's pants."

I laughed. "It's not a big deal."

"It is to me. You always do this." Her anger was gone. It looked like she was about to cry.

What had I done to her? I suddenly actually felt cold. I tucked my hands into the front pocket of the hoodie. The more I learned about the person I had become, the more I hated her. I didn't know how I had become this monster. All I knew was that Penny Hunter was clearly not a good person. It was just more reason to leave. "I'm sorry. I'll take them off. Just give me a few minutes, okay?" I left the room without waiting for a response.

When I got to my room, I pulled the duffel bag over my shoulder. I was about to go hide when I realized this was exactly what a monster would do. Leaving without saying anything was harsh. I didn't want James to worry, I wanted him to let me go. I grabbed a piece of paper off the nightstand and left a quick note.

James,

I'm sorry. I can't do this anymore. This is better for both of us. Please forget about me.

-Penny

I dropped it in front of the bathroom door and then ran out of the room. My whole body froze when I heard James' voice from downstairs. Him being home ruined everything. *Shit, shit, shit!*

"I assumed you knew," he said.

"Why would you assume that? I was completely blindsided today, James," Melissa said. "You asked me to help her try to remember you, but how can I possibly do that when I don't know anything about you."

"She never told you?"

"No." They were both quiet for a moment. "So it's true? You're an addict?"

"I…I'm good right now."

"You don't look good, James. Honestly, you look terrible and…"

"How do you think you'd look if Josh almost died? I'm dealing as best I can. And I'm not using."

"Do you swear?"

"Yes."

"Good. Because you'll need your A-game tonight. Penny's lost her freaking mind. She stole Josh's pants and then pretended it wasn't weird at all and then ran away to take a bath because apparently she's freezing cold."

"She never takes baths."

"Yeah, well, she's not exactly acting like herself. God, I barely recognize her. I've known her longer with you two together than I ever knew her when she was single. I'm used to you two being solid."

"I'm going to go check on her."

"Let me," Melissa said with a sigh. "She used to always wear Tyler's sweatpants when she'd come over. I may have snapped at her because it reminded me of that."

Man of my dreams Tyler? I bet I did want to be in his pants. I almost laughed at the thought. There was no way I had tried to steal Melissa's boyfriend. She had to know that.

James laughed. "Yeah. I hated when she'd do that too."

"Why didn't you tell her to stop then? You could have saved me from a huge fight we had."

"I was trying to be less...possessive. I trusted her."

"So not cool, James."

There was a pause.

"I noticed that you used the past tense there," Melissa said.

"I'm trying to hold on." He sounded so defeated. "But I'm tired. I want to wake up and for all of this to be over."

Me too.

"Well, let me go check on her. Sit down and relax. That's why I came...to help."

"Thanks, Melissa."

"I'll be right back."

Oh my God. I looked both ways and then ran to the hall closet and jumped inside. I didn't even have time to close the door when I heard her footsteps on the stairs.

"Penny?" she called as she went into the bedroom.

Please work. Please don't see me.

I heard her knock on the bathroom door. "Penny?"

Silence.

"Penny!" she screamed at the top of her lungs and banged on the bathroom door. "Penny, let me in!" She banged harder. "Open the fucking door, Penny!" More banging. "Josh! Josh, get help!" she screamed down the stairs. "Someone help!"

Commotion, shouting, footsteps pounding on the stairs.

"Penny!" James yelled. "Penny, open the door! Baby, please." It sounded like he was dying. Like his heart was breaking.

I thought about what I had written and cringed. I told him I was sorry. I told him I couldn't do this anymore. That this was better for both of us. That he needed to forget about me.

"Penny!" Pure agony coated every syllable. "Penny, don't do this! Let me in!"

I could barely understand him through his sobs. And I knew what he thought. I hadn't meant the note to make it worse. But it had. He thought I was trying to kill myself. Maybe he thought I already had. Guilt seeped into my bones, paralyzing me. I should have been running. But I couldn't make myself leave when he sounded so distraught. It physically pained me.

"I thought she was downstairs." I recognized one of the security guard's voices. "We saw Josh go into the room..." his voice trailed off. "When the hell did you go back downstairs?"

"I never left my room," Josh said.

"Oh, fuck." More footsteps on the stairs.

"Penny!" James yelled as he pounded his fist against the door. "You can't leave me!" he sobbed. "Baby."

I wanted to curl up in a ball and die in that closet. His pain tore me in two. His words shattered me. But the crack of wood breaking pulled me out of my trance. They were breaking the bathroom door, which meant they were about to see that I wasn't in the bathroom.

It was now or never. *I'm sorry.* I burst out of the closet and ran as fast as I could. And I didn't stop. I ran away from the pain in his voice. The pain in my chest. I ran as fast as I possibly could away from the life I didn't want. *I'm sorry, James. I'm so so sorry.*

PART 2

CHAPTER 17

Saturday

I pressed my hand against the passenger window.

"Don't put me through that again, Penny." James kissed my neck as he moved my hips faster and faster.

"Never." His hands slid to my ass and he slammed his cock into me. I moaned as his fingers dug into my skin. I loved the way he knew exactly what to do to make me completely surrender my body to him. He pulled me closer to him.

"Promise me."

"I promise," I said breathlessly. It was a promise I knew I could keep.

The seat belt buckle hit my knee and I quickly pushed it aside. The angle in the car was awkward but the sensation of him inside me was all that mattered.

"You're mine," he growled.

"Yes! I'm yours!" I moaned.

Someone knocked on the car window, but all I could see was fogged up glass around my handprint.

The knocking grew louder.

My eyes flew open. I was alone in the car. And someone's face was practically pressed against the driver's side window. I jumped, slamming my elbow into the horn. "Sorry," I mumbled, even though I knew the guy standing outside my car couldn't hear me. My dream had felt so real. I could barely calm my rapid heartbeat just thinking about it. I took a deep breath. The dream meant nothing. I probably just had it because I was sleeping in a car. A car fantasy for my current predicament. It had nothing to actually do with James.

"Move it along!" he yelled through the glass and pointed toward the exit of the parking lot.

I wiped the drool off the side of my face as I watched him walk away. He was wearing an apron with a logo that matched the pharmacy. I was lucky he hadn't called the cops on me. But if I had been in a beat up old Chevy or something, he probably wouldn't have even noticed me. Instead, I had accidentally swiped the most conspicuous car. When I pressed the unlock button in the parking garage I had cringed. I had basically stolen the Batmobile. So much for being discreet.

Which was exactly why I had pulled over in the middle of nowhere for a few minutes of shut-eye. I was hoping no one would notice. But a few minutes had quickly turned into a few hours. Fortunately, pharmacy man didn't seem to be interested in calling the cops on me.

I put the key into the ignition and pulled out of the parking lot. I had no idea where I was going. No cell phone meant no GPS. But I was trying to stay off the highway so that there was less of a possibility of being pulled over. And I was generally heading south. *I think.*

There was only one realistic possibility of where I could go. My parents' house. They were staying in the city as far as I knew, so they wouldn't be home.

But the safety of my childhood home wasn't calling to me. I watched the trees rushing by. It was summer. Not many students would be around campus. Maybe going back there would help jog my memory.

No. I didn't want my memory to come back. I wanted to forget. I wanted to move on. But where else could I go? I looked down at the gas meter. I only had a quarter of a tank. Eventually my gas level would decide for me. That was the best way. Leave it to fate.

I drove for awhile longer and saw a sign for I-95. If anything felt like fate, that did. I was sick of the winding roads. I'd just be careful not to speed. And I'd at least know where I was.

I merged onto the highway. And despite trying to just drive for the purpose of getting farther away, I found myself following signs to Newark. It was like I was being drawn toward the University of New Castle. Maybe I just needed to see it for myself. See the changes around campus to further prove that I had lost seven years of my life.

***

I drove along Main Street looking for somewhere to park without a meter. I didn't have any money, so I'd be sleeping in my car again tonight. It would be best if I wasn't outside someone's house that would call the cops.

I pulled the car to a stop on one of the side streets. I looked out the window. Melissa had dragged me to a frat party here once. All the occupants were probably home for the summer. And even if there was anyone living there during summer semester, I doubted that they'd care about my car being here. They'd probably take pictures with it and pretend they met Batman. Or call for it to be towed away.

But I didn't have much of a choice. The car was running on empty. I wasn't going anywhere until I found a pawnshop to sell the watch I had stolen. I cut the gas and climbed out of the car, pulling my duffel bag with me. I couldn't afford to let it get towed away with the car. My only possessions were in that bag. *Sort of.* I didn't recognize any of the clothes I had packed. And judging from my supposed life, I certainly hadn't paid for any of my clothing. None of that mattered though. I was finally free. I smiled as I started walking along Main Street. Everything felt so familiar.

The only time I had been to the University of New Castle in the summer was when I came to tour it before applying. Not that I needed the tour. I always figured I'd come here. Both my parents had. And it wasn't like I had the urge like so many other Delawareans to get the hell out of town. I liked it here. No, I loved it here. I breathed in a deep breath of fresh air. *So much better than New York.*

I turned off Main Street, down the familiar path toward my dorm. I felt more like myself here than I ever had in New York. No expectations. No stranger trying to force me to remember a person that wasn't me.

The thought of James' voice when he was banging on the bathroom door clouded my mind. He'd know I didn't kill myself once he saw that bathroom was empty, right? When he saw one of his cars was gone? He'd know.

I didn't want him to be depressed that I'd died. I wanted him to move on, knowing that I chose to leave him. He clearly needed a fresh start. He needed someone that could make him laugh more. I smiled at the thought. He had a nice laugh.

Why am I thinking about him? I looked down at the brick walkway. Part of me did think I'd suddenly remember everything once I stepped back on campus. I thought it would come back in a rush. My meeting James. Falling for him. Deciding to leave everything I knew and loved.

But all I remembered was studying nonstop. And wishing Austin would like me as much as I liked him. I kept walking. Maybe seeing Austin would change things. I shook away the thought. It wouldn't. Seeing Melissa hadn't changed anything, and she knew me better than anyone. Life as I knew it was over. But I had a chance to be anything I wanted now. I wasn't tied down in a place that didn't feel like home. I was free.

I came to a stop in front of a huge statue of a book in the middle of a circular walking path that I remembered being statue-less. *What the hell?* It was the stupidest thing I had ever seen. You used to be able to stand in the middle of the circle and clap, and you could hear the clap under a tree off the side of the path. It was awesome and like a secret University of New Castle student and alumni thing. Now? *Ruined.* Everything was ruined.

I turned around in a circle. There were new dorm buildings in the distance. And everything seemed to have been added on to. Why couldn't anyone see that it was fine the way it was? I barely even recognized parts of campus anymore. I felt tears pooling in the corners of my eyes. Why had I come here? I couldn't remember anything. And the campus had kept growing without me. It was different, and stupid, and ugly. Nothing was the same.

Maybe my dorm will be. I picked up my pace and followed the path. If I kept my eyes on the bricks beneath my feet, campus felt the same. They hadn't changed, even though everything else had. I looked up in order to cross the street and my feet stopped. My dorm was the same. But right behind it was a new massive twenty-some-stories dorm building. My dorm even looked like it was being shaded by the monster building. It was probably only a matter of time before it was knocked down and replaced by something new and shiny.

Screw this. I didn't need to be here to be reminded that my memory was missing key parts of my life. I started walking back toward Main Street. A fresh start meant going somewhere I didn't know. Maybe I could go to California. The thought was preposterous. And that's how I knew how right it was. It was something I'd never do, and therefore the perfect thing to do. I could reinvent myself. And no one would know who I was. I'd disappear.

I thought about James screaming again. Would he let me disappear? Would he try to find me? *Stop thinking about him.*

"Penny?" called a deep voice from behind me.

Son of a bitch. I hadn't been on this campus in years. Who could possibly recognize me? I picked up my pace. I wasn't going to have anyone dragging me back to New York. Hopefully they'd think they had the wrong person.

"Penny." He put his hand on my shoulder. "I thought that was you. I didn't realize you were even out of the hospital yet. How are you feeling? When I heard what happened, I was so worried. Did you get the flowers I sent?"

"You have the wrong person." I shrugged his hand away without looking at him.

He laughed. "I think I know the beautiful Penny Hunter when I see her. I was at your wedding for Christ's sake."

My tears had already been threatening to spill. And hearing him call me Penny Hunter was the tipping point. "That's not my name." I felt my tears streaming down my cheeks. "My name is Penny Taylor. And I'm not married. I've never been married. And I'm not even sure if I ever want to be married now." I doubt he could even understand me through my sobs. Finally, I looked up at him and wished I wasn't crying. I wished I had brushed my teeth this morning and hadn't slept in a car. He was beautiful.

But not as beautiful as James. The thought hit me like a ton of bricks. It made more tears come. Had I made a mistake by running? The memory of James' broken sobs made me cry harder. I knew I hadn't. I knew getting out of New York City was the right thing to do. So why was I crying?

"Penny? Jesus, what happened? What's wrong?"

I didn't care who he was. He knew me. Or at least, a version of me. And I was almost out of gas. I had no phone. Nowhere to sleep. No food. No money. And no pawnshop to trade the watch I had stolen for cash. It felt like we were supposed to run into each other today. He had to help me. I didn't have anyone else to turn to. "I need your help."

"Of course. Whatever you need. Is James here too?" He looked over my shoulder like he was waiting for James to appear.

"No." I shook my head. "And he can't know that I'm here. Please, don't tell him."

"Why? What happened?"

"I just need some cash. If you write down your name and address I can repay you as soon as I get settled. I touched my shoulder, for some reason thinking a purse had magically appeared there. But I only had my duffel bag and I knew for a fact that I didn't pack a pen or notepad. "I don't have a pen or paper. But if you have a pen, you could write it on my hand. I swear I'll pay you back. I promise."

He just stared at me.

"I have a good memory. You could just tell me. I promise I'll give you back every penny. I just...I need to get to California. A few hundred dollars should..."

"What the hell is in California?"

"A fresh start. Please, if we're friends..."

"If? Penny, look at me."

I tried to remember. Despite what everyone thought, I had been trying to remember this whole time. But all I saw was a stranger. He was the exact opposite of James. His hair was light instead of dark. His skin was much tanner. And he was rugged looking, instead of sophisticated. A five o'clock shadow covered his jaw line and it was hard to look away from his sharp features. I blinked. But I had no freaking clue who he was. "I don't remember you."

His Adam's apple rose and fell as he studied me. "I'm going to call James. He needs..."

"You can't." I grabbed his arm and took a deep breath. "Please, you can't. I don't want to go back to New York. I can't go back there."

"Penny..."

"I don't love him. I'm not...I can't. Please don't make me go back to him."

He studied me for a moment, like he was trying to determine if I was telling the truth. "Okay."

I locked eyes with him. "Okay? You'll give me the money?"

"No, I'm not giving you money to flee to California. You can stay with me."

I stared at him. He had light brown hair. Not dirty blonde, but close. Age changed people. And he wasn't really looking at me like just a friend. He was looking at me like he truly cared. Like maybe at one point we were something more than just friends. *Tyler.* This had to be him. I breathed a sigh of relief. I could trust him. I knew it. I could feel it in my bones.

Sometimes fate had a funny way of working out. It made me get back onto I-95. It made me come to Newark. It made me walk around campus for just the right amount of time, because then I ran into him. Maybe this was my second chance at doing things right. Tyler had clearly been the right choice for me all along. Melissa had even said so. Now I got to fix everything.

"Do you promise you won't call James?" I asked.

"We can discuss that once you get settled in."

"I'm not coming with you unless you promise." I knew I was being juvenile. But I had bit back the pinky swear promise line from coming out of my mouth.

"Fine. I promise I won't call your husband. If that's really what you want, Penny. But you have to tell me what's going on. Are you in some sort of trouble? After everything that happened, I never imagined you'd run off by yourself. Isn't the man that hurt you still out there?"

I don't know. My stomach growled. I hadn't eaten since I had picked at my dinner with James. "I'll tell you everything if you buy me lunch."

He laughed. "I'll do you one better. I'll cook us something."

He was handsome and could cook? Why had I not chosen him all those years ago? I was clearly messed up in the head. Who knew that losing my memory was the only way to set me straight?

CHAPTER 18

Saturday

"So you really don't remember anything?" he asked.

I took another bite of steak and shrugged. "Nope. Nothing. And honestly, I think it's for the best. That whole life seemed…stifling. I couldn't bear to be there for another second. That's why I left."

"And you came here. It's where you and James met. Do you think you were drawn here because of that?"

"No, not at all. I came here because being on campus was the last thing I remembered. I think a small part of me thought everything would go back to normal if I came here. But obviously I was wrong. There was also the issue of not having any money. And of course I stole a car with less than half a tank of gas. It's pretty much empty right now. Which is why I asked to borrow money from you."

"But you can't seriously be willing to leave your family. Let me take you back home."

"God, they might technically be my family, but they don't feel like my family. What if I made a mistake all those years ago? What if I was never supposed to marry James? I feel like I've been given a second chance at the life I want."

"And what kind of life is it that you want?"

"I don't know…" I let my voice trail off as I looked around the apartment. "This is nice."

He laughed. "This is the life you gave up to move to New York."

"And I think I made a mistake."

"Then just tell James that. I'm sure he'd be willing to move back here. He never sold his apartment."

"He didn't?" Maybe I could stay there. It wasn't the independent life I wanted, but it would give me some time to get back on my feet. And there was no reason for him to look there for me. He didn't know where I was. "Well, I could stay there instead of here then. Where is it?"

"Top floor."

"Of this apartment building?"

"Yup."

"Interesting."

He smiled. "And why is that?"

"You just don't look like the type of person that would like the same kind of apartment as James Hunter."

"I do alright for myself, Penny."

"That's not what I meant. I mean, obviously you do." I gestured around the apartment. When I lived on campus, these apartments were being sold for millions. They were most certainly not intended for students. "I just mean you look more…real."

"I don't know whether that's a compliment or an insult." He leaned forward slightly, resting his elbows on the table. It was just further proof that I was right. James would probably never get caught dead with his elbows on the table.

"It's definitely a compliment."

He shook his head. "James is probably worried sick about you. I think I should give him a call."

"You promised you wouldn't."

"Well...I didn't pinky promise."

I laughed. "You know, I thought about asking you to do that, but stopped myself because it seemed so childish. But that's the problem. I don't feel like a grown up." *Besides for the fact that I get tired more easily.* It must have been a symptom of old age that I wasn't used to. I touched my stomach. It was significantly less bloated than it had been in the hospital, but it definitely wasn't back to normal. And then there were the unexplained scars. I wanted to know what had happened to me. "You do pretty well for yourself, right?"

He looked taken aback by the change of topic. "I do."

"Okay, here's the new agreement. I'll let you call James and tell him I was here. *If* you take me to see a doctor. And if you give me...$500 and a 12 hour head start before you call him." I stuck out my hand.

"Why do you want to go to the doctor? You were just in the hospital for weeks."

"No one would tell me what happened." I kept my hand outstretched.

"I'm not letting you go to California alone."

"Then come with me."

He laughed.

"I'm serious. We had something once, I know we did. This can be our fresh start."

"James is my friend, Penny."

And my husband. So why didn't I feel as guilty as he seemed to? "Come on, it'll be fun."

"No deal. And I'm calling James." He stood up from his chair.

"Melissa told me that once I made a pro-con list between choosing you and James. You won. Hands down.

And I have no idea why I didn't listen to my list. I love lists. I make them all the time. All I can guess is that I lost my freaking mind when I stopped being a teenager. Or James drugged me. Or…I don't know. But I should have chosen you. This is where I want to live, not some stupid, loud, crowded, gross city. And you're my type, not him. Never in my wildest dreams did anyone like James make an appearance. I swear there is nothing left for me in New York."

"I think 20 year old you was smarter than you realize. And I'm positive that you never liked me all that much."

"I disagree. I'm pretty sure that I did. I must have, I mean look at you. And I know you loved me once too. Tyler, I…"

"Tyler?" He started laughing. "Wow, this makes so much more sense now." He shook his head. "My name is Brendan. We shared two kisses, years ago. And I promise, you never loved me. Not even a little bit. You couldn't have turned me down any faster. Now come on. I'll take you to the doctor and then I'll call James."

Brendan? Who the hell is Brendan?

***

I had confessed my deepest secrets to a man who lived in James' old apartment building. A practical stranger who I kissed twice, apparently only to try to move on from James. And now the two of them were friends and he had zero feelings for me? *Crap, crap, crap!*

I tapped the back of my heels against the exam table. Coming here was a huge mistake. Trusting Brendan was an even bigger mistake. For all I knew, he was calling James right now. I had been tempted to insist that he come back here with me, but I doubted we were close enough for that. Not only was my escape going terribly wrong, but I was more curious than ever who Tyler was.

There was a knock on the door and a doctor came in. He was about my dad's age.

"It's nice to meet you, Gwendolyn Alabaster," he stuck out his hand.

That was the one thing Brendan agreed to let me do. Give the doctor a fake name. I quickly shook his hand. "Thanks for seeing me on such short notice."

"It was no issue at all. Now what can I help you with, Gwendolyn?"

"I had surgery a few weeks ago, and I can't remember what for. I was hoping you could tell me."

"You can't remember? Was it minor surgery, or…"

"I'm not sure. I was blacked out." Drinking seemed like a good excuse for this. I didn't want him figuring out who I was and calling James or something. I was hoping there was still some way to prevent Brendan from calling him.

"I see." He wrote something down in his notebook. "Do you often blackout after you've been drinking?"

"No, it was just a one-time thing. I was deeply depressed. But I woke up with these scars on my stomach." I lifted up the bottom of my shirt.

He lowered the glasses that were on the top of his head and bent down to take a closer look. "That wasn't minor surgery, Gwendolyn."

"So you know what it was for?"

"The location of the sutures are consistent with a bilateral oophorectomy. But I can do a more thorough exam…"

"No, that's okay. I don't really have time." I didn't trust Brendan on his own out there in the waiting room. "What does it mean? Bilateral oopho…what was it again?"

"A bilateral oophorectomy."

"Yeah. That."

"Well, I can't be certain that's what it was. It's highly uncommon with someone your age that doesn't have any other health issues to need such a surgery. And you've said you've never been pregnant or have had any type of cancer?"

"No, I haven't."

He frowned. "Are you certain you've never been pregnant? The stretch marks on your stomach would usually indicate that you…"

"Are you calling me fat?"

"No, ma'am. Not at all. You're quite thin. I'm merely suggesting that you may not have even realized you were pregnant. That's not unheard of, especially for someone's first pregnancy when it's not planned."

I was pregnant? No, that's impossible. I'd know. I'd feel different. "I'd think I'd know if I had a kid. Wouldn't I be…leaking?" I gestured to my breasts. Milk wasn't spilling out of them. Clearly I didn't have a baby to breastfeed.

"It's likely that you had a miscarriage then. It's my best guess for why you'd have a bilateral oophorectomy, especially since you have no familial medical history of ovarian cancer."

"Okay." *Okay?* Nothing about this conversation was okay. "But what does that mean? What does the surgery involve? Are there any complications that I should be looking out for? Is there anything I can't do now?" I felt fine. I really did. I was already pulling my shirt down, ready to get as far away as possible from this doctor. I didn't even believe him. There was no way I'd had a miscarriage. But maybe that would explain the grief in James' eyes. It would explain why he was so broken.

"The surgery entails the removal of both your ovaries."

"Okay." *Why did I keep saying okay, damn it?* I swallowed hard. "What does that mean?" But I knew what ovaries were for. At least, what I had learned in health class in high school. Ovaries made eggs. They controlled hormones. They were really important. Why had they removed both of mine? Why not one? I started blinking fast. "That's okay, right? I can take medicine to control my hormones?" God, maybe this was why I kept crying.

"Of course. Your lifestyle won't change at all after you've healed a few more weeks. It's very manageable. But..." his voice trailed off. There was kindness in his eyes as his face morphed into a look of pure sympathy.

"What?" my voice came out as a whisper. I knew it was bad. I knew it, but I needed him to say it.

"It also means that you won't be able to have any children, Gwendolyn. I'm so sorry."

There was a lump in my throat that wouldn't seem to go away. I blinked fast, willing my tears not to spill. There was never a time in my life when I hadn't thought I'd be a mother one day. Not now. Of course not now. But one day. I played with dolls way longer than my other friends growing up. I loved the idea of kids and babies, even though I hadn't spent much time with them. No time, really. But I wanted them. Desperately. I knew it, because now that I had been told I couldn't, I felt like I was breaking.

"I know this is hard to hear. Especially if you just suffered through a miscarriage. I have a counselor I can recommend you to see. It's good to have someone to talk to as you digest this information."

"That's okay." I slid off the exam table.

"Ms. Alabaster, do you have someone you can talk to?"

I flinched at my fake name. "Of course." But I didn't even believe the words out of my mouth. I didn't expect him to believe me either.

"Your boyfriend perhaps? The man waiting for you in the living room?"

"Yeah."

"If I was the father, I'd want to know." He gave me a kind smile.

Did James know? I bit the inside of my lip. Was he even the father? He said I wasn't happy. What if I had cheated on him? There were too many what ifs. And really, none of the questions running through my head mattered. The baby had died. And the one thing I wanted in life had just been stripped from me. I'd never have children. Ever. "I have to go." I fled the exam room without waiting to see if he had any more to say.

"Everything good?" Brendan asked as he set down the magazine he'd been flipping through.

"Peachy." Again, I didn't believe my own words. I didn't know how to numb the pain I was feeling. Leaving wouldn't help. Moving to California wouldn't erase my medical history no matter how sunny it was. Drowning my sorrows in booze for one night wouldn't help either. But it would certainly make me feel better right now. "I need a drink."

He frowned as he stood up. "Was it bad news?"

Everything I learned about my current life was bad news. One thing after the next. I took a deep breath. But Brendan wasn't the person who I could open up to. It should be James. He was the one that cared about me. Did he know all of this already?

James was handsome. And rich. And super successful. I was so much younger than him. A classic trophy wife. If he knew I couldn't have children, he wouldn't have been trying so hard for me to remember our lives together. He'd be trading me in for a younger model. That's what people like him did.

"Do you have James' number?" I asked, ignoring his question.

"Yeah. Have you changed your mind about calling him?"

"I thought about what you said, and you're right, I do need to let him know that I'm safe. But I want to call him from a pay phone. And I want to be a few drinks in when I do it. Let's go to Kildare's."

"Kildare's closed a few years ago."

"What do you mean Kildare's closed? It was the best! What the hell happened to this campus? It's gone to shitsville. None of the changes they've been making are necessary."

He laughed. "I know. But the university doesn't have control over which establishments stay on Main Street. And there are plenty of other bars we could go to."

"Let's do Grottos then. And don't you dare tell me Grottos closed too. I'll lose it."

"It's still open. But we could go somewhere a little fancier if you want. Iron Hill maybe?"

"But I love Grottos. They have the absolute best pizza. And what's better than pizza when you've been drinking?"

He smiled. "Grottos it is then."

CHAPTER 19

Saturday

I was wrong before. Drinking away your sorrows worked wonders. Not one thought of unborn babies entered my mind. Nor did the prospect of never having children. I just felt good. So good.

"My arms are so heavy," I said with a laugh. "Do your arms get super heavy when you drink too? I think all the liquid must go straight to my biceps." I turned my arm to examine my muscle and accidentally poured some of my drink on the table. I stifled a laugh. "Party foul!"

"You've had way too much to drink." Brendan grabbed my glass away from me.

"No I haven't. We only just got here."

"We've been here for over an hour. And by the way, you promised you'd call James."

"But I don't have his number."

He tapped the napkin in front of me. "I wrote it down for you as soon as we got here. Remember?"

"Huh. No." I lifted it up and examined it. "I don't remember and I also don't like numbers that start with anything other than a 302 area code. I'm not calling this stupid New York City number."

"Penny, you pinky promised."

"I did?"

"You did. Twice."

"I think two promises cancel each other out. It's a fact. It's not my fault you don't understand the rules."

"No way." He handed me his phone. "Call him. Before I do."

"He'll know I borrowed your phone. He'll recognize your number. I need to use a pay phone."

"There are no pay phones anymore. At least, not that I know of."

"There used to be one here…" I looked over my shoulder. Hadn't there been? It was one of maybe three on campus. *Where are you, elusive pay phone?*

"Penny, that was a long time ago."

I sighed. "Well I can't call him on your phone. I revoke my offer to call him. No deal."

"I'll be right back. Don't move, okay?"

I didn't agree, but I didn't plan on moving anyway. As soon as he left, I pulled my drink back to my side of the table. It turned out that Brendan was a little bossy too, just like James. James, James, James. Why did I keep thinking about him? I leaned down to put my straw in my mouth, but missed completely. The straw hit my cheek. *Ow.* I laughed and tried again.

Did James and I ever come here? We must have. I loved Grottos. Still did. Always would. It was the best pizza on the planet, and no one could tell me any differently. I grabbed another slice and took a huge bite. Cheesy, delicious perfection. I sighed.

"Here," Brendan said and tossed a cell phone down on the table in front of me. "Now you can make that call you promised you'd make."

"Whose phone is that?"

"I borrowed it from the bartender."

That was a good idea, why hadn't I thought of that? "Okay. I'll call him. Why was I calling him again? I don't want to talk to him."

"At least let him know that you're safe, alright?"

"I can do that. But I'm not leaving."

"You can stay as long as you want."

I smiled as I lifted up the phone. It finally felt like I had someone in my life I could trust. Someone I felt like myself around. I bit the inside of my lip. That wasn't true. Rob had been so nice. I had truly felt comfortable around him. And James. I was starting to get used to him. As a friend. Not whatever we were supposed to be. And as a friend, he deserved to know that I wasn't dead in a ditch. I punched in the number Brendan had written on the napkin and put the cell phone to my ear.

"Hello?" James answered after one ring. He sounded out of breath, like he was running.

What was he doing? "I'm safe. I just wanted you to know that."

"Penny?"

"Yeah…"

"Where are you?" There was a dinging sound on his end, like he had just walked into a convenience store. The same noise sounded just a few seconds after the first one.

"I was just calling to let you know that I'm okay and you don't have to worry." But I wasn't okay. Even with alcohol coursing through my bloodstream, I still felt empty. I had felt that way ever since I left the doctor's office. Or maybe I had felt that way ever since I left New York. Which made zero sense.

"Penny, I've spent almost 24 hours thinking you were dead. So don't fucking tell me not to worry."

I winced at his words. "I left you a note to explain…"

"You didn't explain anything." He exhaled loudly. "You promised you'd hear me out. I was going to tell you everything last night. Just…tell me where you are so I can bring you home."

I shook my head, but then realized he couldn't see me. "I'm not coming back with you."

"Penny, where are you?"

"My favorite restaurant." I had a feeling he had no idea what that was. So I was safe.

"You're in Philly? Fuck," he mumbled. "I thought that La Patisserie closed at like 3 or something?" There was a muffled noise and his voice sounded far away. "Ian, get the car."

I guess he knew me better than I thought. *Better than I knew myself.* La Patisserie was my favorite restaurant. "No, I meant my other favorite restaurant."

"In Wilmington or Newark?"

My heart started racing. There were Grottos in Wilmington and Newark. But there were also some in Rehoboth. Maybe he didn't know I was referring to Grottos. "James, it doesn't matter. Brendan made me call you to let you know I'm safe. Now I have. Please just move on with your life."

"You're with Brendan?"

Shit! Was he psychic? "How did you know who I was with?"

"You just told me. Penny, are you drunk?"

Oh God. I ended the call and threw the phone at Brendan. "He somehow knew I was with you. It's like he can read my freaking mind."

"I heard you tell him you were with me." Brendan's phone started ringing. "He's going to kill me for not calling him sooner." He went to answer it but I slapped it out of his hand.

"Penny, I'm not going to avoid his calls." His phone started ringing again.

"Don't you dare answer it."

"I have to. I can't just ignore him."

"Fine, answer it, traitor. But we need to get out of here, I'm pretty sure he knows where we are." I tried to gracefully slide out of the booth, but I ended up toppling out of it. The floor looked like it was moving. Maybe Brendan was right about me drinking too much.

"Whoa, are you okay?" Brendan put his hands on my waist to steady me. "Take it easy."

I placed my hand down on the table so I could support myself. I hoped I wasn't about to be sick. My stomach felt like it was spinning as much as the floor.

"Are you alright?" Brendan asked.

I shook my head.

"Penny!" someone yelled.

It was like I could still hear James' voice in my head. Why couldn't I stop thinking about him? First the dream, now this? I needed to forget about him like I was asking him to forget about me.

"Penny!" someone yelled again.

Brendan removed his hands from my hips and I almost fell over.

I smelled James before I saw him. The comforting smell of his cologne washed over me. And then his strong arms wrapped around me, cocooning me in warmth. And I didn't know why, but it felt like I was finally home. The thought made tears prick the corners of my eyes.

"Baby." His breath tickled my skin as he nuzzled his face into the side of my neck. "I thought I lost you." The tip of his nose grazed my skin. "I thought I lost you," he said again. And then his lips grazed my skin, setting my body on fire. His fingers pressed into the small of my back, drawing me even closer to him. It was like I was living my dream. He breathed me in like I was the only sustenance he needed.

It felt wonderful. And perfect. And wrong. So so wrong. His distress wasn't for me. His kisses weren't for me. His touch wasn't for me. My stomach rolled. "James." I hated that my voice came out airy and needy.

He held me even tighter, which was comforting, but at the same time it squeezed my stomach.

I pulled away from him just as everything I had eaten decided to make a reappearance. All over his shoes. *God.*

I had the faintest recollection that he was wearing a pair of sneakers instead of dress shoes. He was also wearing jeans and a zip-up hoodie. It was like he had transformed into the non-serious man of my dreams. And he didn't even flinch when I vomited all over his shoes. He just rubbed his hand on my back.

"It's okay, Penny. I'm here. I'm here now and everything's going to be okay."

I believed him. Or at least, I wanted to believe him. But my stomach didn't. I hunched over and threw up again until my stomach was as empty as my heart. He wouldn't be looking at me the same way once I told him I couldn't have children. Those words would erase everything we ever had. It was an easy out. But I wanted him to hold me just a little longer. I wanted him to kiss the side of my neck again. I wanted him to breathe me in like I was the air that filled his lungs. Just one last time so I could ingrain it in my memory. Being loved seemed like a wonderful thing. Maybe one day I'd find out what loving someone felt like.

CHAPTER 20

Sunday

"You said you were tired of hearing everyone talking about the same people in their lives. You said to think outside the box. That's what I did. This," I held the paper up again, "is bullshit, Professor Hunter."

"Please take a seat," he replied calmly.

I ignored him and walked behind his desk so that I was right next to him. I picked up the paper and quoted him: "You failed to harness your audiences' attention. I was one of the last people to go, and I still made them laugh!"

"Penny..."

"It was unclear what your point was," I quoted him again. "My point was that I choose who gets a chance at inspiring me. I said that several times, Professor Hunter. Maybe you weren't listening."

"Penny..."

"And this C- used to be an A. I can see it through the whiteout. You changed my grade. You changed it because you overheard Tyler say that the speech was about him. Well it wasn't about him. It was about you." I poked him hard in the middle of his chest. "I don't know why I ever let you kiss me. Is this a game to you, Professor Hunter?"

He drew closer to me. He looked so angry. "Penny, I'm fully aware that this isn't a game. This is my career that we're talking about."

"And this is my G.P.A." I crinkled the paper in my fist and threw it on the ground. My heart was beating fast. He was glaring down at me from under his thick eyebrows. The hunger in his eyes was a temptation I could no longer resist. I had been lying to myself this whole time. I wasn't a good girl. I was bad. And boldness suddenly came easily to me.

I reached up behind his neck and pulled his head down. Without hesitation, he tilted his head the rest of the way down and kissed me deeply. When our lips touched my whole body tingled. He placed his hands on my back and slowly let them drift to my ass. I loved his hands on me. He squeezed my ass hard and lifted me up. I wrapped my legs around him as he shoved my back against the adjacent wall. He buried his face in my neck and let his lips trace my collarbone. It sent shivers down my spine. I slid my fingers through his thick hair.

He lifted his head. "I told you to stop thinking about me." His breathing was heavy. He pressed his body even more firmly against mine.

"I can't possibly."

"You're infuriating, Penny," he whispered into my ear.

"Then punish me, Professor Hunter."

I sat up in bed, panting. *Ow.* It felt like my head was going to explode. I lifted my hand to my forehead and unceremoniously slapped myself in the face. *Ow.* I leaned forward, resting my forehead against my knees. Another dream. I knew that's all it was. Because I couldn't remember anything before or after it. James had told me he was my professor. So I had a professorly dream. A *really* amazing dream. I squeezed my eyes shut. But it felt so real. Like if I reached out, I'd be sitting on the edge of his desk instead of a bed.

A bed. My eyes flew open. Where the hell was I? I scrambled off the mattress, ignoring my pounding headache. As soon as my feet hit the floor, everything came back in a rush. *James' shoes. God, I had thrown up all over his shoes.*

I turned around in the bedroom. It had the same light gray walls and hardwood floors as Brendan's apartment. Fingers crossed I was still there. I wandered out of the bedroom and knew immediately that I wasn't in Brendan's apartment anymore.

James was standing at the kitchen counter with his back turned toward me. He was wearing the same jeans from yesterday and a fresh t-shirt. His cell phone was balanced between his shoulder and ear.

I felt like I could still taste his lips from my dream. Still smell his cologne. Still feel his hardness pressed against me. *Stop.* What the hell was I doing? My dreams were mixing with my reality, messing with my head. I didn't know James. My reaction to him wasn't real. It was just a fantasy. It meant nothing.

"I'll be back tonight, okay?" he said into the phone as he pulled out something from the toaster oven. He waved his hand in the air like he had just burned himself. "I know. Everything's going to go back to normal soon, I promise. But I have to go, pumpkin."

Pumpkin? I immediately swallowed down my jealousy. I was glad he had someone else in his life. It's what I wanted. I hoped that he'd get back together with his ex-wife. Was that who he was talking to? I wondered if their talks had been going on longer than I was injured. Maybe he was cheating on me. But I didn't believe the thought. He didn't look at me like he wanted someone else. He looked at me like I was his whole world. Not that I knew from experience what that look was. It was possible that I had it all wrong. Maybe he wished I had died.

"I love you too," he said into the phone. "Be good okay?" He laughed at something that was said on the other end. "Then tell Soph I say hi too. I'll see you both later." He hung up the phone and ran his hand through his hair, like the secret he was hiding was excruciating. He didn't need to feel bad. I kind of hoped he was cheating on me. It would make all of this so much easier.

"Pumpkin?" I asked.

He turned around. "No…that…"

"It's okay. Really." I shrugged my shoulders.

"It was just…Rob." He sounded so much more tense than he just had on the phone. Whoever was on the other line made him much happier than I did.

It was true, I didn't know him, but I could still tell he was lying. Obviously. "You call your brother Pumpkin? That seems highly unlikely."

He pressed his lips together.

I broke eye contact with him and my gaze landed on his bare feet. "I'm sorry about your shoes."

"I don't care about my shoes. I'm just glad you're safe."

"Yeah." I folded my arms in front of my chest. "You didn't have to come."

He just stared at me.

"Where's Brendan?"

"In his own apartment." His words came out harsh.

I hugged my arms tighter against my chest. "You don't have to be mad at him. He didn't do anything wrong." I was messing everything up. I didn't want to make his life worse by screwing up his friendships too.

"You were with him all afternoon and he didn't call me. I have a right to be pissed."

"At *me*. Not him."

"I'm not upset with you."

"Well, you should be, James. I was the one that left. I was the one that didn't want to call you. I was the one that wrote the note, which I'm sorry about by the way. For some reason, I didn't think through how it would look. But regardless, you should be upset with *me*, not Brendan."

"I'm trying my best…"

"I'm not asking for your best. I'm asking you to be real. If you're mad at me, tell me. If you want to yell at me, yell at me. Don't take it out on someone else…"

"I don't know what you want from me, Penny. Do you want me to say that I hate that you don't remember me? That you don't remember us?" He walked over toward me. "That I feel like I'm living in a daze? That I don't understand how you could possibly run away from what we have? That it felt like I died last night when I couldn't find you?" He stopped a few inches in front of me. "What? Is that what you want? Then fine. I'm furious with you. But I can't hate you because I love you too fucking much." He looked up at the ceiling like he didn't want me to see his expression. When he titled his face back toward me, his eyes were closed. "It hurts to look at you when you don't look at me the way you used to."

With love. I looked at him like a stranger would. Because that's what I was. A passerby in his life. Nothing more. I wasn't sure what made me do it, but I reached out and touched his cheek.

He inhaled sharply. As if my touch shocked him like his shocked me. Like it ignited something inside of him. Images of my dream returned. His lips on mine, his fingers on my skin. I immediately removed my hand.

"Come home." It wasn't a command. It was a plea. He opened his eyes and stared at me.

"I feel more at home here than I do in New York."

"Maybe that's because we lived here together for a short time."

"You mean in this apartment? And you kept it?"

"Rob moved in for a while. But when he left, I couldn't make myself sell it. Sometimes we come here to reminisce."

"That's not why I feel at home here. I remember being here for school. I remember loving classes. This campus was the last place I felt like I belonged."

"It's also where we met."

Why wasn't he understanding? I wasn't drawn to Newark because of him. I was drawn here to get away from him. "But I don't remember that. I'm sorry."

"Let me try to remind you."

I shook my head. "You told Rob you'd be back tonight. I'm not going to keep you."

"I do need to be back tonight. But it's only 11 am. We have all day. Please, Penny. Just give me one day to try to remind you of what we have."

His dark brown eyes looked so hopeful. He had handed me his broken heart and was waiting for me to put the pieces back together again. I needed to tell him that I didn't know how. I needed to tell him that I wanted time and space, but then he grabbed my hand.

"Please, Penny." He ran his thumb along the inside of my palm. "All I'm asking for is one chance."

My heart felt like it was going to burst out of my chest. It was beating so loudly I swore he could hear it. "And I can stay here tonight if I want?"

He smiled, but it looked pained. "I would never force you to come back with me. If what you want is here…" he squeezed my hand and shook his head. "Promise me you'll try." He looked down at my lips and then immediately looked back at my eyes.

I took a deep breath. "Okay."

The smile that broke over his face was real this time. "Okay." He dropped my hand. "First up, waffles. Home-made Eggo waffles."

I laughed. "Are they homemade or are they Eggo waffles?" I sat down at the kitchen island.

He grabbed two plates and brought them over. "Well, I toasted them. They may be slightly freezer burnt because we haven't been here in awhile. But I'm sure they're fine."

"You really know how to woo a girl."

He put his elbows on the counter and leaned forward. "You have no idea."

The way he said it was suggestive enough. But then his eyes gravitated to my lips again. And God, I wanted nothing more than for him to kiss me. I remembered what it was like to be kissed by him and there was no better feeling in the world. I looked down at my waffle. No, I didn't remember. I had dreamed of it. There was a huge difference.

I took a huge bite of my waffle and kept my eyes glued to my plate. I didn't deserve the way he looked at me. Because it didn't matter how today went. Tonight, I'd tell him about my surgery. I'd tell him it was best he moved on. And we'd part ways forever.

CHAPTER 21
Sunday

I didn't know why I was nervous. This wasn't a real date. It was a re-do of something I didn't remember. But I felt a sense of peace as I pulled the sundress over my head. I was giving James what he wanted. He'd be happy all day. *Before I pull the rug out from under him.* I shook away the thought as I turned toward the mirror. It was the third dress I had tried on. This one flared out slightly above my waist, which hid my bloated stomach. I touched my belly. Not bloated. I had been pregnant. It still didn't seem real. It felt like I'd remember such a momentous occasion. It was the only time I'd ever know what it was like to carry a child. And I couldn't recall any of it.

I let my hand fall from my stomach. That wasn't something I wanted to think about. Not today. I had the rest of my life to come to terms with it. Today was about…well, I wasn't sure what it was about. Goodbyes? A fresh start? Maybe it depended on the day. I reached up to try and zipper the back of the dress, but I could barely reach it. I couldn't manage to zipper it more than halfway. I turned to the mirror to see if I could find a better angle.

The reflection staring back at me looked more like me than it had when I had first woken up in the hospital. I looked sad and broken now, but the white sundress with blue flowers looked good. The blue matched my eyes. It almost hid the fact that my eyes looked as sad as the rest of me. I sighed, abandoning the zipper. Today wasn't going to repair anything. But it could lift my spirits. I slid on a pair of sandals and walked out of the bedroom without another glance at my reflection.

James was standing at the windows in the living room, staring out at Main Street below. His hands were in the pockets of his jeans. He had added a button down shirt over his t-shirt. And he was wearing shoes again. Dress shoes, not sneakers. But they looked good. He certainly didn't look like he had a stick up his ass today. *Stop looking at his butt.*

"Hey," I said.

He turned around. "You look beautiful."

I smiled. No one had ever said that to me before. Austin always said I looked hot. Or sexy. But never beautiful. I felt the color rise to my cheeks. "You don't look so bad yourself."

He abandoned the window and walked over to me. "Are you ready to go?"

"I couldn't reach…" I gestured to the back of my dress. "I mean, could you maybe…" I let my voice trail off. Usually I made Melissa zip me. I had never asked a boy to do it before. I swallowed hard. Not a boy. James was all man. A very handsome man that was way out of my league.

He didn't say anything, he just brushed my hair to the side. His fingers slowly trailed across my skin, igniting it like only he seemed to be able to. I was almost disappointed when he was finished zipping my dress the rest of the way up, because his touch made me feel so warm. Safe, yet alive at the same time.

"You ready?" He held his hand out for me.

I don't know. I ignored my annoying thoughts and placed my hand into his. I felt like he could show me what living was. I felt like he could show me everything I'd ever wanted out of life. The thought was just as electrifying as it was terrifying. "I'm ready."

***

We pulled up to a huge building. There was a tennis court to the right and a pool beside it. Behind them I could make out a golf course in the distance.

"Where are we?" I asked.

James smiled. "This is where we had our first real date."

"What do you mean by real date?"

He cut the engine. "It took a little time for my head to catch up to my heart. I wanted to give you what you deserved instead of just taking what I wanted. We started things a little backwards. I wanted to show you that you meant more to me than one time in my office."

I swallowed hard. *His office?* It was just like my dream. "You mean, we had sex before you took me on a date?"

A valet came to my door and opened it for me before James had a chance to reply.

"Welcome back, Mrs. Hunter," he said and put out his hand for me to grab. It was the first time I didn't grimace at the name. I took his hand and he pulled me out of my seat and closed the passenger side door.

James stepped out of the car and the valet walked over to him. "Mr. Hunter," he said with a huge smile. "It's been awhile since you two have visited."

"Much too long," James said. He handed the valet the key. "Hopefully we'll be back more often. Penny's just reminded me how much we love it here." He walked over to me and put his hand on the small of my back. "Right?"

I nodded. He was right, in a sense. I loved Newark. But I literally had no idea where we were right now. And my mind was a little preoccupied by the fact that he said we slept together before he took me on a date. Apparently I had become quite the slut in my late teens.

James escorted me into the building as my thoughts wandered. But I quickly abandoned what I was thinking about when we stepped inside. The floor was pure marble. And the biggest chandelier I had ever seen hung from the ceiling above.

A woman walked over to us. "Mr. and Mrs. Hunter. Your table is ready." She seemed nervous to be talking to us.

We followed her down a hallway and entered an elegant restaurant. I wasn't dressed nearly fancy enough. Most of the women wore lace dresses and the men were in suits. It felt like they were all staring at me. But as we made our way to the back of the restaurant I realized that they were staring at James. I didn't blame them, he was so handsome. But I felt a little jealous again, and I had no idea why. I had no reason to be jealous. I glanced at him. At least he was dressed casually like me. It made me feel a little more comfortable.

The woman showed us into a private room in the back. There was a roaring fire, despite the fact that it was summer, and an elegant loveseat to one side. In the middle of the room was a table with a beautiful flower arrangement in the center. A bottle of wine and two glasses were already on the table. *Oh no, they're going to ask me for my I.D.* I almost laughed out loud. First of all, I didn't have an I.D. As far as I could tell, James was keeping it from me. But it didn't matter anyway. I was old.

Instead of questioning my age, the woman said, "Your waiter will be right with you," and walked out of the room, closing the door behind her.

I turned to James. "So where are we exactly?"

"Our country club."

I stared at him. *Our country club?* I knew he was wealthy. But I wasn't exactly used to the idea that I was wealthy. My parents did well enough to pay my tuition. But this? I looked around the room again. I really owned a part of this?

James walked over to the table and pulled my chair out for me.

"No one's ever pulled out a chair for me before." I sat down and stared at him as he took the seat across from me. I was experiencing a lot of firsts today. And I'd be lying if I said I wasn't enjoying it. Really I just wanted to hear him say I was beautiful over and over again. A girl could get used to that.

"Then you haven't been dating the right people."

Dating. James and I weren't technically dating. We were married. But in a lot of ways this felt like a first date. Not that I had ever had a date like this before. More like a first date from my dreams. "And I've never been to a country club before. Do we come here often?"

"Not as often as we used to."

"Why?"

"Life I guess." He stared at me intently. "But I'm going to start prioritizing us again. I'm going to put you first. Always."

He was right before. I had no idea what it was like to be wooed. Because this felt amazing. I truly felt like I was the center of his attention. It was easy to feel that way when his eyes never left mine.

Just at that moment the waiter walked in and hurried over to the table. "Good evening. It is my pleasure to be serving you tonight, Mr. and Mrs. Hunter. It's so good to see you both again."

I glanced at his name tag. *Jerrod.* I was about to tell Jerrod that we weren't married and then I realized it wasn't true. I was James' wife. He was my husband. We were so much more than a first date.

Jerrod started telling us about their daily specials but I couldn't stop staring into James' eyes. It was impossible to look away. There was so much love there. And I didn't care if I didn't deserve it. I wanted it. Desperately. Jerrod uncorked a bottle of wine and poured us each a glass while he was talking.

After Jerrod was done his spiel, James said we would need a minute to look at the menu. I skimmed through mine, trying to find the cheapest thing as Jerrod left the room. Most of the meals were as much as the used textbooks I always bought for classes. I didn't feel comfortable letting James pay for this. Or…I guess we were paying for it? I shook my head. Even though we were married, it was pretty clear that it was all his money. I couldn't make him pay for this when I was planning on leaving him at the end of the night. *Am I still planning on that?*

"Penny?" He reached over and grabbed my hand.

"James, I've never had food that costs this much." I picked up my glass with my free hand and took a sip of the wine.

"Actually, you have."

An exasperated laugh escaped my lips. "But I don't remember. You told me how we met. You told me that you fell in love with me. But you never explained why, James. Why me? I'm incredibly…uninteresting."

"That's entirely untrue. I find you fascinating."

The way he said it made me blush. I was suddenly very aware of the fact that he had already seen me naked. He had already had me in the most intimate way. I didn't remember, but he did. He knew me. He knew my body. He knew everything about me. I took another sip of wine. I felt so nervous under his gaze.

"So why is it that you don't feel like you're interesting?" he asked.

I gulped and looked up at him. It was because of Austin and all the times that he made me feel insignificant. "Honestly, you're the first person that's ever made me feel like I'm the only girl in the room. I'm not used to feeling like I matter."

Jerrod came in to take our order. I looked back down at the menu. I scanned the options for something that wouldn't get stuck in my teeth. James reached his hand out and grabbed mine again.

"Penny, the crab cakes are wonderful here."

I breathed a sigh of relief. He truly did know me. I loved crab cakes. I smiled, relieved that I didn't have to choose. "That sounds perfect."

James ordered for us. When Jerrod left the room, James put his elbows on the table and leaned in slightly. "When we're together, I can assure you that I don't see anyone else in the room. You always have my undivided attention."

"That must have made grading other student's speeches quite difficult." I wasn't sure what made me say it. But it seemed like it would be true. I still didn't understand how I could have possibly dated a professor. It seemed outlandish.

James laughed. "It did. It was almost impossible."

His words should have comforted me, but all I seemed to be able to focus on was when he had said, "when we're together." I was reminded of his ex-wife. *His pumpkin.* He was clearly talking to her this morning. He still loved her. I could feel it. I didn't have his undivided attention. And I didn't understand why he was lying. I was giving him an out. Why was he fighting for us if I wasn't even the one that he wanted?

James reached in his pocket, pulled out a penny, and slid it across the table. "A penny for your thoughts?"

I laughed. "Very funny." I said it sarcastically, but I was still smiling. This was why we were here. To talk about what we wanted. "Austin didn't believe in labels. I'm used to not being put first. You say all these things like I have your undivided attention..." I let my voice trail off. I had no right to be questioning him. But I couldn't seem to stop. "But I know you're seeing someone else. Your conversation after our dinner the other night? Whoever you were talking to this morning? You're in love with someone else. Why are you pursuing me? I'm giving you an out. You can go back to your ex-wife if that's what you really want. It's okay."

He looked down at our intertwined fingers. "You're worried about my ex-wife?"

"I'm not worried about her at all." *Well, maybe a little.* "I just think maybe you're still in love with her."

"I never loved her." He locked eyes with me. "I already told you that."

"And yet...the phone calls. It's obvious that you still care for her."

"Penny, there is no other woman in my life."

"You don't have to lie."

"I'm not lying. I'll prove it." He pulled out his phone. He showed me the screen as he clicked on Rob's name and put it on speaker phone.

"Hey, you on your way back yet?" Rob asked.

"Hey, pumpkin," James said and then awkwardly cleared his throat. "Not yet, but we'll be heading back soon."

Rob laughed. "Um...okay, honey muffin. Cutie pie. Buttercup. Snickerdoodle. I could go on. But why exactly are we doing this?"

"Because we always call each other cute names," James said. "You know. Since forever." There was an edge in his voice.

"Whatever you say, sugar buns."

"Okay, I'm going to go now," James said. "See you in a bit."

"Later, Cuddles. Crap, I ran out of good ones."

"Bye...pumpkin." James ended the call and slid his phone back into his pocket.

I just stared at him.

"See," he said.

"See what? That was the most awkward conversation in the world."

He shook his head. "Nope. That was normal. It's just what Rob and I do."

"I can tell that you're lying. That whole thing was just bizarre. It proved my point, if anything. He had no idea why you were calling him pumpkin. Just admit that you're still in love with your ex-wife and let's call it a day."

"I'm not."

"Yes you are."

He lowered both his eyebrows as he stared at me.

"Is it so hard to tell me the truth?"

He exhaled slowly. "My ex-wife is dead, Penny."

God, his life was a disaster. So much hurt and I just kept stabbing him. Figuratively, of course. I felt like a monster. "You're a widower?"

He shook his head. "No. She died after we were divorced. Actually, it was shortly after you and I got married."

"Oh." *Oh? What kind of reaction was that?* I was supposed to say sorry for your loss. Or something heartfelt. But if he was telling the truth, he didn't love her. Surely he cared that she died though? "What happened?"

"It doesn't matter."

"It does to me." I stared at him, willing him to tell me his story. I wanted to know everything about him, yet nothing at all.

He sighed and broke his eye contact with me. "She tried to have me killed."

"On our wedding night?" I knew that he had been shot on our wedding night, but I didn't know the story. His ex-wife? Seriously? That was insane.

"She was a monster."

I bit the inside of my lip. I had just thought of myself as a monster. Was I the same as his ex-wife? I shook away the thought. I had never tried to kill anyone. I was just tiptoeing around breaking James' heart.

"And when she didn't succeed, she came after you. Briggs shot and killed her when she attacked us again."

I swallowed hard. Apparently my life was always in danger when I was with him. "So you're not cheating on me?" I didn't even know why those words spilled out. Maybe it was the wine. But maybe I truly wanted to know how strong our relationship was.

"Penny, I would never, ever cheat on you. You're my whole world. I swear to you, I have always been faithful. I've never ever thought about cheating on you. All I ever think about is you. You're it for me. As soon as I met you, my heart was yours."

He was staring at me so intently I felt like I was going to combust. I wasn't sure what compelled me to do it, but I reached my foot out and rubbed it against his shin. I wanted to be close to him. I wanted to taste him. I wanted to see every inch of him. *Fuck, what am I doing?* I was about to move away when James reached under the table and put his hand on my thigh.

His touch made me feel numb, yet set my whole body on fire at the same time. God, he owned me. I didn't remember a thing about him, but his touch possessed me. My body remembered him, even though my mind didn't.

I swallowed hard. "James." I stared at him. "I don't...I've never..." This wasn't coming out right. My mind was screaming at me to excuse myself to the restroom to try and clear my head. But I couldn't deny the fact that my body desperately wanted him. I wanted to beg him to make love to me. I wanted to know what it felt like. I wanted him to ruin me for anyone else.

But Jerrod killed the moment. He walked in with the food and I immediately removed my foot. I retreated back to my side of the table like it had never happened. It was like I had closed a curtain on the idea of us being intimate. And I hated myself for it. Because my dream of him? I wanted to live each second of it.

CHAPTER 22

Sunday

I took a bite of the crab cakes before Jerrod even left the room. "This is amazing." I had completely forgotten the heated moment we had shared. I took another bite of the crab cake.

"You've never what?" James asked.

I finished chewing. "Nothing." I had a moment of weakness. I just wanted to enjoy my meal, not talk about the fact that I had never been in love before.

"You can tell me." He wasn't eating, he was just staring at me, holding his empty fork in the air.

I took another bite to stall. He had no idea how hard this was for me. But what did it matter if I told him the truth? "I've never been in love," I blurted out. "I mean, no one's ever made love to me." *What the actual fuck?*

His fork clattered against his plate as it fell.

"I mean…God, I don't know what I mean."

"Believe me when I tell you that I've made love to you, Penny. Countless times. In every possible way."

I was pretty sure my whole face was red.

"It kills me that you don't remember. All I want to do is remind you."

He was making me wet with just his words. I remembered him pressed against me in my dream. I remembered running my fingers through his hair. It was like I had actually felt his lips grazing the side of my neck. And like I truly knew what it was like for him to whisper dirty things into my ear. "Why haven't you?" My heart was beating so fast it felt like it was going to burst through my ribcage. "You haven't even kissed me."

His eyes lowered to my lips again. "Trust me, I've wanted to. It's all I can think about."

I felt my face begin to flush. I hoped he thought it was because of the fire. I had been wondering if sex was at all on his mind. He said he had made love to me countless times. In every way imaginable. I still barely knew him, but I knew a part of me wanted him. I had no doubt that it would be the best sex of my life. It wouldn't even be comparable to anything I had with Austin. Austin was like a jackrabbit. He always finished in just a few minutes. I didn't even know what an orgasm felt like. But maybe I was about to.

There was just one problem. I had no idea how to get what I wanted. Zero experience in asking. Austin always just...took. And took. And took. He gave me nothing in return. I knew I deserved better. I just didn't know what better was. I stared at James. Maybe better was sitting right in front of me. Perfection in human form. My eyes dropped to the neckline of his dress shirt. I'd seen a glimpse of his abs of steel a couple nights ago, a perfect match to the rest of his hard features. But I wanted to see more of him. Why was I fighting this? There was no better fantasy than him.

"What do you want, Penny?"

I watched his Adam's apple rise and then fall. Was this love? I didn't know. Maybe it would be someday. But today?

He knew me, but I didn't know him. It was like he was waiting for me to say something. I just had no idea what. I wanted him to kiss me. To hold me. To tell me everything was going to be okay. But I wasn't sure if that was what he was offering.

"I don't know…" my voice trailed off. "What did we do here on our first date?" Maybe he could recreate the whole thing for me. I wanted to remember now. I wanted to wake up and know who I was again.

His chest rose and fell but I didn't hear a sigh. "We talked," he said.

"That's it?" I felt as naïve as the 19 year old I thought I was. I kind of thought he was going to say he banged me in front of the fire.

He leaned back in his chair, a memory taking over his mind. "The taste of you was better than any dessert they serve here."

Oh my God. I melted into my chair.

"And I fell harder for you in a few hours than I had ever fallen for anyone else in my entire life."

"I guess the sex was good then?" I was startled by my own words. I grabbed my wine glass and took a huge sip.

He laughed. "Stars in your eyes good. But we have always had more than just a physical connection, Penny. I can be patient when I need to be. And I know you're not ready, despite how badly I wish you were."

That was a subtle way to turn me down. I took another sip of wine and lowered my voice. "Did we have sex in this room?"

Again his Adam's apple rose and fell. The action made me cross my legs under the table. *So fucking sexy.*

"It depends on your definition of sex." His voice was husky. He wanted me again. Maybe as much as I wanted him.

I thought his Adam's apple was sexy. But his voice? *Kill me now.* I could barely even focus on what he was saying. "What exactly is your definition of sex?"

Jerrod found that moment appropriate to walk in carrying two dessert menus. "Are either of you interested in dessert this evening?" He placed the menus down in front of us.

"I've heard the dessert here isn't very good," I said.

James laughed.

But Jerrod frowned. "Mrs. Hunter, you love the chocolate lava cake. It's the best in town."

Do I? Hmm. "Actually, that does sound pretty good. Do you want to share a slice?" I asked James.

"That sounds perfect," James said. "We'll split one chocolate lava cake."

"Very good, sir." Jerrod collected the menus and walked back out of the room, leaving us in silence.

I couldn't get James' words out of my head. He thought I tasted better than any dessert here. Had he actually just meant a kiss? Or did he mean something else? I could actually feel the silence as it settled around us. I wanted to break through the awkwardness. I wanted to taste him. But I had no idea what to say.

"Do you want some fresh air?" James asked.

It was like he had handed me a get out of jail free card. "Yes." I tried not to sound too excited. "That sounds perfect." I didn't know exactly what he had in mind, but I grabbed his hand and let him pull me to my feet. It was easy to follow him, like I had done it countless times before. He kept my hand in his as he led me out of the private dining room. It seemed like everyone in the restaurant turned to look at him again as we walked through. He squeezed my hand and smiled down at me. God was he sexy. I found myself thinking I would follow him anywhere.

We exited the restaurant in the back and stepped onto a huge terrace. Even though it was summer, the dusk had brought a chill. There were only a few people standing by a fire with glasses in their hands, enjoying an after dinner drink. James escorted me past them and we made our way down a set of stairs. His strides were longer than mine and it was hard to keep pace with him. If I walked any faster I'd be jogging.

We reached a row of golf carts. He leaned in and turned the key. "This will do." He smiled at me.

"Are we allowed to use those? We're going to get in trouble." I looked both ways, waiting for someone to stop us.

James laughed and got behind the wheel. "Get in."

Of course he could use them. He could do whatever he wanted here. He owned the place. I climbed in next to him and as soon as my butt hit the seat he pressed down on the gas pedal. He stuck to the small paths and wooden bridges on the course for awhile and then veered off into the grass. We rolled up next to a small waterfall and he cut the engine. Lightning bugs flittered in the darkening sky around us. It felt like I was in a dream. And even though we were surrounded by fresh grass and beautiful flowers, all I could smell was his sweet cologne. Every inch of me felt alive when I was next to him.

I got out of the cart and walked over toward the little waterfall. The water splashing against the rocks was surprisingly loud. I saw James' reflection in the rippling water as he came up behind me and wrapped his arms around me. I stopped breathing as he moved my hair to one side and kissed the back of my neck. My whole body tensed. It was exactly what I wanted him to do when he had zippered my dress. His lips felt better than his fingers. *Oh my God, he wants me right here. In the middle of the golf course. Fuck this is hot. Why do I think this is so hot?*

"I'm sorry." His lips were off of me almost as soon as they had landed against my skin. He took a step back from me, like he was appalled by himself.

I could barely control my rapid breathing. "Did I do something wrong?"

"No." He shook his head. "No," he said more seriously. "I'm supposed to be taking things slowly and I…" his voice trailed off. "I'm sorry." He started staring at the waterfall instead of me.

I wanted him to wrap his arms around me again. I wanted him to kiss my neck. I wanted all of it. But he didn't feel the same way. I blinked fast, removing the tears from my eyes. "That's okay. Really." I turned away from him. There was a weeping willow close by. *How appropriate.* It seemed like a good place to hide away before I let my emotions take over. I walked over to it as fast as I could.

"Penny!"

I kept walking until I was hidden in the darkness of its branches. I hunched over and let the tears fall. Why was I crying? I put my hand over my mouth to stifle my sobs. So what if he didn't want me? I didn't even know if I wanted him. God, that was a lie. He was sexy and handsome and thoughtful. I wanted him. He just didn't want me back. How had this day turned everything upside down?

"Penny."

I stood up, trying to hide my tears. I wiped them away just in time.

"Oh, Penny." He cupped my chin in his hands and lifted my face so that I'd be looking at him.

My tears were gone, but he still saw me. "I don't know what I'm doing wrong. I'm trying. Isn't that what you wanted? I'm…"

"You're not doing anything wrong." He traced his thumb beneath my eyes.

"Then why won't you kiss me?" I hated how distressed I sounded. I hated how the page had turned and I was the one that desperately wanted him.

"You think I don't want to kiss you?" His hand slid to the side of my neck.

I stopped breathing as his fingers traced my clavicle.

He leaned forward, his lips brushing against my earlobe. "You have no idea how badly I want to kiss you. But this wasn't where we had our first kiss."

"It could be our first kiss…now."

He pressed his forehead against mine. "I'm going to do this right. Because I need you to remember. I need you to remember everything."

I breathed in his exhales. This had to be what love was. I wanted to tilt my face up to his so that our lips would touch, but I resisted. He didn't want to kiss me like this. Had something else happened on this golf course? He had to restrain himself near the waterfall. I breathed in another of his exhales. "What did we do out here?" But I knew the answer. I didn't have that much experience with men, but his body language all pointed to one thing.

He leaned forward slightly, pushing my back against the tree behind me. I swallowed hard.

"It's more a question of what didn't we do."

There was a scene playing in my head of him grabbing my ass, lifting me up, and pushing my back against the trunk of the tree. I could picture him raising one eyebrow and thrusting his length inside of me. Filling me. I didn't want the image to disappear. I wanted to tell him I remembered. That I remembered everything. But the fantasy disappeared as quickly as it had come, reminding me that it wasn't a memory. I was just getting caught up in the moment. I'd always had an overactive imagination.

Thunder rolled above us. I looked up, even though the sky was hidden by a canopy of leaves. "I didn't know it was supposed to rain tonight. I love when it rains." I laughed. "I honestly have no idea why I said that. I don't love the rain. It makes my hair all frizzy and Melissa always makes fun of these bright red rain boots I wear whenever it rains." I smiled. I could picture her look of distaste so easily.

James' eyes searched mine, like he was waiting for something.

"She doesn't like them because she thinks they're the epitome of un-sexiness." My rambling nonsense was filling the awkward tension and I couldn't seem to stop talking. "But you try walking around on wet brick in flip-flops. You wouldn't guess it, but they get so slippery. It's like walking on ice. The one time Melissa convinced me not to wear my rain boots, I almost slid to my death."

He pulled away from me.

I guess that's not what he was waiting for me to say. Who would be waiting for me to talk about wet, slippery bricks? *I'm so bad at this.*

"I want to show you something else." He put his hand out for me.

The thunder rolled again. "What is it?" I didn't hear the rain yet, but I knew it was coming. And even though I said I hated the rain, every inch of me wanted it to pour. I couldn't explain it. Maybe my first reaction was right. Maybe I loved the rain now. But why?

"Penny, I'm asking for you to trust me."

I did trust him. And even though the thought was terrifying, I put my hand into his.

CHAPTER 23
Sunday

"I've been here before," I said as James pulled to a stop in front of the coffee shop on Main Street. Austin had introduced me to this place. They had amazing pastries. I honestly wasn't a huge fan of coffee, but I was trying to get used to it. Always trying to fit in even though I never seemed to be able to. I glanced over at James as he put the car in park. Did he truly understand me?

He smiled, like he somehow knew exactly what I was thinking. "This is where we met."

He had told me the story when we had dinner the other night. I looked back out the window. This was the place that changed the course of my life? I unbuckled my seatbelt as James climbed out of the car. All I felt when I looked at this storefront was slightly sick. How many times had I sat in there while Austin flirted with other girls right in front of me?

James opened my door and put his hand out for me.

Could James really have erased all that pain? Could he have made this one of my favorite places? Could he have made me feel like I was worthy of more than being second? There was one way to find out.

I let him take my hand and help me out of the car. Another first. No one had ever opened a car door for me, let alone taken my hand and helped me out. Except for the valet earlier. It truly felt like I was a princess in some Disney fairy tale. As memories from college began seeping in, I was starting to remember more than just happily studying all the time. I remembered feeling lonely. I remembered feeling like I just didn't quite fit. It wasn't all rainbows and sunshine like I was trying to believe. Maybe I had needed a knight in shining armor more than I realized.

My life certainly hadn't been perfect. I had a sort of boyfriend who I was pretty sure cheated on me. Not that you could cheat if we technically weren't an item. I cried myself to sleep a lot. Sometimes I was homesick for Wilmington. The only real friend I had made was Melissa and she was always busy with social activities that I wanted nothing to do with. I usually took my food to go from the dining hall so I didn't have to eat alone. Looking back on everything, I don't think I was really that happy. I think I was pretending to be. Maybe James had saved me, not the other way around.

I looked up at the sky. It had been drizzling when we left the country club, but the storm had ceased. The clouds were still threatening though. Maybe it would start pouring any minute. What was my sudden fascination with the rain? James squeezed my hand, pulling my attention back to him.

"So, I was walking in when you were walking out," he said as he opened the door for me. "The door collided with your cup and you started to fall. You got coffee all over yourself, but I caught you. And I don't know how to explain it exactly, but when you were in my arms it felt like all my problems went away. Nothing mattered but you." He smiled down at me. "That feeling has never gone away."

I stood in the doorway, waiting for the memory to flood back. But it didn't. Not one single heartfelt part of that story made me remember him. It was romantic and perfect and almost too good to really be true.

"You were wearing those red rain boots that Melissa hates. And I have to respectfully disagree with her. I'm pretty sure they're the epitome of sexiness, not un-sexi-ness."

I laughed. But he wasn't laughing. Wait, was he serious? "I was wearing my red rain boots when I met you? And you still fell in love with me?"

The saddest smile I had ever seen was on his face. I had never seen a smile hold so much pain. "You really don't re-member." He didn't phrase it as a question. His voice was as broken as his smile.

"I'm sorry, James."

He shook his head like he didn't believe me. "Okay, you walk out while I walk in. And pretend to slip when the door opens. We'll recreate it. You'll remember everything." He walked out of the coffee shop before I had a chance to stop him.

This was ridiculous. I wasn't going to suddenly remem-ber. But he was already walking in, trying to recreate a scene that was only in his memory.

What did he want me to do? Slip? It wouldn't hurt to play along. At least he'd know I tried to remember, even though I had been trying all night.

"Oh me, oh my, I'm falling." I placed the back of my hand on my forehead like I was a damsel in distress and tee-tered to the side. I was pretty sure I looked more like a drunk person than someone slipping.

Before I teetered too much, I felt his strong hands grab my waist, holding me steady.

"I'm so sorry. Are you alright?" he asked.

"I'm fine." I kept my eyes on the ground. Ever since the golf course, I had wanted him to hold me again. Not just a hand. But hold me like he needed me. That's how I felt right now. Like he truly needed me.

His hands slowly fell off my waist. "I'm afraid I've ruined your shirt."

I looked at my dress, trying to remember the story he had told. *Coffee.* He said he had spilled coffee all over my tank top. "Oh, crap," I said. "That's...very unfortunate. Rats." *Rats?* God, I was being so weird. I awkwardly snapped my fingers, which made it so much worse. There was a reason I was never cast in plays growing up. Although, it probably had nothing to do with my awkward improv and everything to do with my shyness.

"Here," he said. He started unbuttoning his dress shirt.

"What are you doing?" I asked. Had he given me a striptease after dousing me with hot coffee? I glanced over my shoulder at the checkout counter. But there was no one there. They were probably calling the police.

"Just play along," he whispered.

I started to shake my head, but then froze when he unbuttoned his shirt the rest of the way. Seeing his perfect six pack again made my whole body feel warm. James just stood there, topless, in the middle of a public restaurant. Even though it was inappropriate, I couldn't stop staring. I didn't even know which was worse – me staring or him taking his shirt off in the first place. I pulled my eyes away from his perfect body and up to his face. It truly looked like he had stepped out of the pages of a magazine. His dark brown hair was still a little wet from the drizzle earlier. The way it was sticking up made it look like he had just run his hand through it. His jawbone was sharp and there were dimples in his cheeks. His eyes were a deep brown like his hair and they were staring at me intently. My heart began to beat fast. He handed me his shirt.

"That's okay. I can't take that," I laughed uneasily. "You should put it back on, James." I moved to the side so he could pass by me. I felt my cheeks begin to blush.

"I insist." He had a slight smile on his face. "First day of classes," he shrugged. "You'll want to make a good first impression."

I took the shirt from him. Had he really walked around without a shirt all morning? "Thank you," I said quietly.

He was staring at me expectantly.

I pulled on his shirt. It was huge but comfortable. The scent of sweet cologne drifted off of it. It made me feel slightly dizzy. I could feel myself staring at him. "I'm sorry, I should probably go. I'm going to be late…for classes I guess." It came out as more of a question than anything. He was so handsome that I was acting even more awkward than usual.

His lips parted like he was about to say something, but then they closed again.

What was he about to say? I waited for a moment, but all he did was stare at me, setting my skin on fire. *I guess that's my cue to leave?* I smiled gratefully and walked out of the coffee shop. Bright red rain boots and a men's dress shirt? Had I really worn that to my first day of class? I'm sure Melissa had loved that story.

I pulled off his shirt as he joined me on the sidewalk, but his the scent of his cologne was still all around me. It lingered on my skin and in my hair. God, just the smell of him made me want to beg for more.

He was staring at me so hopefully.

"That was…nice. I can see why I couldn't forget about you." I held the shirt out for him but he didn't take it.

"Did that bring anything back?"

I shook my head. "I'm sorry." I pushed the shirt into his hands. "Did you really give me your shirt? What happened to no shirt, no shoes, no service?"

"I gave you my sweater. I was wearing a dress shirt underneath."

That made more sense. I looked down at the dress shirt in his hand. "You should put that back on before you get arrested."

"We're the only ones around."

"What about the owner of the coffee shop?"

"I'm the owner. It's closed right now. I just had them leave it open for us."

"You bought the coffee shop where we met?"

"I didn't want it to change. I wanted everything to stay exactly the way it was when we ran into each other." He looked down at the shirt in his hands. "And it wasn't just where we met. It's also where I proposed to you. Where you said yes."

That was so sweet and romantic and wonderful. I bit the inside of my lip. But I still didn't remember. Coming here hadn't triggered anything. I could see myself falling for him one day. But I hadn't already fallen. He was so much further ahead of me, I knew I'd never catch up. None of this was fair to him. I needed to tell him I was staying here. It was so hard to find the words.

"You'll remember. I know you will. You just need more time." He pulled his dress shirt back on and slowly buttoned it, hiding his perfect abs beneath the fabric.

Say it, Penny. Tell him you're not going back to New York. A big fat raindrop landed on the tip of my nose.

"Let's get back to the apartment," he said.

At least he hadn't said it was time to go back to the city. I'd tell him I wanted to stay here. I just needed a little more time to gather up the courage to do it.

James reached out to open the car door for me, but stopped as soon as his fingers touched the handle. He looked up like he had just felt a raindrop too. And in a matter of seconds it started pouring.

Instead of opening the door for me, he just stood there, staring at me as the rain soaked us. It was like he was waiting for something. Waiting for something exciting to happen.

"James…"

"Call me Professor Hunter."

I swallowed hard. Would that make me remember? It didn't matter if it did. Just the idea of calling him that when our bodies were so close made me want to rip all his clothes off. Maybe that's how this whole thing had started. The forbiddenness of it all had made us cross the line. And I was close to crossing it again. So close. "Professor Hunter."

The look he gave me took my breath away. It was like he was hungry for me. He leaned forward and placed his hands on the car, on either side of me. Our mouths were less than an inch apart. He opened his lips slightly like he was about to say something. I could feel the heat of his breath in the rain. He drew a fraction of an inch closer.

"Was this how our first kiss happened?" I whispered. "In the rain?"

Instead of responding, he quickly grabbed the back of my neck and let his lips meet mine. His kiss was full of passion, passion that he had been holding back just as much as I had. He pressed his body against mine and lightly pushed me so that my back was on the cold, wet steel of the car. He leaned into me. The contrast of the heat from his body and the coolness of the car sent a spark through me. I had never wanted someone so badly before. I let my hands wander beneath the neckline of his shirt. His skin was so soft.

His lips pulled away from mine and he groaned softly in my ear. "I've been haunted by the night I first kissed you. I couldn't resist. And just one taste was never enough. It never could have been." He leaned down and kissed me again. Softer this time. Slow and loving. And it was somehow even more intense than his rough, passionate kiss. I had crossed the line. And knew I needed to step back before I was too far gone.

I pressed my hands against his chest, pushing him away. "I can't."

He cringed. "I'm sorry. I should have waited. I just…"

"No." I tried to steady my breathing. "The kiss was amazing. That's not…" I let my voice trail off. "James, I can't come back with you. I can already see myself slipping into this life that I don't know. I can see myself falling for you. I can see you becoming my whole world."

"And why does it sound like you think that's so horrible?"

"Because it's a life I've been given. Not a life I found." God, this was coming out wrong. My mind was all foggy from the kiss. I shook my head. "I'm staying here. I don't want to go back to New York. That's all that I'm trying to say."

"If you're staying here, then so am I. I'll figure out a way. We just need more time. I believe in us. We…"

"How am I supposed to find myself if everything's already carved out for me?" I wiped away the tears beneath my eyes before they had a chance to mix with the rain. "I don't know how to be in this world. Your world. I need to find myself."

He placed his hand on the side of my face. "Find yourself with me."

"James…"

"You'll search your whole life and never find anything as good as what we have. I promise you. I swear it's true. Just give our life together a chance."

"I have. That's what today was all about. And it was wonderful, but I didn't feel like me. I don't know how to explain it." I shook my head. "Maybe you're right about everything. But I'm not going to force you to take that journey with me as I find myself."

"You wouldn't be forcing me. I'm offering to stay."

"What about your obligations?"

He dropped his hand from my face, like he knew I was right. He had a life outside of me. And he needed to get back to it.

"It's for the best, James." The rain between us made this feel final. We were already drifting farther away from each other.

"In no world is us being apart for the best."

In this case it was. Time healed everything. It would put his heart back together again. He'd be fine without me. I took a deep breath. "One day you're going to want a family. And I can't give that to you." He was older than me. Certainly he was thinking about having children sometime soon. Telling him that was my way out. But hearing the words out loud made it seem so real.

"You can. You just…don't want to with me? Is that what you're saying?"

The pain on his face made my tears fall faster. I prayed he thought it was the rain instead of me falling apart. "No." *Maybe.* "I can't have kids. Ever. With anyone."

"Why would you say that?"

"I saw a doctor about the scars on my stomach. He told me about my surgery."

James shook his head. "That doctor is wrong. We'll get a second opinion. We can…"

"You didn't know?" I searched his face. How had he not known? Wouldn't the doctors have told him when I was unconscious?

Something seemed to dawn on his face. "They told me they removed something. That some of the damage was ir-reparable. But I wasn't listening. I was more focused on whether or not you were going to wake up."

"They removed both my ovaries. I'll never be able to have children." I tried to keep my voice flat, even though all I wanted was for him to hug me and tell me everything would be alright. Everything could never be alright for me. But it could be for him.

He looked as devastated as I felt. And he stayed completely silent, like he was already slipping away from me. It wasn't easy to walk away from him. But I had to.

"It's pretty clear that kids are something that you want. It's something I wanted." I looked down at my hands. "So you're going to go back to New York and I'm going to stay here. Well, not here. I'll probably go home to my parents' house until I get back on my feet. And you can forget all about me. It's for the best."

"Baby." He tilted my face back up to his and wiped my tears away with his thumbs. "I could never forget about you." His hands felt so warm compared to the cool summer rain.

"You have to. I don't know who I am. And the only thing I knew I wanted in my future was just taken away. I can't focus on a relationship right now. I need to figure out what I want, uninfluenced by anyone else. I have to start over."

He pressed his lips together. He didn't say anything at all. But he also didn't let go of me.

"It's late, James. You promised Rob you'd be back."

"I wasn't actually talking to Rob this morning." His voice sounded strained.

"I know. I'm not an idiot. And I'm telling you it's okay. I just want you to be happy."

"I fucked this whole thing up." He let go of my face and ran his fingers through his hair. "I was told that I should wean you into your life slowly. And I thought it was a good idea, because I wanted you to remember me. Just me. But it's not just about me."

"James…"

"You can't leave, Penny. I can't do this on my own."

"Of course you can…"

"But it's not just me that needs you. We already have two beautiful children."

What?

"Our daughter is the spitting image of you. You met her in the hospital. But you were freaking out. And everyone said it was best if I waited to tell you. But she misses you. You have to come home. For her, not for me. And you have a son. A newborn. He was born early and…" his voice broke. "We don't know if he's going to make it. That's what I've been doing when we're not together. I'm visiting our daughter at my brother's apartment. And I'm spending every other second at the hospital soaking up any moment with my son that I can because I don't know if he's going to wake up tomorrow. And you can't leave me. You can't leave us."

I felt like I couldn't breathe.

"And you were right, I've never called Rob pumpkin in my life until this afternoon. I was talking to our daughter. I'm not cheating on you. I'd never cheat on you. And I don't care if you can't have any more children. The ones we have are all I need. And we need to go home so that we can spend time with them. They both need you way more than they need me."

It was raining, and I couldn't be sure, but it looked like he was crying.

Everything he said made sense. The doctor I had talked to said he thought I lost a baby. But I hadn't lost him yet. He was in a hospital somewhere, waiting to meet me. Possibly dying. And I remembered the little redheaded girl. It felt like my veins turned to ice. I thought I had dreamed about her. I thought I was seeing myself from my past. Was it possible that she was real? She had called me Mom. She had looked at me with so much love. And she ran to me like there was no one in the world she loved more.

"I can't." I was surprised that those two words came out of my mouth. James had just put everything on the line, and I said: "I can't"? I shook my head. "I…" I tried to swallow down the lump in my throat, but I couldn't seem to.

"I know that was a lot to drop on you. I know you're scared. But you're stronger than you know."

I closed my eyes. "I can't." Why did I keep saying that? It wasn't a choice now. I had to go back. It wasn't about whether or not I loved James. It was so much more than that. I had kids?

"I'll sleep in one of the guest rooms," he said.

That wasn't why. I shook my head. I liked waking up to his arms around me. I liked the way he smelled. I liked the way he looked at me.

"I won't touch you at all, if that's what you want."

I opened my eyes. And I definitely liked when he touched me. His skin against mine made me feel alive. Like he ignited a spark in me I didn't know existed. So I don't know why the word "okay," came out of my mouth so quickly. I don't know why I agreed. It wasn't what I wanted.

"So you'll come back?" He sounded so hopeful and distraught at the same time.

I stared at him getting soaked in the rain, looking as helpless as I felt. "For them." Again, I didn't know why I said it. Was I purposely trying to hurt him? Or was I trying to convince myself that he had nothing to do with my reason for going back to New York?

"Of course. For them." He stepped back toward me, but didn't take me in his arms. "Let's go home."

PART 3

CHAPTER 24

Sunday

A change of clothes hadn't taken the chill out of my bones. I glanced over at James.

His hair was dry now, but the rain had made it curl. He looked handsome. And so very tired. He hadn't touched me once since he promised not to. He didn't take my hand to help me out of the car this time. He didn't touch the small of my back to guide me toward our apartment.

We'd had a lovely evening until I broke everything. And now I was back, and our relationship was more broken than ever. But I didn't know how to fix it. And I was too consumed by nerves. I felt like I was going to be sick.

"Are you ready?" he asked.

I swallowed hard. "Is she already home?"

James nodded.

I wasn't ready. I wasn't sure I'd ever be ready. But he had given me a short rundown of my daughter. Her name was Scarlett. She was three and a half. She had red hair like me but brown eyes like him. She was outgoing and a little spoiled. When he told me that, I think he expected me to laugh. But nothing about this situation was funny to me. How was I supposed to be a mother when I didn't even remember my daughter.

"You can wait until the morning, if you want. It's pretty late, I can put her to bed."

"No." I shook my head. "I can do this."

He didn't wait for me to change my mind. He opened the door and walked into his apartment. *Our apartment.* How was I ever supposed to get used to any of this? I could barely get used to him. Let alone...

"Mommy!"

All I saw was a blur of red hair and panda pajamas before my leg was attacked in a hug. I looked down at her mop of red hair. She was so cute. "Hey, Scarlett."

She looked up at me with her big brown eyes. They looked exactly like James'. But hers weren't stormy. Or tormented. "I missed you." She pressed her face against my leg again.

"I missed you too." It wasn't even a lie. It was like I missed her even though I hadn't known she existed. I squatted down to look her in the face. "Did you have fun with your aunt and uncle?"

She nodded. But she didn't look as happy to see me as she had a second ago. It felt like she was examining me. She squinted her eyes slightly as she stared at me. Maybe she needed glasses? "Do you want help getting ready for bed?"

She squinted her eyes a little more before opening them wide again. She took a step back from me. "No, I want Daddy to help me."

I saw how it was. She was a Daddy's girl. And there he was a few hours ago claiming my kids needed me more than him. What a lie. Scarlett didn't really seem happy to see me at all.

James lifted her up in his arms and peppered her face in kisses as she giggled. "Your mom's going to help you, pumpkin. I'll be up in a minute to tuck you in."

Pumpkin. It truly had been her that he was talking to on the phone earlier. He really wasn't cheating. I felt a wave of relief, and I wasn't really sure why.

She squeezed her arms around James' neck as she stared at me. "No." She looked back at him. "I want you to help me. And to read my bedtime story. And to tuck me in." She glanced back over at me and squinted her eyes again.

Was she glaring at me? Well, James had warned me that she was spoiled. Was I a bad mother? Is that why she was looking at me the way she was?

He kissed her forehead and then looked over at me. "It's been a long day. Is it okay if I just…"

"Of course." I honestly had no idea how to help a kid get ready for bed anyway. My babysitting skills were limited at best.

I watched them walk away. And I felt…empty. Did my daughter hate me? I wrapped my arms around myself so that I wouldn't fall apart.

"Hey, sis," Rob said as he walked into the foyer. He was holding a little girl about Scarlett's age on his hip. She was fast asleep, her head pressed into his chest.

"Hey," I said, despite the fact that he didn't look happy at all to see me.

"Didn't take you for a flight risk. Here I thought we had a fun afternoon, and the whole time you were planning on being an ass."

His wife elbowed him in the side. I didn't remember her name, but I remembered her from the hospital. "What he means to say is that we're glad you're back. We should probably get going." She reached over and tucked a loose strand of hair behind her daughter's ear.

"Of course. Thanks for watching Scarlett."

She looked up from her daughter. Her eyebrows pinched together for a moment before she rushed over to me and gave me a huge hug. "Don't cry. Rob didn't mean it. He was the one being an ass."

I laughed. "It's not that. Well, maybe it's partially that."

"Then what's wrong? You look devastated."

"Does Scarlett hate me?"

She immediately shook her head as she let me out of her embrace. "No. She talks about nothing but you. And whenever James came to visit her all she asked him was when she could see you. I know all of this has been hard. And I'm here if you need me. I know you don't remember me, but we're friends. If you need to talk about anything…"

"Then talk to her instead of leaving," Rob said.

"Rob, you're not helping. Can't you see that she's upset?"

He looked at me almost the same way Scarlett did. "Well, she shouldn't have left. You didn't just worry James. You worried all of us."

"I'm sorry, Rob." And I was. Just thinking about the note I had left made me cringe.

"Yeah, I'm not the one you should be apologizing to. Next time you think about making a run for it, try thinking of someone else for a change. You're not the only one that got hurt, you know."

"Rob." She grabbed his arm. "I'm so sorry. We're going to go before my husband decides to be even worse. Call me if you need anything. Really, anything." She gave me a small smile before she pulled her husband out the front door.

She seemed nice. But I couldn't call her. I didn't even know her name. All I could think about was the fact that Rob had said I wasn't the only one that had gotten hurt. He had to be talking about James. There was still so much I didn't know. James had promised me answers before I had run out on him.

I walked into the family room to wait for him to come back downstairs. Melissa and Josh were sitting on the couch reading a newspaper. It was the strangest thing I had ever seen. Not just because I had forgotten they were visiting, but because I had never seen Melissa read anything but a textbook or magazine.

"Hey guys," I said.

Melissa looked up from the paper. "I don't know whether to hug you or give you the silent treatment."

"I'm sorry." All I could do tonight was apologize. I had messed everything up.

"I thought you killed yourself."

James hadn't said the words out loud, but Melissa had never shied away from how she was feeling.

"I didn't think about how it would look," I said. "I just wanted you to think I...you know...slipped and was unconscious."

She stared at me. "Are you kidding? You took my example of why the cameras were a good thing and used it against me?" She shook her head. "Never mind, silent treatment it is."

"Melissa."

"Don't Melissa me. We were up half the night looking for you all over the city. Speaking of which, we're exhausted." She tossed the newspaper on the coffee table. "We're going to bed."

"I'm sorry," Josh mouthed to me before he followed her out of the family room.

I sighed and sat down where they had been sitting. I hadn't thought about how much my actions would hurt everyone. But in my defense, I hadn't planned on coming back.

Laughter drifted down from upstairs. Hearing it put a pit in my stomach. I expected to feel an instant connection with Scarlett. And I kind of had, until she gave me that strange little scowl. The way she studied me reminded me of her father. Maybe it was that they had the same eyes.

What if she never warmed up to me? What if she never liked me in the first place? I had no idea how to win her over because I didn't know anything about her. Tomorrow was a new day. I'd try harder.

But no matter what I thought, the pit in my stomach only seemed to grow. It wasn't just Scarlett I had to win over if I stayed. I had created this awkward tension between me and James. His brother hated me. Melissa hated me. And I had a son I still hadn't even met.

I put my face in my hands. Tomorrow wasn't going to be an easier day. I'd have to go see my son. Liam. James said he was born two months early. He had a lot of health problems. The doctors worried that if he made it, he'd have some kind of disability. The kid was doomed from the start.

I wanted children. But not like this. I wanted two healthy children that loved me as much as I loved them. Maybe that was the problem. I didn't feel like I loved them yet. Scarlett was this tiny little stranger that happened to look like me. And in my mind, Liam was this tiny sickly thing hooked up to scary tubes.

James said they needed me. But who was I kidding? I could barely take care of myself. I had run away from home like a child. I still felt like a kid myself. My last memories were from when I was a teenager. I wanted kids someday, but way way in the future. I bit the inside of my lip.

"She's sound asleep."

I looked up at James. He was holding a pillow and a folded set of sheets. He was making good on his word to sleep in a separate bed. Just like he had been making good on his promises by not touching me for the rest of the evening.

"I can sleep in the guest room," I said. "Really, I don't mind."

He shook his head. "That's okay. You'll be more comfortable upstairs."

Wouldn't he be too? But he didn't look like he wanted to negotiate. Actually, it didn't look like he wanted to talk at all. I shrugged my shoulders. "Thank you for today. For trying to remind me."

"If you need anything, I'll be down the hall."

"Okay."

He took a step and then stopped. "Sometimes when Scarlett's scared, she climbs into bed with us. But I told her I'd be down here, so she shouldn't be bothering you." He looked over his shoulder toward the stairs. "It might be best if you lock the door, just in case she forgets."

"It's okay, I don't mind."

He nodded. "I'm going to head to bed."

I wanted to ask him what happened to us. I wanted to know if I was still really in danger. But he looked so tired. And sad. I knew how badly he wanted to walk away right now. So I needed to let him. The pit in my stomach kept growing. "Goodnight, James."

His eyes locked with mine. "Goodnight, Penny." He waited the briefest of moments before dropping his gaze down to the blankets in his arms and walking away.

I knew he was hoping a switch would go off in my head. That I'd suddenly remember. I wanted to remember. For my kids. Maybe for him too.

The apartment felt empty and cold when he disappeared down the hall. I wrapped my arms around myself. I hadn't even realized I was shivering. And I had the oddest feeling that if things didn't change, I'd always feel this cold and alone. But how could I change them when I barely understood the woman I had become.

I brushed away a tear as I made my way up the stairs. One of the doors that had been previously locked was open. I tiptoed toward it, almost afraid of what I'd see on the other side.

But it was just Scarlett's bedroom. A nightlight was pretty bright in the small room, casting way more light than shadows. She was already sound asleep, hugging a stuffed animal close to her chest. I smiled. When I was little, I used to always sleep with a stuffed animal too. And with a nightlight. I was basically scared of the dark until high school.

I watched her peaceful little face. And I felt drawn to her. Like a piece of my heart belonged tucked against her chest instead of that stuffed animal. It was the oddest sensation when I didn't even know her. Maybe my heart remembered even though my head didn't. I hoped that was true. I hoped that I was able to connect with her.

Scarlett sniffled in her sleep and turned away from me. I tiptoed back out of the room and stared at the door next to hers in the hall. I walked over and tried to turn the knob, but it was still locked. I had my suspicions of what it was. Liam's room. A cute little nursery for a baby that might never even see it.

I let go of the knob and wiped away more tears. My family was broken. I needed to figure out how to fix it. I had to try.

CHAPTER 25
Monday

Despite what James said about our room being more comfortable, I couldn't sleep. I tossed and turned for hours until I couldn't take it anymore. I needed fresh air. Maybe a walk or a run. But that was probably out of the question. I shoved the blankets off and climbed out of bed.

There were still towels all over the bathroom floor where I had let the tub overflow. My note had even been on the vanity last night, mocking me. James had left everything in disarray when he came to find me. Or maybe he wanted me to see this. To remind me to stop being selfish. I knew I had been. I didn't need a reminder.

Either way, I wanted today to be a fresh start for all of us. I grabbed the towels off the floor and headed downstairs. The last time I had done laundry, I was paying for it with quarters in my dorm. Nothing nearly as fancy as the washer and dryer here. I turned a bunch of knobs and prayed I was doing it right. The last thing I wanted was to cause any more trouble. *Or water damage.*

As I waited for the laundry to finish, I stared out at the skyline. The city lights were starting to dim as the sun rose. The park in the distance looked even prettier at dawn. Maybe I could get used to this. Apparently I had before. I just needed to remember.

James had mentioned a book that I had written. I had always wanted to write a book. Was it any good? I glanced down the hall. Where would it be? Probably in an office if I had one. I abandoned my view in search of the documents that would reveal everything I had forgotten.

After a few wrong turns, I walked into a beautiful library. Floor to ceiling books. Every inch of shelf space was covered. There was even a fancy stone fireplace to one side. I felt like Belle from Beauty and the Beast. I turned in a circle, taking it all in.

There was a small desk in the corner. A notebook was sitting on top of the desk, but I wasn't sure if it was mine. It said *Ivy Smoak* on the front and there was an outline of sorts. It did look like my handwriting. A pen name, perhaps? Why would I want a pen name? I had never disliked my name. But I had a different name now. Penny Hunter. It was going to take me a lifetime to get used to it. Hunter. Mrs. Hunter. God, it didn't even sound good. I sat down in the office chair.

There wasn't much left on the desk. Just a sleek laptop and a few pens and pencils. I glanced in the waste bin next to the desk. There was an envelope torn in two with James' name on it along with a few crumpled up pieces of paper. It looked like my handwriting on the envelope. I glanced at the door, knowing well enough that no one else was awake, before lifting the torn envelope and the pieces of paper out of the trash.

I put the two sides of the envelope together. *Definitely my handwriting.* I un-crumpled the pieces of paper and realized it used to be one sheet. I placed both sides together and read the letter.

James,

If you're reading this, we both know what happened. I don't need to say it. And all I can say is that I understand what you're feeling. Like your heart hurts. Like you don't know if you'll ever smile again. Like the world has stopped. Like the only thing you can see for miles is darkness.

You see, I almost lost you once. I know that feeling. My mother found me falling apart in a bathroom stall at the hospital. And she told me something that really stuck with me. She told me that you have to keep living in order to keep the memory of those you love alive. And I'm asking you to do that for me. Remind Scarlett of who I was. Tell stories to our son. Don't let me disappear to our children. Don't let them forget how much I loved them.

Maybe that seems like the hardest thing in the world. But what I'm about to ask you to do, it may just be harder. I need you to keep the memory of me alive to our children. But I need you to let the memories of me with you fade. Because I need you to keep your heart open. Keep loving. Keep living. I need you to let me go.

All I've ever wanted was for you to be happy. And even though it feels like the world has stopped, it hasn't. Because despite what you think, there is so much light in this world. There's so much light in you.

Remind Scarlett that I love her. Tell our son I wished I could have met him. And find a new love for yourself. You've always been stronger than you realized. But it's okay to lean on your family and friends. Let them help you. Let them in. Don't shut out everyone who cares about you. Because despite how it feels, you are not alone. You're strong.

You're good. You're whole. You're loved. You are so loved, James.

Now smile,

Penny

Smile? Seriously? I realized my hands were shaking as I smoothed the two sides of the note against the top of the desk. What had I been thinking?

I folded the letter in half to hide the words. Clearly I hadn't been thinking. This was a suicide note, wasn't it? And it seemed like James had seen it. His name had been on the envelope. He saw it and tried to destroy it. He didn't want me to see just how depressed I had been.

I thought about the conversation I had overheard between James and Rob a few days ago. He said he used to catch me crying and I'd wipe away the tears and pretend I was okay. He admitted that I wasn't happy. I looked down at the note. But this unhappy?

Or maybe there was another explanation. *If you're reading this, we both know what happened.* I shook my head. The whole thing was about death. I was saying goodbye. Why? I looked around the library. What was so awful about this life?

This version of me was married to a handsome man, had an adorable daughter, and another kid on the way. I had written a book. I was wealthy beyond my wildest dreams. *So what was so horrid? What was I missing?*

Because my current life seemed worse. I had no memory of the life around me. I had a son who was dying. I'd never have any more kids. I took a deep breath. Penny Hunter was a lot better off than Penny Taylor. She had it all. But I was terrified to remember. Not just because it meant giving up my current state of mind, but because it might spiral me into a horrible depression.

I folded up the letter again. And again. Until it was a tiny piece of paper in my hand. James tried to hide parts of my life from me. So what else was he hiding besides the children? What other secrets was he keeping?

I stood up from the chair. I didn't care that it was early. We needed to talk. I needed to understand everything if I had any chance of fixing this. I wandered out of the library and down the hall to the guest room he was sleeping in.

"James," I said and tapped lightly with my knuckles.

No answer.

"James?" I knocked again.

No answer.

I heard whistling down the hall. It didn't sound like him. It sounded more like a woman. I abandoned the door and wandered back into the living room. An older woman was standing in front of the couch fluffing pillows and humming.

I glanced at the camera in the corner of the room. *Please be watching.* "Hello?"

The woman jumped. "Oh, Penny. You gave me a fright, dear. How are you feeling? I made you your favorite breakfast. And I saw that you did a load of towels. You know I would have done that for you. Really, you should be sitting down." She stepped away from the couch.

"Who are you?" I tried my best for it to not come out rude. She seemed pleasant enough. She reminded me of my mother. But I had no idea what she was doing in James' apartment.

She put her hand to her chest. "Ellen. Oh, my. James warned me of this but…" she shook her head like she was trying to shake the tears away. "It's hard to believe without seeing you in person. Please sit. I'll bring your breakfast to you. You need rest. And fluids. Plenty of fluids." She bustled off toward the kitchen.

Ellen? Who the heck was Ellen? It sounded vaguely familiar, but I couldn't place it. Before I even realized what was happening, I was sitting on the couch with a huge omelet and freshly squeezed orange juice in front of me. I didn't know what to say. I had already asked her who she was and her explanation hadn't helped at all. "Um…where is James?"

"He's used to going for a run every morning. So he's been…" her voice trailed off. "You can ask him yourself when he gets back. He'll be home shortly. Aren't you hungry, dear?"

That was weird. But it wasn't worth asking her about it. There was no way she'd tell me what he was doing instead of running. Everyone loved keeping me in the dark. And she asked me if I was hungry in a terrible segue for a reason. I looked down at the omelet. Honestly, I was a little hungry. But I was a little more suspicious. "So…what is it that you do?"

She smiled and sat down next to me. "You know, the little things to help make everything run smoothly here. I cook and clean. And I take little Scarlett off your hands whenever I get a chance. We go to the park all the time. She loves the park. And especially the zoo. She's an adorable little girl. Just an absolute pleasure. Oh my, I feel like I'm going on and on. I don't need to tell you about Scarlett, you already know all that." She cleared her throat. "I mean, you will soon. You'll remember. I know you will. You must. Now eat up. You need your strength."

This woman was the adorable one. Not Scarlett. Scarlett leered at me. Ellen was simply wonderful. Or she was an intruder that creepily knew way too much about my family. I was willing to take my chances though, because the omelet looked amazing.

"This is fantastic," I said after taking my first bite.

Ellen stood up. "At least your taste buds haven't forgotten what they like. That's probably a good sign. I'm going to go make sure we have all the ingredients for your favorite meals all week. After all, if one sense comes back, surely the rest will follow."

I wasn't sure if that was true. But I hoped she was right. She could be. I hadn't remembered liking mushrooms and peppers in my omelets. Yet, here I was devouring this one. I stopped mid-bite, my cheeks full of food, when I heard the front door open.

I swallowed down my bite without fully chewing and almost choked. I had no idea why I was nervous to see him. Maybe it was the letter I still had folded up in my hand. Or maybe it was the fact that I knew how badly I'd messed everything up. I just wanted today to be better.

James stepped into the living room in just a pair of running shorts and sneakers. No shirt. All the abs. Sweat dripped down the muscles in his chest. If I still had food in my mouth, I'm pretty sure it would have fallen out because my mouth was probably hanging open. *Calm down.*

Despite his hotness, he looked nervous, like he hadn't expected to see me. And pale. His face looked really, super pale. "Hey," he said.

"Good morning," I said at the exact same time, blurring out his hello.

He smiled for the briefest of moments before it disappeared again. "Is it okay if I use the upstairs shower?"

"Um...yeah. Of course. I cleaned up the towels on the floor."

"You didn't have to do that. Ellen would have this morning."

Good, he does know her. And then her name finally clicked in my brain. But not because I remembered her from before. It was because Rob had mentioned her to me. He had joked around and pretended Ellen was James' other wife. It all made sense now. "Yes, Ellen seems very nice. But there's no way I would have made her clean up after me. It was my fault." I thought about the letter I had read. If I had tried to kill myself, the stunt I pulled in the bathroom was a thousand times worse.

He raised his left eyebrow at me. "She doesn't mind, Penny. It's her job."

"But still." The letter was burning a hole in my palm. *Ask him.*

"You're supposed to be taking it easy. For a little while longer."

I nodded. "Okay."

He took a deep breath, his chest rising slightly. That's when I noticed the faded scar on his ribcage. And the one on his stomach. But they weren't as alarming as the scar right above his left peck. It didn't look old at all. I was pretty sure there were still stitches in it. How had I not noticed that yesterday when he kissed me in the rain? I swallowed hard. Well, I had been rather distracted.

I looked back up at his pale face and he immediately looked away from me. Like he didn't want me to realize he was staring. Or maybe it was something a little more than that. *Stop hiding things from me.* "Where were you?"

He ran his fingers through his hair. "I've been doing physical therapy a few days a week."

I tried to force myself to stop staring at his perfect hair. "For?"

"Penny, I'm fine. I'm not the one you need to worry about. You made it pretty clear why you came back."

There was more to that sentence and we both knew it. *You made it pretty clear why you came back, and it wasn't for me.* He was right. I came back for Scarlett and Liam. But I was pulled to him too. It was like we were two sides of a magnet and he was drawing me in with his six pack abs and brooding smile.

"I'm going to go take that shower," he said.

"When are you going to tell me what happened?" I stared at his pale face, willing him to tell me the truth.

"It's not a long walk to the hospital. After I shower, maybe we can talk on our way over to see Liam?"

Liam. I bit the inside of my lip. I thought I'd have a bit more time to process everything before meeting my son. But I'd take what I could get. I nodded. "Yeah, that sounds good."

He didn't say anything else. He just walked away, giving me a wonderful view of his strong back and firm ass. I sighed and leaned back on the couch. James was the perfect storm. Giving me just enough to need more. I could feel myself being pulled closer to his chaos.

Him saying he wouldn't sleep in the same bed as me? Now I couldn't seem to sleep without him. Him saying he wouldn't touch me? Now I wanted him to. Desperately. I couldn't just erase how I felt yesterday in his arms. I looked down at my half eaten omelet. I was decidedly not hungry for anything but James.

***

I kept my arms folded across my chest so that I wouldn't be tempted to reach for James' hand. Not that I could've even if I'd wanted to. He was keeping his distance from me. A whole person could fit between us on the sidewalk. And sometimes they did, almost knocking into me. *God I hate New York.* It was loud and crowded and…I glanced at James…*lonely.* I hadn't expected it to feel so horribly lonely.

"Scarlett will be up in about an hour," James said. "I'd like to be back before then. She hasn't had a normal day in quite some time."

"Of course." It had been like this ever since we started our walk. He wasn't giving me anything. If I was going to learn about what happened, I needed to steer the conversation. The hairs on the back of my neck rose as a chill ran down my spine. I glanced over my shoulder. It was the same sensation I'd had in the apartment. Like someone was watching me. Two of our security guards were a few paces behind us. Certainly they were watching us. *It's just in my mind.*

I turned my head back before I gave myself a chance to collide with anyone on the sidewalk. This was my chance at getting answers, not pretending I was being followed. "So someone tried to hurt me?" I wasn't even sure if I believed that anymore. I was pretty sure I had tried to hurt myself. The note in my pocket was proof enough of that.

James looked straight ahead. "Dr. Nelson. Your OB-GYN. While you were pregnant with Liam, he said he found a heart murmur that had been there all along that was getting worse the longer you carried our son. He claimed your last OB-GYN was negligent not to tell us. But he made the whole thing up."

"I don't have a heart murmur then?" I didn't know what that meant so I was happy it wasn't true.

"You didn't until him. He successfully gave you one as he slowly poisoned you and our son."

Poisoned?

"Your heart murmur is mild again now, after the delivery. Your cardiologist believes you'll have a normal, healthy life without any surgical intervention. We were lucky we figured out what was going on when we did. Before it was too late."

All I heard were the words *surgical intervention* and *before it was too late*. I had almost died. This crazy doctor had poisoned me. And for what? "Why would a doctor do that? I don't…"

"We think he wanted his practice to be number one. The OB-GYN you had for Scarlett retired, but his practice was still considered the best in the city, even though Dr. Nelson was now considered the best OB-GYN. He couldn't shake the reputation of the practice, so he tried to deface them. By blaming your death on them."

But I didn't die. Right? I pinched the inside of my arm. I still had trouble believing this life was real sometimes. I couldn't just embrace it as easily as everyone wanted me to. "You know all this and he's still not in custody? Was it not enough proof?"

"No. We have all the proof we need. We have the whole thing recorded."

"So what's the problem?"

"The police think he skipped town. There's a warrant out for his arrest."

I glanced over my shoulder again. Was that why I felt like someone was watching me? Was it possible that Dr. Nelson was out there right now? I shook away the thought. "Do you think he'll try to hurt me again?"

"We don't know. But even if he does try, he won't succeed."

I should have been freaked out. I should have had more questions. But I didn't. Maybe because part of me still felt like I was dreaming. That none of this was real. Besides for that nagging feeling that someone was watching me, I didn't find his story alarming at all. I didn't even really know if I could trust his account. I had a note that explained everything a little differently. "So let me get this straight. A crazy doctor drugged me in an attempt to make it look like I had a slowly growing heart murmur that would lead to my untimely death?"

James finally looked over at me. "I guess that's the gist."

I laughed.

He scowled.

"That's the stupidest plan I've ever heard. He walked into our house with cameras everywhere and spiked my pills? He must have known he'd be caught. What a whack job. Hold on, so if I was poisoned, what happened to you?"

"Ellen swapped our weekly pill holders in our suitcases. I took a few days worth of the pills."

"You didn't notice the difference?"

"I thought Ellen just got a new brand of multivitamins. I didn't think anything of it."

He was absentminded. That much was clear. And apparently he relied on Ellen a lot. I wondered if he relied on me as much. "So I went into a coma, delivered a premature baby, and lost my ability to have any more children in my lifetime. What happened to you?"

He grimaced. I just wasn't sure which part had upset him. "I'm fine," he said.

"You're not fine. I saw the stitches on the side of your chest. Your face gets pale when you exercise. And you keep running out of breath. You're out of breath right now." I grabbed his arm to stop him.

"I'm going to physical therapy. I'll be fine soon enough."

"Tell me what happened."

"Why? So you can make a joke of the whole thing like it doesn't matter? *You* were in a coma. *You* delivered a premature baby. *You* lost the ability to have more children. It's not all about *you*. There's another side to the story. My wife who I love with every ounce of my being was in a coma for weeks. I thought I was going to lose her. And she delivered a beautiful, helpless, broken little boy into this world without her. I had no fucking idea what I was doing without you.

I don't know how to take care of a baby by myself. Let alone one as tiny and sick as him. And you didn't just lose the ability to have children. *We* lost the ability, Penny. *We*. There is no you and me, we're an us. We can't have any more children. If we lose Liam, that's it. We don't get another chance. So don't make light of this situation. It's not just your life, it's ours."

"I'm sorry." It was a lame apology. It made it seem like I hadn't listened to a single thing he'd said. Like his pain hadn't shaken me to my core. "I'm sorry," I said again, but it sounded just as lame as the first time.

He pulled his arm out of my grip and ran his fingers through his hair. "It's fine."

But it wasn't fine. There was nothing fine about his demeanor. I had hurt him. Yet again. Apparently it was all I was capable of doing.

He started walking again and I had to jog to catch up to him.

"James, I do care. I didn't mean to joke around about what happened. But of course I care."

"I'm not asking you to care about me. You've made it pretty clear that isn't something you want. All I'm asking is that you're here for our son." He stopped again and took a deep breath.

I tried not to cringe. I had the oddest sensation that I was just as likely to lose him as I was to lose Liam. And not in the loving sense. Clearly I had already lost him there. But he looked ill. Was he dying?

James leaned forward. For a second I thought he was going to kiss me. My heart started beating so fast I thought it would break out of my ribcage. The one kiss we had shared was seared into my brain. I wanted another. I wanted him to press my back against the car again. I wanted to feel the rain on my skin. I wanted to feel alive. He leaned even closer.

And then he opened up the door behind me, breaking the spell. He moved away as quickly as he had drawn close, and stepped inside of the building. More questions than answers swirled in my head. And now I was the one left out of breath.

CHAPTER 26
Monday

The bustling and beeping of the hospital died away when I looked into the window of the NICU. I thought I'd recognize my son right away. But I had no idea which baby was Liam. I swallowed hard. The instant connection wasn't there. I couldn't even tell which squirming blob was my son.

"You ready?" James asked.

But I barely heard him. I blinked fast, trying to remove the threatening tears. What if I held him and felt the same way? Like he wasn't a part of me?

"Penny." James' voice was gentler. He put his hand on my shoulder.

It was like his touch emanated strength. I took a deep breath and turned toward him. He was touching me. He had promised not to, yet here he was. And I was happy that he had broken his word. I nodded my head. "I'm ready."

He gave me a small smile and then removed his hand in a rush. Maybe he had just remembered his promise. Or maybe my touch did the opposite to him. It zapped the strength out of him instead of reviving him.

I followed him into the room. The first thing I noticed was how much warmer the air was. It wasn't a pull to my son. Or a realization of which baby he was. No, it was just the sensation that it was warm.

There was a nurse writing something down on a clipboard. She looked up as we entered and a smile crossed her face. "Good morning, Mr. Hunter. Our strong-willed warrior is doing well this morning. He's been sleeping better at night." She set her clipboard down and walked over to one of the little incubation cribs.

"Strong-willed warrior?" I asked.

The nursed looked up like she hadn't seen me. "Yes. That's what Liam means."

I wasn't sure why I was glaring at her instead of looking at my baby. But the way she had said that was so condescending.

"And he needs to be strong right now." She pulled him out. "Don't you, little man?" she said in a babyish voice. She looked back up at me with her perfect smile that matched her perfect long blonde hair and perfectly tanned skin. "You must be Mrs. Hunter. Would you like to hold him?"

"I…" I looked back and forth between the baby and James. "What is that mask on his face?"

"It's a CPAP. His lungs weren't fully developed when he was born so it's helping him breathe a little easier. But he'll be breathing on his own in no time." She looked down at my son. "Won't you?" she said in her baby voice. "Yes you will, yes you will."

I swallowed hard. He was so tiny. So so tiny. And he wasn't just attached to one machine. There were all sorts of tubes and wires everywhere. If I held him, I was afraid it would be like holding a robot.

James didn't wait for me to decide what I wanted to do. He walked over and took Liam out of the nurse's arms.

"Hi, Liam," he said as he stared down at the baby. "You slept better last night, huh?" He wasn't using a baby voice like the nurse. But his voice was softer. Gentler than it was with me. Loving.

I couldn't look away from the two of them.

"Your sister said you were a good boy yesterday. I'm sorry that I couldn't be here. I won't go that long without seeing you again, okay? I promise."

I thought the baby looked small before, but he looked even teensier in James' arms. Or hands, more accurately. Liam practically fit in his hands.

James rocked Liam back and forth slowly. He looked up at the nurse. "He looks bigger than the last time I saw him." The smile on his face was brighter than I had ever seen. So much brighter than when he smiled at me.

"I told you he was doing well. All it took was a good night's sleep." She reached over and adjusted Liam's blanket. "Let's take his mask off for a few minutes too." She carefully unstrapped the contraption. "Isn't that better?" she cooed.

James and the nurse stood close, staring down affectionately at Liam. I shouldn't have been jealous. I was standing right here. But I couldn't help it. This stranger was a better mother to my child than I was. I didn't even feel compelled to hold Liam because I was scared he might break in my hands.

"Who else has been to visit you while I was away?" James said gently to Liam. "Rob and Daphne. Your grandparents." He rocked the baby in his arms. "You didn't miss me at all, did you?"

"Aw, I'm sure he did," the nurse said as she adjusted the blanket again. "Matt was here too. And Tyler and Hailey stopped by to spend some time with him."

I had no idea who Matt was. But I recognized the name Tyler. *The Tyler.* The perfect male specimen that Melissa said I passed on. We were still close enough that he visited my baby? Everyone had been here. Everyone had held him but me. And that nurse wasn't Liam's mother. *I was.*

The nurse placed her hand on James' bicep. "But he's never as happy as when you're here." She leaned down into Liam's face, keeping her hand on James' arm. "Isn't that right?" She and James stood there smiling down at Liam. The perfect little family. They had no need for me. And it wasn't lost on me that James didn't flinch at her touch. He seemed way more comfortable around her than he did around me.

"You're going to get out of here so soon," James said in his calming voice. "You're going to come home and everything's going to be okay. Just keep breathing for me, Liam. Keep breathing."

"You heard your daddy," the nurse said. "Keep breathing for us."

Us? Hell no. This random nurse wasn't a part of *us.* "Can I hold him?" I asked.

James looked up. He seemed surprised that I was standing there. Like he had completely forgotten I existed. Which was exactly how I'd felt watching him with Liam and the nurse. Invisible. Yesterday he had sworn he saw me. Today? It felt like he was trying to prove how alone he could make me feel without him.

I walked over to them without waiting for a response. James slowly maneuvered Liam into my arms, being careful with all the cords.

"You have to support his head. Careful of his blanket, he needs to stay warm." The nurse kept chirping orders but I ignored her. I'd know how to hold my son. I'd just know.

For just a moment, James kept his hands beneath Liam too. And for the first time I felt like we were a family. But then the warmth of this hands disappeared. It was just me and Liam. Me and…it felt like I stopped breathing as I stared down at him. His dark hair. His nose. He was the spitting image of James. But then he opened his little eyes and looked up at me. And I saw myself. He had my blue eyes. I knew that most babies had blue eyes, but I was hoping that they'd stay blue. That there would be one thing about him that was a reflection of me.

"Hi, Liam." I tried to keep my voice calm but not baby-like. I didn't want to sound like the nurse. I wanted to sound like me. I wanted him to remember. He would have heard me talking all the time while I carried him in my belly. He'd know I was his mother. "Do you remember me?"

His face scrunched up for a moment like he wanted to cry. But then his features softened. And he blinked. The tiniest, cutest little blink.

I took that as a yes. And I felt guilty about it, because I didn't remember him. It wasn't fair for me to expect so much from him. He was a baby, after all. I was the grown up. "I'm going to remember you too. We can do it together."

I felt it in a rush. The same as I had with Scarlett. That a piece of my heart belonged with him even though my mind didn't remember giving it away. "You look just like your father," I said. I gently touched the side of his face. "So handsome."

While I held him, I wondered what kind of mother I was. Did I read to my belly at night? Did I sing to him so he'd recognize my voice? Did I eat the right things? Did I care as much as I hoped I would?

None of it really mattered. Because I was going to start caring right now. Holding him in my arms turned my world upside down. He was so small. And he needed me. He needed me and I was going to be there for him.

"I'm not going anywhere this time," I said. "I promise. We're going to figure all of this out together. I've always wanted a baby. And you're perfect. You're so perfect."

He squirmed in my arms. *Aw.* My heart felt like it broke into a million little pieces as I stared down at him.

I lowered my voice. "Don't let any nurses or doctors tell you any differently. You're perfect, little Liam. And I'm going to take care of you. We're going to be okay. We can get through anything together, you and me." I wasn't sure why I felt compelled to align my future with this tiny little baby's. James had told me the odds. All the statistics about what his life would be like if he ever got out of here. And Liam was clearly small. But he didn't seem sick to me. He seemed healthy. Just small and misunderstood. *We're okay, baby boy. We're okay.*

James already had opinions of me. Scarlett already had opinions of me. Everyone already had opinions of me. Except for this baby. Liam had only just met me. And he seemed to like me well enough. I just knew in my heart that we were going to get through all of this together.

"You're a strong-willed warrior, huh? Well, me too." I leaned down and placed a kiss on his forehead. "Me too, baby boy."

CHAPTER 27

Monday

"Daddy!" Scarlett screamed when he opened the front door. She flew into his arms as soon as he got down on his knees to catch her.

"I thought you disappeared," she sobbed into his shoulder. "You weren't here when I woke up. I thought you left like Mommy."

Ouch.

"I'm right here, pumpkin." He slowly stood up, hugging her close. "And I'm not going anywhere. We've talked about this. People don't just disappear, okay? I'm right here. And your mom is here too."

"We talked about that. But you also promised you'd be here when I woke up. You promised, Daddy." She was holding on to him so tightly I thought she might be strangling him.

"I know, I'm sorry. We were visiting Liam and it took a little longer than we thought."

"You could have taken me with you. Don't leave me again." She sniffled.

He ran his hand up and down her back. He looked stressed, and strained, and tired. She was angry with him and it was my fault. I was the one that had kept saying one more minute when I was holding Liam. It was my fault that he broke his promise.

I gently touched Scarlett's arms. "It's my fault, Scarlett. It was my first time meeting him. He's cute, isn't he? It's hard to leave him at the hospital when he's so cute."

She lifted her head over James' shoulder. "You left me."

Oh, Scarlett. That wasn't what I meant at all. I watched her blink her tear stained eyes. "I'm back now. And I'm not going anywhere."

She shook her head and hid against James' chest.

I guess she didn't believe me. I had broken her trust. And I didn't know how to get it back. Because I didn't know her. "What do you want to do today, Scarlett?" I asked. "We can do anything you want. You just name it."

James started shaking his head back and forth.

"The zoo!" she screamed.

James sighed and looked up at the ceiling. He needed a break from sick kids and demanding ones. I was here to help. And I wanted to spend time with Scarlett.

"How about just us girls?" I asked. "It'll be fun."

"I don't think that's a good idea," James said.

Couldn't he see that I was doing it for him? He needed a break. "It'll be fun. Scarlett, do you want to go get ready? We'll leave in a few minutes."

She practically leapt out of James' arms and ran toward the stairs.

James was glaring at me. I doubted he had any idea how handsome he was when he glared. I certainly wasn't going to tell him. Him looking hot as sin was the one thing that made the daggers he was throwing with his gaze bearable.

"Penny, I really don't think it's a good idea."

"I saw your face when she mentioned the zoo. I know you don't want to tell me what's going on with you, but I can tell you need rest. Let me do this."

"I'm not comfortable with you taking her by yourself."

"Why?"

"Why? Because you ran out on us a couple days ago. Because..."

"I didn't know about her."

"That's fair." His Adam's apple rose and fell. "You ran out on me. Not her. But that doesn't change the fact that you don't know anything about her. You're taking her to a crowded public place. She likes to run off when she's excited."

"She has red hair. It'll be hard to lose her."

"It's more than that. When she gets grumpy in the afternoon it's because she needs a snack. And not just any snack. She likes the little fruit ones that come in the blue bags. And she's obsessed with panda bears. She always asks a million questions about panda bears at the zoo and doesn't understand why they don't have one here. We always tell her one is coming soon because it makes her happy."

"So you're worried I'm going to tell her the truth about pandas not coming to the zoo here? That's what you're worried about? Letting the truth about that slip is probably for the best."

"You don't get it, Penny. You can't just jump in and be a parent."

"I don't know what you want from me then. This is what you asked me to do."

He pressed his lips together. "You're right. Being a good mom is all I've asked from you. But..." his voice trailed off. He ran his hand through his hair and looked away from me.

But what? I wanted him to say he was wrong for asking that. Because it wasn't all he wanted. He wanted me too.

"It would make me more comfortable if you let me come with you." He was still not looking at me.

That wasn't what he was about to say. He was about to say something heartfelt and real. And he replaced it with nonsense. I wasn't going to lose our kid. And I wasn't going to randomly tell her all sorts of stuff that didn't align with our parenting decisions. I was trying to win Scarlett over, not upset her. "I'm giving you a free pass to do whatever you want this afternoon. For a few hours you don't have to worry about kids and obligations. I'm trying to do something nice *for you*." I emphasized the last words because I wanted him to know that I cared. That a part of me came back for him too.

"Will you at least ask Melissa if she'll go with you?"

"Sure." Now that was a suggestion I could get behind. This was going to be fun. "If you tell me what you were about to say before. You said being a good mom is all you've asked from me. But...your voice trailed off. What were you going to say?"

He shrugged his shoulders. "Honestly, it doesn't matter. Anything I say will just make this worse."

"This as in us?" I asked. He wasn't the only one aware of the fact that we were having a conversation standing several feet away from each other. He wasn't the only one that wanted the distance to close.

"I'm doing the best I can. I made you a few promises, and I'm trying to stick by them. That's what you want, right? For me to keep my distance?"

Now was my chance. I could tell him I wanted to kiss him again. That I wanted to wake up in his arms. That I wanted my dreams of him to become a reality. "James, I have no idea what I want." *Not true. You're a liar, Penny!*

"Well, I know what I want." His gaze dropped to my lips. "And that's why it's good I made you those promises. Because our ideas of what this is between us couldn't be more different." He looked back up at my eyes. "We'll be friends. Nothing more. And as a friend, I hope you have fun today. Thanks for the break." He didn't say it sarcastically, but I heard it that way.

Yesterday on our date he stared at me like he loved me. I felt like he loved me. And today it felt like he didn't care one way or the other whether I stayed or went. No, that wasn't true. It felt like he hated me. Like he wished I was out of his house and out of his life for good.

"Porter and Briggs will accompany you too." His voice was all formal now. Any trace of emotion from earlier was completely gone. "I assume you'll be out for lunch. Will you be back by dinner?"

"Do you want me back for dinner?" I felt juvenile and stupid. He had confessed his love every which way. And I had told him to stop. I had messed all of this up. Yet I was the one that was angry at him. I could clear it up. I could tell him I wanted to be more than friends. But my mouth wouldn't open except for stupid snide remarks I didn't mean.

"It's whatever you want, Penny. I just want to know so I don't worry." His gaze dropped to my lips again for just a moment. I would have missed it if I hadn't been looking.

I shook my head. I doubt he'd worry with Porter and Briggs following us all day. "Ellen said she was cooking. So we'll be back for dinner."

"Good. I'll see you around 6 then."

"Fine."

"Great." He walked away without another word.

Again I found myself staring at his ass. My stomach twisted in a knot. That whole conversation had been angry and hostile and…hot. *Hot?* Why the hell did I think him being pissed off was sexy? But God, it was. I wanted to grab the back of his neck and pull him into a kiss. And rip his clothes off. And bite his skin. I wanted to know what it actually felt like for him to thrust inside of me.

God. What the hell is wrong with me? I had completely lost my mind.

CHAPTER 28

Monday

"And that's a red one like me," Scarlett said and pointed to the red panda with her free hand. Her other hand was holding Melissa's. It had been ever since we had left the apartment. Scarlett would barely look at me. At least it seemed like Melissa had forgiven me for running away. I wasn't sure what I'd do if they both hated me.

"It is like you," Melissa said with a laugh.

"But they come in big sizes when they aren't red. The black and white ones are huge. But I've never seen one here. Daddy says one's coming soon. But I don't know when soon is. It feels like I've been waiting forever." She stepped forward to get an even better look at the red panda.

"Real pandas are cool, but do you know what's even better?" Melissa asked.

Scarlett shook her head.

"Red ones." She crouched down and tickled Scarlett's side, sending her into a fit of giggles. "You know, I bet if you crawled in there you could blend in."

"Really?" Scarlett looked so excited. "Do you think I'm allowed to go in to play with them?"

"Only if your dad says yes. Next time he's here with you, definitely ask him. You can tell him I said it was okay." She winked at Scarlett.

Scarlett nodded enthusiastically and then looked back at the exhibit.

Melissa was so good with her. I could have gotten mad at her for digging that hole with James. Next time Scarlett came here she'd think she was allowed in the red panda exhibit. But I wasn't upset at all. Melissa was just being a good aunt. Her first instinct wasn't to tell Scarlett that pandas would never come to the Central Park Zoo. She had just casually changed the topic to distract Scarlett. It was brilliant. And I was a little jealous that they were the ones bonding. This was my chance to get closer to Scarlett and I was holding back. I wasn't even sure why.

A chill ran down my spine and I glanced over my shoulder. Porter and Briggs were standing a few paces away, watching us. I wasn't sure I'd ever get used to that feeling. It gave me the creeps.

"Hey…you." Scarlett poked my knee.

Speaking of little creeps. Why didn't she call me Mommy? Her most affectionate term for me was *you?* That was so weird. "What's up, Scarlett?"

"Daddy said if I got hungry you'd have a snack for me." She did that squinted eye thing at me. "That's me now. Hungry."

"Oh. Right." I opened up my purse and pulled out the blue snack pack of gummies. "Here you go." I handed it to her.

She looked at it and then lifted her head back up to me. "No. *My* snack." She tried to hand it back.

"This is your snack."

She shook her head back and forth.

"Yes it is. It's a fruit gummy snack in a blue bag. Just like your dad said you liked."

"It's not the right one. This says…" she scrunched her mouth to the side as she looked at the package. "Fib…fibey…fieb…"

"Fiber fruit snacks," I said.

"Mine aren't fibey snacks. Mine are shaped like animals. These are yours and Daddy's."

How different could they be? "Do you want to try one? You might like it."

"No."

I laughed. "I'm sure it tastes the same as yours. Just try it."

"I don't want to. I want my animal snack. We're at the zoo. At the zoo you eat animal snacks."

That wasn't very sound logic. She was basically implying that you should eat the animals at the zoo. What a little carnivore. I crouched down and took the bag away from her. "Here, I'll show you that these are good too." I opened it up and ate one. They were fine. "See, it's good. Try one."

Scarlett shook her head as she looked at me. "You're not very good at this thing." And then she grabbed the bag and ran back over to Melissa.

What thing? Being her mother? I sighed and stood back up. Why did this kid hate me so much? But at least she was eating the fruit snacks. She liked them just fine. She finished them within a few minutes and then ran back over to me.

"Here," she said and tried to hand me the bag.

"I'm sure there's a trashcan around here somewhere. Let's go find one."

"That's your job." She threw the empty bag at my feet.

This was not going well. I needed to turn things around somehow. "Did you want more fruit snacks?" I asked. "I have a few more packs." I pulled the rest of the bags out of my purse.

She stared at me. "I can have all those?"

It was only three more packs. She was acting like I was giving her the biggest treat ever. "Of course." I handed them to her.

She immediately grabbed them and ran back over to Melissa, leaving me with the trash at my feet. I guess I had been diminished to a human waste bin and food dispenser. *Great.* I needed to turn this day around. As soon as I found a trashcan. I turned in a circle but didn't see any. Well, Scarlett already thought I was a waste bin. Might as well prove her point. I picked up her trash, put it in my purse, and then ran over to catch up to them.

"Do you guys want to go to the tropic zone?" I asked. I fumbled with the map as I pulled it out. "It's supposed to be creatures of the rainforest. Like lemurs and frogs and snakes."

"Snapes?" Scarlett tried to hide behind Melissa.

"No, snakes," I said. "With a 'K'."

"I don't like snapes," Scarlett said.

"Okay. Well, there's also these fancy rainforest pigeons and…"

"Me and *my* mommy both hate snapes together. I don't want to be anywhere near snapes."

Snakes. With a K, Scarlett. I sighed. I wasn't about to correct her. She already hated me. "Okay, fine. What would you like to see next?"

"Red pandas."

"But we just saw the red pandas. How about we…"

"I want to see them again. Can't we, Aunt Melissa? Please?"

"How can I say no to that face?" Melissa said. She laughed as Scarlett pulled her back toward the red panda exhibit.

I was not giving up on today. This was my chance to connect with my daughter. And I was going to find a way to do it. When we reached the red pandas again, I crouched down next to Scarlett. "You know, I used to love red pandas when I was little too. I thought it was so cool that their fur matched my hair."

Scarlett took a moment to stop staring at the animals to glance at me. "My mommy used to say that." She gave me a small smile and then turned her attention back to the red pandas. "She loved red pandas too."

Why did she keep saying stuff like that? Was she implying that I wasn't her mother? I placed my hand gently on her shoulder. "Scarlett, I'm right here. And I promised you I wasn't going anywhere."

She looked at my hand and then my face. "My mommy promised me that too. But she hasn't come back yet." She threw her empty snack bags at my feet. "I don't believe in promises anymore."

There was so much wrong with what she had said. What kid didn't believe in promises? And I was literally right here. I was even willing to pick up after her littering little self. I picked up her trash and shoved it in my purse. I was here for her. "Pumpkin…"

"Only Daddy calls me pumpkin." She shrugged her shoulder to make my hand fall away. And then she scrunched up her face. I thought she was about to cry but then she screamed, "I need the potty!"

"Okay, well…" I opened up my map. "I think there's one…"

"Aunt Melissa, Aunt Melissa!" Scarlett yelled and ran over to her, ignoring me and my map that would tell us exactly where to go. "I need the potty!"

Melissa lifted her up and started walking as quickly as she could with a kid in her arms. The two of them disappeared into a public restroom a minute later.

I sighed and sat down on a bench to wait. Scarlett didn't even trust me to take her to the bathroom. Did she really think that I wasn't her mother? That couldn't be it. She could see me. She could see that I was the same. I put my chin in my hand.

It might help if I didn't call her pumpkin again. I basically confessed to her that I was a fraud. Why didn't I call her that if James did? Was there another nickname I didn't know of? Today was going horribly, horribly wrong. What could be worse than your own kid not trusting you?

I just needed to ask James more questions about her. I didn't know any of the facts that a child would expect me to know. Her favorite color. Favorite food. But even the things I knew I kept messing up. I knew her favorite animal and I'd tried to make her look at other things. And I knew her favorite snacks but brought the wrong one. What a freaking disaster. God, what could I do to make her like me?

It would be so much easier if I was just being the fun, cool aunt like Melissa. Well, maybe. I wasn't exactly fun or cool. If I was being honest, it seemed like Scarlett would hate me as an aunt just as much as she hated me as a mother. There had to be something I could do to make her like me.

Ice cream! Ice cream always fixed everything. At least, it did for me. And if she was my daughter, she was probably obsessed with it too. She clearly liked snacks. Sweets could be my ticket to her liking me. I opened up my map again. This would definitely make up for the non-animal fruit snacks I had brought. She was going to freaking love me.

"We had a bit of an incident," Melissa said.

I looked up. Scarlett was in her arms. Pants-less. There was just a bunch of paper towels wrapped around her waist in a make-shift skirt. She looked like a mini barbarian.

"What happened to her pants?" I asked as I stood up, abandoning my map and any thought of ice cream fixing anything.

I heard Scarlett sniffle. I looked at her tear stained face just in time, because she immediately turned away from me.

Oh, sweetie. All I wanted to do was hug her.

"Her pants couldn't be saved," Melissa said. "We didn't quite make it to the bathroom."

"So you threw out her pants? Where? I'll go clean them real quick. I'm sure a little tinkle from such a tiny little girl…"

Melissa cleared her throat. "It was more of a number 2 issue."

"Oh."

"Yeah, oh," Melissa mouthed silently. She pressed her hand against Scarlett's ear that wasn't snug against her chest, so that Scarlett wouldn't hear. "Is she on some kind of juice cleanse I'm not aware of?"

"No…"

"Then what the actual hell? I've never even had a poop explosion like that. Do you think she's sick? Should we take her to the doctor? Did she somehow get into something that would make her crap everywhere? Like some kind of medicine?"

"Oh shit." I immediately placed my hand over my mouth. I knew cursing was bad around kids, but luckily Melissa's hand was still covering Scarlett's ear. I cleared my throat. "I may have given her the wrong fruit snacks."

"A little snack wouldn't cause something like this. I think she's sick. We should definitely take her to a doctor."

"Would a super fibrous snack cause something like that to happen?"

"What do you mean?"

I pulled one of the wrappers out of my purse.

"You gave her a pack of fiber gummies? Kids can't handle that much fiber all at once. There's enough fiber in those to regulate adults. Not infants. What were you thinking?"

"I…I don't know. I wasn't thinking. She wanted fruit snacks so I gave her fruit snacks. Several packs actually."

"More than one? Seriously?" Melissa shook her head like I was the most incompetent person she had ever met. "We need to get her home. It's probably going to happen again and she's out of pants." She lifted her hand off of Scarlett's ear. "How are you feeling, Scar? Do you want to head home?"

"I don't feel good. My tummy hurts."

"Yeah, I know." Melissa tucked a loose strand of hair behind Scarlett's ear. "You're going to be okay. We just need to get you home."

Scarlett nodded.

God, James was going to kill me. I'd told him I could handle this. And I had basically caused a poop explosion. I was bringing back his daughter without pants. "Do you think there's time to stop somewhere and get her another pair of pants real quick?" I asked.

"My tummy hurts," Scarlett said again. "I want Daddy."

Fuck me.

CHAPTER 29

Monday

My hand was practically shaking as I unlocked the door. I felt like I had soiled my one chance. Literally.

I glanced at Scarlett. Porter was carrying her now. He gave me a sympathetic smile.

That just made me more nervous. Was that sympathy because he knew I was about to experience James' wrath? Or because he thought I was a terrible mom? Probably both. *Here goes nothing.*

As soon as we were inside, Porter set Scarlett down and disappeared back out the door.

I was probably supposed to yell something like, "Honey, I'm home!" But James wasn't my honey. Besides, I was hoping to sneak Scarlett upstairs and wrassle her into a pair of pants before James saw us.

"Let's go change," I said to Scarlett and held out my hand.

She held on to the paper towel skirt for dear life.

"Melissa, can you help me get her upstairs?" I asked.

"James is going to find out one way or the other. Scarlett still doesn't feel well." She tussled Scarlett's hair.

Traitor.

"Daddy!" Scarlett yelled.

They were all a bunch of traitors. *Damn it!*

James walked into the foyer. He pushed his hair off his forehead, like he was trying to look more presentable. As if he ever looked un-presentable.

"I didn't expect you back so soon..." his voice trailed off when he looked down at Scarlett. "Pumpkin, what happened?"

Scarlett immediately let go of her paper towel skirt, sending it to the floor, and ran over to James. Her little naked butt was the biggest traitor of all.

"What happened to your pants?" James asked as he lifted her into his arms.

"She fed me a bad snack." The little traitor pointed directly at me.

"It was just a tiny accident," Melissa said. "We didn't make it to the bathroom in time. No big deal."

Thank you, Melissa.

"My tummy hurts," Scarlett said.

Was she trying to get me in trouble?

"She gave me fibey snacks. And they made my tummy hurt."

James looked up at me. "What is she talking about?"

This time Melissa didn't come to my rescue. I was on my own. "I grabbed the wrong fruit gummies. She wanted a snack and I only had the fiber ones. Apparently those aren't for kids. But I had no way of knowing that, James. I seriously thought it would be okay, or else I wouldn't have fed them to her."

"It doesn't matter." But the way he said it didn't make me believe him. His tone screamed, "It matters a lot, you incompetent idiot." He adjusted Scarlett onto his hip. "Let's go get you cleaned up, pumpkin."

I sighed as they left the foyer.

"So that went well," Melissa said. "He didn't even seem that mad."

"Are you kidding? He was so pissed."

"Really? He said it didn't matter." She shrugged.

She couldn't tell that he was mad? Maybe I knew him better than I thought. *Or maybe I'm remembering.* I shook the thought away. If I was remembering, I'd know what to do around Scarlett. I'd be a good mom. I clearly wasn't remembering anything.

"So, I'm supposed to meet Josh for dinner in a bit. I thought I'd leave you to get better acquainted with your family tonight."

"You're abandoning me?"

She laughed. "No. But family dinners are something you always do. Maybe it'll trigger a memory." She smiled. "Is it okay if I go get ready?" She was already backing away.

Maybe she wasn't abandoning me. But it felt like she was. "Yeah, that's fine."

"Don't worry about today. It happens to the best of us."

I knew that wasn't true. She had said that she had never even experienced such a big bowel movement. I sighed. I just hoped tonight would get better. I walked into the living room and froze.

The room wasn't the same at all. There were no longer any empty hooks in the walls. There were pictures everywhere. Images of me and James. Pictures of Scarlett. Photos of us with our friends and family. Ones with all of us together. And in every single one we were all laughing and smiling.

Scarlett's laughter drifted downstairs. It was foreign to me. Just like the pictures on the wall.

James had removed the pictures to help me ease back into my life. He had tried to erase everything we had. And I wasn't sure why. I tried to wipe away the tears in my eyes, but they just kept coming. These images were proof of what we had. The majority of them weren't professionally done or posed. They were candids. And I could see it on my face. I could see the love. In several photos, I wasn't even facing the camera, I was staring at James like I adored him. Like he was the only person I ever wanted to see. Like I lived to wake up next to him. And to fall asleep in his arms at night.

"Penny?"

I turned to see him standing there, watching me. He looked happy that I was staring at the pictures. Like I was doing exactly what he had planned. And he was shirtless again. He kept doing that. It was so distracting. It was almost like he was trying to...*God.* I was so dumb. Of course he was trying to make me notice him. I thought about earlier when he said he just wanted for us to be friends. How angry I had gotten. He knew how to push my buttons. He knew it would turn me on. He knew me.

He hadn't given up on us being more than friends. Because there was more than my love in those pictures. There was his love too.

But there was also one huge problem. Just because I could see the love in the pictures, it didn't mean I felt it. Just because he knew how to trick me into wanting him, it didn't mean I actually did. Him angering me? Him walking around without a shirt? Him putting up these pictures? He was trying to trick me into falling in love with him again. And my heart couldn't just flip a switch and feel everything he wanted it to feel. Love didn't work like that. He had to know that. He had to know I needed more time. Just because he knew me, it didn't mean I knew him. Or that he understood what I was going through.

"I'm not upset about what happened with Scarlett," he said. "I was a little at first, but it could have happened to anyone. You don't have to cry. I'm sorry if I overreacted. I didn't mean to snap at you."

I could see it on his face. He wanted to comfort me. But he was worried I would freak out. He was trying to keep his word. And it was killing him.

"I'm not crying about that." I wiped my tears away. "I mean, yes, I'm sorry I wasn't more careful. I should have known better. But I'm crying because..." I couldn't look at him. Instead, I stared at one of the pictures of us. "I'm crying because you love me. And for some reason, you decided it would be fun to pretend you just want to be friends even though you obviously want more. And you keep doing that." I waved at his six-pack without looking at him. "And you keep pushing my buttons. And it's not fair that you know more about me than I know about you. You're messing with my head."

"Is it working?" James asked.

That was not the reaction I had expected. I was almost positive that he'd deny it. I finally made eye contact with him, just in time to see him run his fingers through his hair. "No, it's not. And that. Stop doing that."

He laughed and lowered his hand to the side. "I don't know what you expect me to do, Penny. I keep having new plans on how to fix everything and you keep derailing them."

"Is that an admission that you're prancing around the house shirtless because you want to seduce me?"

"I'm not trying to seduce you. I'm actually trying to get you to want to seduce me."

I stared at him. "Seriously? That's the master plan I derailed?" That was never going to happen. My eyes wandered down to his six-pack. *Fine.* Maybe it would have happened eventually if he kept looking so amazing.

"It wasn't that horrible of a plan. You should have seen your face earlier when I said I just wanted to be friends. You looked like you wanted to kill me."

"I did not."

"Yes." He stepped closer to me. "You did. Can't you just admit that you're starting to fall, even if you're not starting to remember? That kiss we shared yesterday…"

"Even if I was starting to fall for you, it's because you're tricking me. You're messing with my head instead of letting me make my own decisions."

"I'm not trying to trick you, Penny. I'm trying to jog your memory. I was trying to make you want me. And trying to push you away at the same time." He sighed. "That's how we started. A little give. A little pull. I thought if I acted that way, you'd remember. And I just ruined it but letting you know you already have my heart."

The way he was looking at me made my chest hurt. "Recreating stuff doesn't seem to help. Can't we just…start over?" I needed a level playing field. I needed to know more about him. "I think that maybe…"

"Story time?" Scarlett said.

I jumped. I still wasn't used to a little kid running around. Where had she even come from? She was standing behind us, hugging a book close to her chest.

"I don't feel well," she said. "Can I have a bedtime story?"

"Hold that thought," James said to me. "I want to keep talking about this. I just have to…" he nodded toward Scarlett.

"Yeah, no, it's fine. I'll just keep looking at the pictures. Even though you put them up to manipulate me, you never should have hidden them. They're wonderful."

He smiled as he glanced at one of our wedding photos. "They really are. I'll be right back."

"No, Daddy. I want her to do it." Scarlett pointed at me.

I was pretty sure my whole face lit up. "Me?"

She nodded.

In a matter of minutes I had turned things around. I had been honest with James about needing to make my own decisions. And he seemed open to letting me figure things out. Or maybe he was just out of ideas on how to trick me. Regardless, it felt like progress. I was excited to talk to him more.

And it wasn't just James I had made progress with. Had I really gotten Scarlett to like me? What the heck was happening? This weird world I had been thrust into was finally accepting me. "I'd love to." I smiled at James before letting Scarlett grab my hand and lead me upstairs.

"I'm sorry that I made you sick," I said, as I tucked her into bed.

"That's okay." She was still holding the book tightly against her chest.

"Do you want me to read that to you?"

She shook her head. "I have questions for you first."

Oh crap. She brought me up here for a pop quiz? I already knew I was going to fail.

"What's my favorite color?" she asked.

I looked at the walls in her room. "Pink?"

"Uh-uh. What's my boyfriend's name?"

She has a boyfriend at her age? That seemed preposterous. I wondered if James knew. "Um…"

"What's my favorite cereal?"

"I…"

"What do you call me instead of pumpkin?"

This wasn't a pop quiz. It was a rapid-fire inquisition. "I really don't…"

"What's my favorite book?"

"Scarlett, I'm sorry. I don't know. But if you give it to me I can read it to you." I held my hand out. I didn't want to play this game anymore. It was making me feel horrible.

"I know you're not my mommy."

Ouch. "Yes I am. Sweetie, I'm right here."

She slowly sat up, reached out, and put her hands on both sides of my face. I didn't know what to do, so I stayed completely still. She ran her little hands over my forehead. And nose. And lips. And chin. And scrutinized my whole face before moving her hands back to my cheeks.

She squished her mouth to the side like she was thinking. "You look like my mommy," she said. "And you sound like my mommy." She shook her head. "But you're not my mommy. I want her back. Can't you bring her back?" Her bottom lip started to tremble.

My heart felt like it was breaking. She was just a kid but she still saw that I wasn't the same. I wasn't who she remembered. "I'm trying. I'm trying to remember. But it doesn't mean I don't love you right now."

"I miss her."

Was she trying to make me cry in front of her? "I know. I miss her too." It was the truth. I desperately wanted to remember her. I needed to remember her. And a piece of my heart knew I wanted to remember James too. If those pictures downstairs showed the truth, then I did love him. Somewhere deep inside of me I knew I did.

"Do you promise not to leave too?"

"I promise."

She let go of my cheeks. "My favorite color is green. My boyfriend's name is Axel. I love cinnamon Chex. And you always call me Scar. Or sweetie when maybe I'm a little bad. Which isn't very often. I'm a very good girl."

I smiled and tried my hardest not to cry. "My favorite color is green too."

"I know."

Right. Of course she knew. "I'm going to remember all that this time."

"Okay. And this is my favorite book. You can read to me now." She thrust the book she was holding into my hands.

I looked down at the cover. *The Ruin of House Hornbolt.* It wasn't a children's book. It seemed like it was probably for adults, or at least teens. It was thicker than most books I'd had to read for school. "This is your favorite book?"

"Mhm." She pulled the sheets all the way up to her chin. Just like I always did.

"Okay then." I flipped to where the bookmark was and started reading aloud:

"He heard someone humming and turned the corner to see Nesta skipping toward him with her arms overflowing with muffins. A small peeping noise fell from little Nesta's lips and she dropped most of the muffins onto the floor. Her eyes grew big as she looked up at him approaching.

"Good morning, my lady," Rixin said with a smile and a nod.

Nesta looked relieved when he didn't scold her. "Do you want a muffin?" she asked and held out one of the ones that hadn't fallen on the floor.

"You saved my day, Lady Nesta," Rixin said as he took the muffin from the young girl. "I'm starving and these look delicious."

She giggled. "Do you want to come see what I've been making?"

"Actually, I..." his voice trailed off when Nesta slipped her hand into his and started pulling him down the hall. Her fingers were sticky from the muffins she had been carrying, and she was pulling him through the hall with surprising strength for her small frame.

Rixin glanced over his shoulder at the pile of muffins and crumbs Nesta had left on the floor. "Shouldn't we clean that up?"

"If we hurry, no one will know it was us." She giggled again as they turned a corner and came to an abrupt stop outside her door. "You wait here. Boys aren't allowed in my room." She unlocked her door and disappeared inside.

I looked up to see Scarlett fast asleep and quietly closed the book. She was a lot like me. Dreaming of princes. She was also a lot like Nesta too. I could see why she liked this book so much. I'd have to make sure to read the whole thing as soon as I could. But there was another book I wanted to read first. The one I wrote. It could be the key to getting my memory back. I just needed to ask James where I could find a copy.

When I walked out of Scarlett's room, I realized that the last locked door was now open. I already felt like I knew what was inside. But seeing it and believing it were two very different things. I paused by the door when I saw James inside.

He was sitting in the rocking chair in the corner of the room with his eyes closed. For the first time, it felt like I saw him. Truly saw him. He wasn't acting a certain way to win me over or help me remember. He didn't even realize I was watching him. I studied the sharp cut of his jaw line. The way his hair curled slightly when it was wet. The scars on his chest and stomach and…bicep. I tilted my head to get a better angle, only to realize that his arm was hiding a tattoo. All I could see was a small line. I wanted to know what it said. I stepped forward and the floor squeaked.

James opened his eyes. They were bloodshot. The first thing I thought about was his addiction problem. My worst suspicions about him sniffing cocaine off the dresser appeared in my mind.

But then he sniffled in the most adorable way. And he looked away from me like he was embarrassed. Had he been crying?

He cleared his throat. "I'll be down in just a second. Dinner will probably be ready soon."

I knew he was asking for me to give him a minute alone. But my feet didn't move. I hadn't truly seen him a moment before. I had studied his beautiful features, but I was so un-connected to him that I didn't realize he was crying.

He leaned forward and put his elbows on his knees so he could drop his face. So he could remain hidden. So he could keep his secrets.

"James?" I wanted to go over to him and rub his back. Or hug him. Or something. I couldn't casually ask him what was wrong. I knew what was wrong. He had a son that might never see his nursery. *We had a son.* My eyes dropped to his clenched fist. He was holding an article of clothing in his hand. "What are you looking at?"

He put it down on his lap and smoothed the fabric out over his thighs. It was a tiny onesie with a Giants logo on it. "You bought this for me right after you found out you were pregnant the first time. You were convinced we were having a boy."

I smiled, even though I didn't remember. "*I* bought something with a Giants logo on it? I'm an Eagles fan. I guess I must really love you." The words kind of tumbled out of me. And they settled around us in all their awkward glory.

"Yeah. You did." He folded the onesie back up and looked at me. "I'm sorry I hid things from you. I'm sorry I tried to trick you into loving me. I'm just...sorry."

I shrugged. "It's okay. I'd probably do the same thing if I was in your shoes."

"Maybe." His smile was so sad. "It's hard for me to be in here. I didn't want to subject you to that when you were having a hard enough time accepting me."

"I get it." I looked around the room. It was adorable. There were stuffed animals everywhere. The only odd part about it was that the walls were bright orange. "Is orange all the rage this season?" I asked.

James laughed and stood up from the rocking chair. "We let Scarlett pick it out. We didn't know whether we were having a boy or girl so we didn't want the standard pink or blue. She had fun choosing."

That was sweet. "You're a really great father, James." He was a much better parent than me.

"We're a great team." He folded the onesie and put it on top of the dresser.

"Speaking of that..." my stomach felt like it was doing summersaults. "I feel like we haven't been much of a team. You know everything about me. And I don't know anything about you. And if all of this is ever going to seem normal...you can't keep me in the dark anymore. You need to answer my questions. You need to tell me everything."

"Where do you want me to start?"

"At the beginning, I guess. Tell me about your family. Tell me what you were like growing up. Were you a jock or a geek? Did you have lots of dates or none at all?"

"I'll tell you everything you want to know over dinner." He grabbed my hand. I hadn't expected him to do it. James had made good on his word of not touching me. He realized his mistake at the same time that I realized how much I truly liked the spark I felt when our skin touched. That the feeling was real. He tried to pull away, but I closed my hand to intertwine our fingers together.

"That sounds perfect," I said and smiled up at him. Any trace of his sadness had disappeared. He was looking at me the way he had in the pictures. The way he had yesterday. And even though it was scary, I didn't want him to stop.

This version of him was so much better than the cold version.

CHAPTER 30

Monday

"I'm sorry, James." I had listened to his retelling of his childhood. And the few funny stories scattered throughout didn't change the fact that it sounded miserable. His parents were God-awful. How had they not seen that he was so unhappy? I barely knew Scarlett and I could tell when she was angry with me. Which was most of the time, but I was improving. I wanted to improve. His parents? They didn't care enough about him to even try. It was heartbreaking.

"It's okay. I met you. I found my love of teaching. I love the life we've made together. Besides, nothing heals the past like time."

"So you're on good terms with both your parents now? I know your father visited me in the hospital. But your mother? How is she?"

"We haven't spoken since everything that happened with Isabella."

"You mean her forcing you to marry Isabella?"

"Well, that and the fact that my mom was trying to help Isabella break you and me up before our wedding. She sided with a monster instead of her own son. I don't know how to forgive her for that."

"Isn't forgiveness the key to happiness, or something like that?"

"Maybe. But I almost died. She almost prevented me from ever being a father."

I nodded. I wasn't an expert on forgiveness. If I ever saw the doctor who had poisoned me I was worried I'd try to stab him or something. He had taken away all my most wonderful memories. Of James, of Scarlett, of Liam. "Then screw her."

He laughed.

I took the pause in the conversation to help myself to another serving of the delicious penne noodles with chicken and vodka sauce. "Don't let me forget to tell Ellen how delicious this is. She's a great cook."

"I actually made it."

I looked up from my fork. "Really? James, it's so good. I didn't know you could cook."

"I can't. Not really. It's one of the only things I know how to make. And in the interest of full disclosure, I made this for you on one of our first dates. I already had the whole night planned before you called me out on my games."

I smiled. He had planned to spend the whole night trying to win me over? How could I not swoon over that? "What else did you have planned?"

"Do you really want to know, or do you want to just play along?" His dark brown eyes were so mischievous.

I laughed. "That convinced it'll work, huh?"

"I just know I can't stop trying. Even when you call me out on it. I tried the whole not touching you thing. And the not sleeping next to you thing. I can say with full confidence that it wasn't for me."

"I'm trying my best to remember. Just, take things slowly with me. I've only ever dated one guy. And I don't know if you can even really call it that. We were never actually exclusive."

"I know."

Of course he knew.

"I believe in us. And I don't care if it takes me the rest of my life to convince you to love me again," he said. "I'll never stop trying."

I'm pretty sure I sighed out loud from how romantic that was. But instead of telling him that, I took another huge bite of food. I still had a lot of questions for him and no good segue. The note I had found in the trash was burning a hole in my pocket. And his scars were still staring back at me.

"How did you get your scars?" For some reason, that question seemed like the easier of the two.

"From when I got shot on our wedding night. Three times." He gestured to his bicep, his stomach, and his ribcage. "My lung collapsed and I had my spleen removed, but I've made a full recovery."

"And the new one? You told me you took some of the poisoned pills too. What happened?"

He immediately looked more tense. "I had a cardiac episode."

"Like a heart attack?"

"Not exactly. It wasn't as severe. Just set me back a little. And I tweaked my knee when I fell down the stairs. But nothing serious. I've been going to physical therapy for everything. I'll be good as new soon enough."

I thought about all the times I saw him take a break from walking. Or put his hand down for balance. "All of it sounds serious to me. They clearly had to operate." I pointed to his chest. "You've been telling me to take it easy, but you should be too. I wasn't the only one that got hurt."

"I'm fine. I've always had issues with stress so…poison didn't help with that."

"Huh. I never would have guessed that you have stress issues. You seem so carefree." I smiled at him as he laughed. "But seriously, James. Are you going to be okay?"

"Yes. When have I ever lied to you?"

"Oh, I don't know. Ever since I woke up?"

He smiled. "Well, I promise I'm not doing that now. The physical therapy is working. I'm feeling stronger every day. How are you feeling?"

"Honestly? I physically feel okay. Nothing hurts. But when I think about everything, I feel so overwhelmed. Do you know that Scarlett doesn't believe I'm her mom? She thinks I'm some imposter."

"Yeah. I've talked to her about that. I can talk to her again."

"No, it's okay. I'll figure it out. But it is upsetting. Dr. Nelson stole my memories. And I know that I have children. But it still feels like I'll never have them. I always pictured a bunch running around, you know? And I expected to remember being pregnant with them. He stole all of that from me."

"I know. I pictured that too."

I bit the inside of my lip. "Do you really think we're safe now? From Dr. Nelson I mean?"

"The police think so. They think he's long gone."

"And you?"

"Our security detail has been very diligent. There hasn't been any suspicious activity. No sightings. Nothing. It's not like the guy is going to be able to practice medicine here ever again. Maybe he went somewhere he could start over."

"That makes sense." I took a deep breath. "So maybe we could get rid of all these cameras? They make me nervous. I feel like I'm being watched right now." I looked up to one of the ones mounted in the dining room.

James ran his fingers through his hair. "Most of them are already disabled. We found out that they were how Dr. Nelson got access to our apartment in the first place."

"He broke into the security system?"

"I thought this was the safest apartment in the whole city. But everything worked against me. I'm updating the software. Until then, there's only a few active ones."

"You're updating it?"

"That's what Hunter Tech does. I thought we were unhackable. I was wrong. We're going back to the drawing board. Well, mostly the company. I've been preoccupied."

"But you mostly teach, right?"

"Yeah. After what happened I took a leave of absence from the university though. Another professor is handling my summer session classes."

"Will you go back in the fall?"

"That depends on a lot of things. How Liam is doing. If you remember me."

I laughed. "You can teach without me remembering anything. Your life can't just stop. You've said that yourself."

"I know. But it feels like it's stopped. It's hard to breathe when I look at you and you don't look at me the same in return."

I was about to say I was sorry when music started playing lightly in the other room. I looked past him to the living room. Melissa winked at me and then disappeared down the hall.

When I turned back to James he was standing beside my chair with one hand stretched toward me.

"May I have this dance?"

This was part of the evening he had planned for me. And I wanted to remember. How could I not want to remember loving this beautiful man? I slid my hand into his and he pulled me to my feet. His hand squeezed mine as we walked into the living room and stopped in front of the amazing view.

"It's beautiful," I said.

He spun me around and pulled me into his chest. Our laughter drifted together. It felt right to have his hands on my waist. I lightly wrapped my hands around the back of his neck. All of it felt right. But there was still a note in my pocket that claimed I didn't love all this. That I wasn't happy even though life had handed me everything I could possibly dream of. I had to ask him about it. But I didn't want to break the spell. "What song is this?"

James spun me again. "Hands Down by Dashboard Confessional."

"And it means something to you?"

He lifted one of his hands off my waist and placed it on my cheek. "To us. We played this song during our first dance at our wedding. It was also the first song we ever danced to when we started dating. We were on a walk in Central Park."

My mouth felt dry. I could picture it so clearly.

We walked slowly back toward the hotel. It was nice walking through the street holding hands like a normal couple. We'd never be able to do this on Main Street. Maybe he was right. Disclosing our relationship would be for the best. I heard music playing in the distance.

A smile spread across Professor Hunter's face. "Come with me." We jogged into Central Park until we came to a guitarist. He was strumming his guitar and singing. I laughed as Professor Hunter twirled me and then pulled me in close.

His hand was on the small of my back. It reminded me of when he had walked me home in the rain. The smell of him and the look in his eyes took my breath away.

"Do you know this song?" My voice sounded airy. I wanted to know what it was so I could find it on YouTube and remember this moment forever.

"I believe it's called Hands Down." He twirled me again and placed both of his hands on my waist.

"Every day I spend with you I fall harder and harder." I looked up into his eyes.

He leaned down and kissed me. When the song ended he didn't pull away. We kept swaying to the loud sounds of the city. "I should get you home."

"Does that mean going home with you? Or are you sending me back to my dorm?"

He laughed. "I'd like to bring you home with me."

"I don't want tonight to end." I put my hands in his hair and brought his lips back down to mine.

There was a quiet groan in his throat as he pulled away. "I love you, Penny."

"I love you, James."

"Penny?" James' voice pulled me back to the present. Or out of my fantasy? Or out of whatever that was.

I felt it. I felt his story come to life. My mind filled in the details. Whether it was memories or fantasies I had no idea. But the image of us in Central Park made my heart pound faster. And my breath catch. It was perfect. Too perfect. It made me sick knowing what would happen to us after that dance. How we'd slowly break.

"Do you remember?" His voice sounded so hopeful as his eyes searched mine. He had seen me leave the present. He had seen my mind go somewhere else.

I shook my head without really even focusing on his question. "I don't know."

"Baby, you have to try. Tell me what you were thinking. Tell me you saw our first dance on our wedding night. Tell me you remember."

My heart pounded faster. *I don't know. I don't know. I don't know.* My mind was spinning.

He pulled me closer, his cologne making it harder to think straight. I felt like I was suffocating.

"I need you to try," he said. "I need you."

All I needed was air. And space. Hadn't I just asked him to take things slow? "Why? Because I'm the light to your darkness? That's what you said, right? James, that's too much pressure. You can't put all your happiness on me. That's not realistic."

"If you would just let your heart…"

"I don't remember, James. I'm sorry. I can't remember." I shook my head and pushed his hands away from me. "And even if I could…I don't know if I'd be happy."

"Why would you say that?"

"Light and dark and black and white isn't what I want, James. That isn't what love is. Dull tones of gray. Love is…" My voice trailed off as I turned to look out the window. Dusk was settling over the city, casting a beautiful sunset over Central Park and between the buildings in the distance. "Love should be more of a…a whirlwind of color." I turned back to him. "And I have to assume that isn't what we had."

The music stopped as James stared at me. "Okay. You're not the light to my darkness. You're my…whirlwind of color. It doesn't matter how I put it. What matters is how much I care about you. How much I love you. Because I do love you, Penny. I love you with every ounce of who I am."

"It's not about that. You can't just change how you describe our relationship. I don't think our life was colorful. I think you had it exactly right. It was black and white and honestly I feel like it was mostly darkness. I…" *God, just rip the freaking Band-Aid off.* "I tried to kill myself, didn't I? That's why you were hiding so much stuff from me? So I wouldn't figure it out."

"What? No." He stepped forward and grabbed both my hands. "Penny, we were happy. You have to trust me on this. I don't know how else I can convince you…"

"I found the note, James."

"What note?"

In that moment, I knew he was lying. He knew which note I was referring to. And he was playing dumb. I couldn't trust anything he told me. All of it could have been lies. "The note where I said goodbye." I kept going because he was still playing dumb. "Where I told you to move on." Still nothing. "My suicide note, James. *That* note."

"Fuck. I thought I threw that away."

"So it's true?" I pulled my hands out of his. "What was so wrong with my life that I'd try to do something like that?"

"You didn't, Penny. You were poisoned. The note was a what if. You tried to add it to our will in case something went wrong during childbirth. That's it. That's the only thing that makes sense. It was just inconvenient timing of when I found it. You'd never try to take your own life. You loved your life. You loved our life together."

"You couldn't possibly know that for sure. Only I would know what that note meant."

"But I know you better than you know yourself right now…"

"No you don't." Screw him. I knew myself. The real me. Not whatever person I had become after meeting him. "No matter what you do to convince me that what we had was perfect, I know it wasn't. Nothing is perfect."

"I never said our life was perfect. Of course we have issues. Everyone has issues."

"Like my severe depression?"

"You weren't depressed…"

"Stop lying, James. Please stop lying. For one minute can't you…"

He grabbed the back of my head and pulled me into a kiss. I tried to push him off, but within a second I was completely captivated by his lips. I couldn't move. I couldn't think. I was paralyzed by that kiss. A hot, passionate, mind-blowing kiss. *God.* It wasn't just a kiss. It was everything. Every. Single. Thing.

He pulled away far too soon. "I can prove to you we were happy. Just…don't move."

When his hands left my body I immediately felt cold. The reaction I had to him was all-consuming. He disappeared out of the living room and I silently cursed myself. I meant to just ask him about the letter. I didn't mean to fight. And why was I so turned on whenever we fought? What the heck was that all about?

I smoothed down my hair and tried to even out my breathing. But all I wanted was his fingers in my hair again. I wanted his hands on the small of my back, pulling me closer. I wanted more. I swallowed hard. There was no way I was ready for more. Besides, he was healing from his cardiac episode. And I was healing too. *Nothing heals the past like time.* That's what he had said earlier. I didn't know if that was true. It felt like every time James and I took one step forward we took two steps back. And he wasn't being patient with me. He was suffocating me. And intoxicating me.

James reappeared with a huge stack of papers in his hand. *No, not just papers.* He handed me my manuscript. *Temptation* by Ivy Smoak. The pages were worn, like he had read through it a lot. "You've read it?"

He pressed his lips together. "Several times. I may have tried to recreate a few scenes. I didn't remember every detail. But you did. When you wrote it."

"And Ivy Smoak is my pen name? Why wouldn't I use my real name?"

"We have enough publicity. You wanted to do this on your own. Anonymity has its perks."

"Do I have a publishing deal or..."

"Read it. We can talk about everything after you've read it. I just need you to understand how we started. How hard and fast we fell in love. How much we love each other. How real everything I've said is. Read it and then we can talk."

I looked back down at the worn pages. He said he had read it several times. That was touching. "What did you think of the writing?"

"It's the best thing I've ever read."

I laughed. "Yeah right."

"It's emotional, and raw, and real. I barely made any notes. And I'm all about making notes. I'm a professor."

"So you didn't go all professorly on me and mark everything up?"

He smiled. A genuine, knee-weakening smile. "Professorly isn't a word, Penny."

"Really?" I scrunched my mouth to the side. "It feels like a real word. I'm the author though. If I want to use professorly, I think it's okay."

"Yeah. I think it's okay too."

My eyes drifted to his lips. "I didn't expect you to kiss me."

"I can only resist so much temptation." He nodded to the manuscript.

"Hence the name Temptation?"

He smiled. "I don't know…you're the one that titled it."

I looked back down at the book. Now that I was holding it, I felt like I finally had all the answers. I didn't know what time frame it covered, but I hoped it was everything I was missing.

"Full disclosure, it's pretty detailed," James said.

I met his gaze. "What does that mean exactly? Too much detail?"

"No, I think it's the perfect amount."

I didn't recognize the look he was giving me. Amused maybe? "If there's something wrong with it you can tell me. It's not like I remember writing it."

He smiled. "Just read it, Penny. I'm going to head back to the hospital for a bit. I'll be back soon."

"Okay." I bit the inside of my lip. Was he going to see Liam or to flirt more with that nurse?

"What?" he asked.

"Nothing."

He laughed. "I know when something is bothering you. What's wrong?"

I hugged my manuscript to my chest, but then immediately pulled it away. That was how Scarlett had held her favorite book. I didn't want James to think of me as a child. I lifted my chest slightly.

The amused look on his face only grew.

Damn it. "Nothing really. I just happened to notice that you seemed awfully close with the nurse…"

He stepped forward. And I held my breath. *He's going to kiss me again.*

But instead, he lifted my hand and placed it on the center of his chest. "Baby, my heart beats for you." He leaned forward, sending my own heart into a fit, and kissed my temple. "And for our children. I've spent as many hours as I could in the NICU. Liam is the only reason I'm going."

"Good." The word came out squeaky and high-pitched.

"Good." He smiled down at me. "So unless there's something else…" His eyes dropped to my lips.

I swallowed hard. "No, that was it."

"You sure?" He moved a fraction of an inch closer.

All I had to do was stand on my tiptoes in order for my lips to brush against his. Instead, I closed my eyes and inhaled the smell of his sweet cologne, willing him to be the one to kiss me.

But instead of his hot breath intertwining with mine, I suddenly felt cold. I opened my eyes to see him a few feet away from me with the biggest smile on his face.

"Have fun reading, Penny." He winked at me and walked away.

I was pretty sure he left me with my mouth hanging open. God, he had me wrapped around his finger. *Temptation.* I looked down at the manuscript. That seemed like a perfectly fitting name. I wandered over to the couch and dove into my book.

CHAPTER 31

Monday

Oh my God, tell him. I read the words as fast as I could. It was a scene I could picture clearly. I wasn't sure if it was because I was a great writer or if it was because it was helping me remember. James had said the book was super detailed. But those probably weren't the reasons I could visualize what was happening so easily. I had walked the green hundreds of times. I knew the campus like the back of my hand. *No! Tell him!*

The chapter ended with the door closing with a thud. And me referring to seeing James again as a date. And leaving the lie of me being at least 21 hanging there. Why the fuck hadn't I just told him the truth? I just wanted to scream at the character, rip her out of the pages, and shake her. *So mortifying.*

I blamed the booze. Vodka was a seductive mistress. I was also horrified that my shirt was see-through in the rain. And that I had just kneed Tyler in the nuts. And that I was drunk and underage in front of my dreamy professor. A girl could lose her senses when all that had just happened.

Regardless, it was pretty clear that I had been smitten with James immediately. Tyler had never stood a chance. Maybe if I had run into him first. But that's not how the story went. I'd met James. And I had fallen head over heels for him despite knowing that it was wrong. Somehow it being wrong just made it even more appealing. To me now and to me then. *Something must be wrong with me.*

I put the pages of the manuscript on the coffee table and stood up to stretch. I hadn't read very much, but my mind was racing. I could feel the chemistry through the pages. It was undeniable. But it was still hard to believe I'd sleep with my professor. That I'd fall in love with someone so utterly unattainable.

And what did James mean by details? I leaned over and flipped the manuscript to a random page and scanned. Nothing unusual. I flipped to another page and my eyes bulged.

He pushed my back against the tile. "Is there something that you wanted?" His voice was so seductive.

I gulped. "Yes." His torso glistened from the water flowing down it. And the steam from the shower surrounded him. God he was sexy. He looked almost ethereal.

He leaned over and took one of my nipples in his mouth and bit it lightly. He pinched my other nipple between two of his fingers. I writhed under his touch.

"And what is it that you want?" He left a trail of kisses down my stomach and stopped right where I wanted it the most. I could feel his warm breath.

"You."

"Do you mean like this?" He stroked my pussy with his tongue.

"Professor Hunter," I moaned.

He put his knees on the tile floor and lifted my thighs over his shoulders. While I was admiring his strength, he slid two fingers inside of me.

I gasped.

"Or maybe you'd prefer that I fuck you with my fingers?" His dirty words made me want him even more.

"Yes!"

He moved his lips to my clit and sucked on it hard. I was pinned against the shower wall, completely immobile. He pumped his hand faster, moving his fingers in and out of me. His tongue continued to stroke my clit, driving me crazy.

"Yes!" I screamed again.

He pushed my thighs even farther apart. The position allowed his fingers to go even deeper. He was licking and swirling his tongue over my clit. I could feel my body begin to shudder in his arms. He placed his lips around my clit again and sucked hard.

"Professor Hunter!"

I threw the pages back down, scattering them across the coffee table. *Holy shit.* My whole body felt hot. James was right about the details. Vivid, mind-blowing details. I swallowed hard. I almost felt like I was drunk like I had been in that scene where James had walked me home. I pushed the pages back together so no one would be able to see the heated scene I had just been reading. I needed fresh air. A walk would help clear my head and cool me off. I walked over to Melissa and Josh's room and knocked on the door.

"Hey, Melissa?"

She opened the door and blew a strand of hair out of her flushed face.

I stifled a laugh. I was almost 100 percent sure she had just been banging Josh.

"What's up?" she asked.

"I was wondering if you could watch Scarlett? She's up-stairs sleeping, so she won't be much trouble. But I wanted to go for a walk…"

"Oh, I can come with you. Just give me a sec."

"It's okay. I wanted to clear my head."

"If I'm being completely honest, I promised James I wouldn't let you go anywhere alone."

That made sense after I'd tried to run away. It was funny that she was in charge of watching me instead of Scarlett, though. I wasn't sure James trusted me with my daughter after today either. I had learned my lesson about fiber. "I'll ask one of James' security guards to come with me."

"Alright. You sure?"

I lowered my voice. "You're clearly busy."

"I am not…" her voice trailed off. "Fine. You caught me. In my defense, I thought you and James were busy too."

I laughed. *No, not quite.* In my manuscript though? *Yes. Yes. Yes!* I could feel my own cheeks blushing just thinking about that shower scene. "I'll be back in a bit."

"Awesome. Maybe we can watch a movie or something like we always used to? Just us. I feel like we need a girls' night."

"I heard that," Josh said with a laugh from behind the door.

I smiled. "I'd like that. No offense, Josh," I added.

"None taken," he said.

"Have fun." I smiled at her and left them alone. A girls' night sounded perfect. Just like old times. Even though they still partially felt like current times to me. But I was getting used to this reality. I was getting used to James and the kids. I could picture myself here now.

I opened up the front door. Ian was standing outside talking on his cell phone.

"Oh, Jen, I have to go, Penny just walked out. Mhm, I will. Take a deep breath, it's going to be fine. I love you too." He hung up the phone. "Jen says hi."

"James' sister, right? And your fiancée?"

He smiled as he slid his cell phone back into his pocket. "You're remembering things now. So, um…what are you doing out here?"

"Actually I was hoping to go for a walk and I was told I needed someone to accompany me. But you're busy. Maybe Briggs or Porter could come? Or…" my voice trailed off trying to remember all the names. "Or William?"

"I'd be happy to go with you, Penny."

"But your phone call…"

"Everything with Jen is an emergency. Our wedding isn't very soon. A flower arrangement disaster isn't even a thing this far out. She'll be fine." He walked over toward the elevator.

I laughed. "What exactly is a flower arrangement disaster?"

"I don't know. I may have been holding the phone away from my ear." He smiled, even though we both knew it wasn't true. He had been listening to every word, crazy or not. I could tell he loved her.

"What made you realize you wanted to get married?" I asked as we stepped onto the elevator.

"Well, a number of things really. I liked Jen for far longer than I'd like to admit. Really since the first time I met her." He smiled. "I hadn't been working for James long and he asked if I'd pick her up at the airport. She's just so full of life. And beautiful. And smart."

We walked through the lobby and out the front doors as I thought about what he had said. He made it seem like it was love at first sight. Was that what James and I'd had? The first few chapters of my manuscript sure made it seem like we had.

"Are we friends?" I asked.

"You and me? Or you and Jen?"

"I was asking about you and me. But now I'm curious about both."

He smiled. "Well, yes to both."

"Can I ask you something then?" There was still something nagging me about the note in my pocket. What James said made sense. But what if he was wrong? What if I was unstable? And depressed. And lonely. If I could get out ahead of it, maybe I could fix it. I was growing attached to this life. I didn't want for it to end.

"Of course."

"Do you think I was unhappy before I lost my memory?"

"I believe you were happy."

"There isn't anything that seemed off about me? Anything at all to indicate that I wasn't?"

It looked like he was deep in thought as we entered Central Park. "Do you want my honest opinion? As a friend?"

"Yes."

"I think you've always struggled a little with self-confidence. You felt lucky that James fell for you and you have a hard time understanding why he's lucky too."

I sighed. "That sounds like me. It's kind of how I feel right now. I mean…what is he doing with someone like me? He could have anyone…"

"He loves you, Penny. And you have no reason to doubt your self-worth. You're smart and funny and kind. He's lucky to have you. And he knows it. You just have to accept that."

The note hadn't felt like I didn't understand James' love. Maybe I did feel worthy of him. Maybe I had finally realized that we were both lucky, instead of just me. James could have been right about everything. The letter was just an unfortunate coincidence.

Ian's phone started buzzing. "Hey, Jen," he said. "I'm working right now. I'll have to call you back…" He paused. "We can find a new florist…" Another pause. "Babe, it's late. We can look tomorrow."

"You can go if you need to," I said.

He pulled his phone away from his ear. "Yeah, I'm not leaving you out here alone. James would kill me."

"It sounds like Jen will kill you if you don't. I talked to James about it earlier. He thinks that crazy doctor is long gone. You've seen no sign that he's around. Trust me, I can take care of myself." I thought about when I'd kneed Tyler in the balls in the chapter I had read. I was kick ass. "And I'll head back now if it makes you feel better."

He glanced at his phone and then back at me.

"Really. Go."

"Are you sure?"

I looked around. It was late, but there were a few people still walking through Central Park. I was safe here. "I'm sure."

He put his cell back up to his ear. "I'll be there in a few minutes, baby. Love you too." He hung up. "Let me just walk you back real quick."

"Ian, I'm fine. See?" I started walking backwards in the direction we had come. "I even know the way."

He laughed. "Okay. I'll see you tomorrow. And thank you. You're right, she was probably going to kill me."

I smiled and waved before he turned and started walking in the opposite direction.

This was what I had wanted anyway. A little time to myself and some fresh air. I took a deep breath. The air didn't seem as stale in the park. I slowly walked back toward the apartment.

The hairs on the back of my neck stood up. I glanced over my shoulder, but no one was there. Why did I keep feeling like someone was watching me? Usually I could dismiss it because I knew the security detail was tailing me. But tonight? Ian was gone. No one else knew I was out here.

I picked up my pace. *So much for a relaxing stroll.* But I had gotten everything I needed from this walk. Talking to Ian was exactly what I had needed. I'd always had issues with self-confidence. It made sense that they plagued me into adulthood. But it didn't mean I was depressed. If anything, it would have just made me want to prove that I was worthy of James. I smiled to myself. That was probably what the book was for. And the pen name. All of it. I wanted to show him that I wasn't just some stupid trophy wife. But James already knew that. I could tell by the way he looked at me.

"Penny? Penny is that you?"

I turned around, expecting to see Ian. But it was an older man jogging up to me. His gray hair was slightly askew and looked in bad need of a cut. Really, he looked disheveled in general. But he also looked familiar. Just like the scenes in the book felt familiar. And the dreams I'd been having.

"Oh, it is you." He smiled. He had a perfectly white, straight smile that did not at all fit with the rest of him. I would have guessed he was homeless before he smiled. But now that he was closer, I could tell he definitely wasn't homeless. He was just a little dirty. Like he had accidentally fallen asleep out here. Or rolled around in the grass. Or something. I studied him as he brushed a leaf off his shoulder.

"I'm sorry, do I know you?" I asked.

"Yes, yes. I'm a good friend of Jon's. We've met before but it's been several years."

"Jon?" I racked my brain. "James' father?"

He nodded. "Indeed. I'm so glad I caught you. I heard about what happened, dear. How are you feeling?"

"Better now."

"Good." He smiled. "Do you want to sit and catch up for a moment?" He gestured to a park bench off to the side of the path.

"Oh, I'm sorry, I can't. I really must be getting back."

He coughed. "I understand." And then he coughed again. And again.

"Are you okay?" I asked.

He kept coughing.

"Do you want me to go get a water bottle?"

"No," he wheezed. "I just need to sit down."

"Here." I helped him over to the bench he had pointed to before.

He collapsed onto it and patted the spot beside him.

How could I say no? I was worried that if I left him alone he'd cough up a lung. I sat down even though all I wanted to do was get back. I wanted to read more of the manuscript. And watch a movie with Melissa. And maybe get a goodnight kiss from James. It was a silly thought. But also a perfect one.

"Sorry, dear," the old man said. "My lungs aren't what they used to be." He pulled out a handkerchief from his pocket, but instead of blowing his nose or coughing into it, he just wrung it in his hands.

I didn't know what I was supposed to say. The hairs on the back of my neck rose again. "I really should be getting back."

He took a deep breath. "Just a minute and I'll be alright." He took another deep breath.

I started to tap my foot nervously. How did James' father know this guy? Jon was fit for his age, and wealthy, and put together. The man beside me was the opposite of all that. Not that two people so different couldn't be friends. It just felt…off. "How did you say you knew Jon again?"

"Old friends." He reached over and placed his hand on my forearm. His fingers were like ice.

Something clicked in my mind. And I almost laughed out loud, but luckily I stifled it. I didn't remember him. He just looked like someone I remembered. Professor Snape from the Harry Potter movies. He had an uncanny resemblance to that actor. "Has anyone ever told you that you look like Professor Snape from the Harry Potter films?"

"Why, yes. Your daughter actually. Last time she saw me she actually called me Snape." He smiled.

There was something off about his smile. It didn't seem genuine. *At all.* If anything it felt menacing. I shifted nervously on the bench as his words tumbled around my head. "But I thought you said it's been several years since you've seen me. Scarlett's only three and a half."

"Several can mean three," he said calmly.

"But if it had been that long she wouldn't have been talking. And..." I tried to remember what James had told me about his parents at dinner. "James' relationship was pretty strained with his parents when we met. I didn't even meet them until just a little before our wedding."

"I thought you didn't remember anything. I guess you can't always trust tabloids. I should have known when they were talking about what designer dress you were wearing when you left the hospital instead of focusing on the real story. Your lost memories."

Tabloids? God, this man didn't know me or my family. I tried to stand up, but his icy fingers dug into my skin, pulling me back down onto the bench.

"Let go of me or I'll..."

"You'll what? Call for help? There's no one around. And you have no phone."

How could he know that I didn't have a phone? Unless he had been following me. I knew I felt someone watching. I knew it. Why hadn't I said anything? Why hadn't I trusted my gut? I knew why. Because I had been fighting my gut this whole time. My gut screamed that I loved James. That I could trust him. That he was everything. But I kept denying it. I had been telling my gut to piss off ever since I woke up in that hospital room.

"You're coming with me," he said and pulled me off the bench.

So I did what I knew I was good at. I tried to knee him in the crotch.

But before my knee made contact with him, he pushed his handkerchief over my mouth.

I screamed but my voice was muffled by the fabric. I tried to move, but my body felt heavy.

"You were supposed to die," he said. "You were supposed to fix my life, not ruin it."

I couldn't breathe. My eyelids started to close. I should have trusted my gut all along. Because images of James were the last thing that flashed through my mind. I loved him. And now he'd never know.

There was nothing wrong with him describing our love as light and dark. I liked the darkness. The sounds of the city died away as my eyes closed. Darkness was everywhere. And I understood what he meant. It was hard to breathe without the light.

ABOUT THE AUTHOR

Ivy Smoak is an international bestselling author. When she's not writing, you can find her binge watching too many TV shows, taking long walks, playing outside, and generally refusing to act like an adult. She lives with her husband in Delaware.

Twitter: @IvySmoakAuthor
Facebook: IvySmoakAuthor
Goodreads: IvySmoak

Made in the USA
Las Vegas, NV
28 September 2021